THE
BOARDWALK
Antiques
SHOP

A **tangerine street** ROMANCE
A NOVEL IN THREE PARTS

THE
BOARDWALK
Antiques
SHOP

A tangerine street ROMANCE
A NOVEL IN THREE PARTS

Julie Wright
Melanie Jacobson
Heather B. Moore

Mirror Press

Copyright © 2015 by Mirror Press, LLC
Paperback edition
All rights reserved

Cover Design by Rachael Anderson
Interior Design by Rachael Anderson
Edited by Cassidy Wadsworth & Crystal Liechty

Published by Mirror Press, LLC
Print edition released April 2015
ISBN-10: 1941145469
ISBN-13: 978-1-941145-46-3

Welcome to tangerine street

Tangerine Street is a must-see tourist stop with a colorful mix of one-of-a-kind boutiques, unique restaurants, eclectic museums, quaint bookstores, and renowned bed-and-breakfasts. The Boardwalk Antiques Shop is an exclusive shop where every antique has a story, and each story possesses the gift to match true love. The customer who buys an antique also buys its story and soon discovers that its story unites the past with the present, creating an unexpected romantic future . . .

Other Works by the Authors

JULIE WRIGHT
Spell Check
Death Thieves
The Newport Ladies Book Club Series
My Not-So-Fairy-Tale Life
Cross My Heart
Loved Like That
The Fortune Café

MELANIE JACOBSON
Not My Type
Second Chances
Twitterpated
Smart Move
The List
Painted Kisses
The Fortune Café

HEATHER B. MOORE
The Aliso Creek Novella series
A Timeless Romance Anthology Series
The Newport Ladies Book Club Series
Heart of the Ocean
Finding Sheba
Lost King
The Fortune Café

Part One

Message in a Bottle

One

Jennifer Day took a deep breath and squinted against the sun backlighting the sign to her inheritance. The rusted metal plating of the sign nailed to the distressed wood fit the entire feel of the place. *The Boardwalk Antiques Shop.*

"Might as well say goodbye before I put you up for adoption," she muttered as she slid the ancient metal key into the keyhole under the doorknob. She turned the knob with one hand, pushed on the door with the other, and was surprised at how solid the wood felt underneath her palm. The lock had looked so fragile because of its age and made the establishment appear easy to break into. But the thick, heavy door with its leaded window proved that a fair amount of strength existed in the framework of her deceased aunt's storefront.

Jennifer gripped the handle of her rolling suitcase and stepped inside the orphaned business.

She'd inherited the Boardwalk Antiques Shop from her father's only sister. While she'd been living, financially-secure Aunt Daisy Day had worn droopy hats and flip flops everywhere she went—even during those long-ago visits to Oregon in the middle of winter, as if she somehow expected southern California weather to trail after her like an obedient puppy. Jennifer hated it when Aunt Daisy came to visit. Those were the weeks when she hid out in her brother's room and pretended to be interested in his online gaming accounts. She couldn't hide in her own room because she was the only neat freak in the family, making her bedroom the default guestroom. And she was never allowed to play her guitar or the piano because Aunt Daisy claimed it gave her a headache.

Everyone said Jennifer and Daisy were twins. They shared the same long blonde hair, the same light sprinkling of freckles across the bridge of their noses, and the same caramel-brown eyes. But the similarities ended at the physical. Emotionally and mentally they were polar opposites. They disagreed on pretty much everything: music, datable men, decorating and design, art, clothing, *everything*.

Jennifer hadn't cried during Daisy's funeral. But she felt bad for not feeling bad. All the other cousins had felt bad. Her own brother had felt bad. Jennifer only felt relieved. She would never again hear her aunt's nasal-toned voice say the words, "Jenn, girl, you need to get some hobbies and interests. You're spinning your wheels and accomplishing nothing. You're never going to get married and have kids if you keep yourself locked away with a guitar all the time."

All that lecturing from the aunt who *wasn't* married and had *no* children. Hypocrite.

Jennifer didn't attend the reading of the will. Why would she? Aunt Daisy and Jennifer had never seen eye to eye on anything. The last thing she wanted was to bear the insult of Daisy leaving her out of the will in front of everyone else. Bad enough that they would recognize the hole in the will where Jennifer's name should have been. She'd stayed in her apartment with her friends and practiced their music—the same music Jennifer hoped someday would be heard on the radio at regular intervals.

Jennifer thought that might be the reason Daisy disliked

her so much. Jennifer lived in the future—in the possibility of tomorrow. Daisy Day had lived in the past—in all the stories of lives that already happened. Jennifer had tried not to think about all that when the will was read, as she strummed her guitar and sang the songs her friend and only male band member, Eddie Findlay, had written.

Except the will reading hadn't gone like she'd thought. The will reading had changed her world, stealing away her possibilities of tomorrow by leaving her stranded in a store full of yesterdays.

Daisy left the antique store to Jennifer.

The cousins, and even Jennifer's own brother, were all furious with their measly inheritances of a few thousand dollars apiece. Jennifer had been gifted with the goldmine of the lucrative business located in prime, touristy beach territory. The back door of the store led straight to the boardwalk and overlooked sand, tide, and sunsets, and everyone hated her for it.

Jennifer understood why they'd all been upset by the will's contents, but none of them understood how hard the inheritance had blasted *her*. The bequest was an eccentric woman in a floppy hat taking one more sucker punch at Jennifer from beyond the grave. She could almost hear her aunt's voice saying, "It's unnatural for a twenty-five-year-old woman to have no solid plans in her life. You're going to end up alone if you don't settle yourself soon."

Daisy had said things like that as if Jennifer was some sort of laze-about—which she totally wasn't. She'd moved out of her parents' house almost immediately after high school graduation and paid her own way through college. Sure, she'd been a music major, and sure, that meant that her job opportunities were tapeworm slim; but even though her job at Musician For Life helping five-year-olds pick out their first violins wasn't glamorous, it paid the bills—most of the time.

3

Jennifer took another breath and shook her head to clear her frustration with the whole situation. She blinked in the dim light sneaking in through the cracks of the closed plantation shutters over the windows and the single window of leaded glass from the door.

Face it. Conquer it. Come home. That had been Eddie's advice when he'd dropped her off at the airport. "I'm facing you," she now told the shadowy collection of antiques tying up space in the store.

The words sounded braver than she felt. She'd "visited" enough times to remember the strange wire dressmaker's mannequin and the creepy, near-life-sized puppet that decorated the store but was never for sale because Daisy had loved them.

Jennifer hated them. They freaked her out. They had that almost-alive appearance that allowed her to imagine being strangled by wooden puppet fingers or maybe being swallowed into the wire belly of the dressmaker's mannequin. Daisy had bamboozled Jennifer's parents into "letting" Jennifer go to California every summer to help out with the store. This meant Jennifer spent several weeks out of her summer every year being terrified.

She flipped the light switch and found that, under the scrutiny of illumination, the shadows stopped advancing on her.

How old was she? To be afraid of shadows and inanimate objects? "Stop being an infant," Jennifer said to herself. She turned to face another person standing in the dim light and let out a yelp of surprise and then a noise of exasperation. A mirror. Only a mirror. And a really pretty one at that—full length with swirls and flowers worked into the silver frame. The faded silvering made her reflection look like an old photo worn at the edges.

"Just jitters," she murmured, squinting at the cardstock placard fastened to the mirror's side. The words were printed in a fancy font she didn't recognize: *I was made in Britain and brought across the sea to Maryland in 1807 as a gift from Henri Stier to his youngest daughter, Rosalie. I remained in Maryland, shining Rosalie's reflection back to her for many years. As I was passed from mother to daughter and then given away for a charity auction, I found my way westward, changing hands from one merchant to the next until the Gold Rush took me all the way to Northern California. The rise of Hollywood brought me to Southern California, where I was owned by the Greta Garbo estate during her time in Hollywood. My favorite owner, however, was a sweet, unassuming woman named Janice Herold who bravely fought breast cancer and had an innate kindness. If I were to declare a fairest of my owners, it would have been Janice.*

Jennifer turned slowly, surveying the shop and its contents. Every item had a story attached to it. Jennifer wondered how Daisy found the history of each and every item in her store. Had she refused to buy an item that didn't come with an ownership pedigree?

"Figures," Jennifer muttered.

It was confirmation that her aunt's meticulous fanaticism over the past had reached an unhealthy level. "Nice that you criticized me for needing to broaden my horizons when your own are so narrow, Daisy." She sketched a quick glance around, half-expecting Daisy's ghost to be glaring down from atop the front counter.

With a shudder, Jennifer pulled her phone from her back pocket and tapped the screen over Eddie's name. She put the phone to her ear and willed him to answer quickly. Even from another state, his voice would be better company than the silence of the artifact cemetery she stood in.

"Eddie!" She felt slightly ashamed at the relief in her voice, at hearing his.

"Jenn, my flower, wassup?"

"I just got here. It's creepier than I remember." She

wrinkled her nose as she glanced around. "And there's all these info cards hooked to each and every item. It's like a sinister history class."

"Worse than American history with Wilson?" he asked.

She smiled at his playful tone, feeling relief at having a conversation with someone breathing instead of feeling like she was tiptoeing around, and talking to, ghosts. "Definitely worse."

"So when are you coming home?" Eddie's voice took on a plaintive tone—almost a whine. "You know if you leave me in charge of your plants for too long, they'll die of boredom."

"You could sing to them," she offered.

"I have no song without you."

Jennifer smiled at that.

"And," he continued, "if the plants don't die from boredom, I might. I need you to entertain me. There's nothing to do around here."

She almost reminded him that they didn't do much when she was around and that she felt pretty sure nothing would change when she returned, but her heart wasn't in the mood for banter. She wanted to be home as much as he insisted he wanted her there. "The real estate agent comes tonight."

Eddie snorted into the phone, the loud noise making Jennifer pull the phone away from her ear before her eardrum was blown out. "Studly the realtor . . ." he sang out. "So, is he as studly as his name indicates?"

Jennifer grunted. "I haven't met him yet. As long as he makes the property look studly, I don't care what he looks like. He'll help assess a value and take some pictures. With any luck, I'll be through with this whole business by next week."

"Good. Face it. Conquer it. And come home."

She nodded even though he couldn't see her. "That's the plan."

"That's a good plan. Let's stick with that one. But, hey . . . Jenn . . . I gotta go. Misti's coming over to play for me so I can practice."

Jennifer's heart stuttered in her chest. "I thought you had no song without me." She kept her tone light, not wanting to seem needy, desperate, or jealous even though she felt a little of all three emotions. Her friendship with Eddie had always only been just that: friendship. He'd been through a parade of girlfriends, but it had been a while since his last relationship, and Jennifer thought that maybe he'd been looking at her differently lately. She hoped so anyway, because she'd been in love with him pretty much since the day she'd heard him sing at the high school talent show.

He laughed at her comment regarding him having no song without her. "Yeah well, don't want the pipes to get dusty."

"Right," Jennifer said. "Wouldn't want that." She really didn't want that. Listening to Eddie's voice was a magical experience, and he had an amazing skill at writing lyrics. Jenn heard Eddie's doorbell through her phone.

"Misti's here! Gotta go. Be brave, soldier!"

Before Jennifer could say any form of her own goodbye, Eddie ended the call.

She rolled her eyes and stuffed her phone back into her pocket. She hated it when he called her soldier, as if the band was a mini-military instead of a seriously-minded music group. She felt an urgency to get back home, before Eddie decided to get comfortable with his new guitar replacement.

"I'm not jealous," she told the life-sized Egyptian puppet who stared at her through dead eyes that had probably been brushed on with a lead-based paint. "I'm not," she insisted and then wondered why she was arguing with an entity from her nightmares. Even if it didn't reach out with its nimble, wooden fingers and try to choke her, she was certain to get lead-poisoning from the thing. She squinted at the card.

7

THE BOARDWALK ANTIQUES SHOP

My name is Cleopatra. I was crafted to call attention to the Egyptian exhibit at the 1893 Chicago World's Fair. I was sold to H.H. Holmes as a decoration in his hotel. You don't want to know the unspeakable horrors I saw in that hotel. From there, I belonged to a variety of theaters and high schools as a stage prop until I made my way west as part of the traveling production of the play Aida. *My right leg broke during a move, and I was left with a stagehand named Nathaniel Davenport who verified my history, fixed me up, and brought me to the Boardwalk Antiques Shop.*

Jenn wondered what kind of *unspeakable horrors* could have happened in a nineteenth-century hotel. That had been an era where women still wore dresses all day long, which, Jennifer supposed, was horrific enough. She looked down at the puppet's left leg, where a hairline crack was visible to anyone knowing to look for it.

She hated to admit it, but the Cleopatra card and the card on the mirror were a little interesting. She'd never taken the time to read the cards when she'd been forced to visit before because that would have required her to pretend to care about Daisy's crazy life.

But Daisy wasn't here now. Jennifer swept her glance over the room to verify this fact, and, satisfying herself that Daisy really wasn't present, she wandered to the next cardstock history lesson and began reading. Then she moved on to the next one, and the one after that.

The jingling bells on the door announced the arrival of another person. Startled that anyone would show up when she wasn't expecting the realtor until that evening, Jennifer glanced up to see a couple in the kind of beach attire covering their pasty-white bodies that gave them away as tourists. "Oh, I'm sorry, the store's not—"

"Charming!" the woman declared over the top of Jennifer's, "not open for business."

Jennifer opened her mouth again to explain that the

store really *wasn't* open for business but then reconsidered. Wasn't her goal to get all this stuff sold? She pasted on her best smile. "Good morning! Welcome to Boardwalk Antiques." She scowled and wondered if the store was supposed to be referred to as Boardwalk Antiques or The Boardwalk Antiques Shop.

"You mean 'good afternoon,'" the woman said. Her floppy hat made her look like a reincarnation of Daisy Day.

"It can't be much past ten," Jennifer said, knowing it wasn't exactly good manners to argue with the customer. Wasn't there a rule on that sort of thing? Something like *the customer is always right*? Who made up stupid rules like that, anyway?

"It's almost one," the man, who really should have used more sunscreen on his balding head, said.

Jennifer looked at her phone and found that it really was almost one in the afternoon. She frowned. "Wow . . . I lost track of time."

The couple laughed as if losing track of time was expected to happen at a beach. Of course, Jennifer wasn't at the beach. She'd been sitting inside a store filled with history cards.

Her frown deepened with the realization that she'd actually been interested in everything she'd seen and read. She'd turned on the music box, wound up the Jack in the box, and inspected the box labeled *dynamite*. The dynamite one had been empty—to Jennifer's relief. She wasn't sure she liked the idea of selling explosives to anyone. Was selling explosives even legal in the state of California? Was it legal anywhere? Jennifer shook her head and mentally chided herself for focusing on the trivial. What did it matter, since no dynamite actually existed?

She opened the plantation shutters to allow genuine light into the store in the hopes of making the place more cheerful, and inspiring the tourists to make a purchase.

Opening the shutters did add a friendly atmosphere to the shop, and within moments, the bell jingled again. More customers.

Not knowing quite what to do with customers in the store, Jennifer maneuvered herself to the only place that seemed logical: behind the front counter. She'd helped Daisy operate the antiquated register many times but figured since it had been a long time, she ought to practice a little before anyone expected her to be proficient.

After several long minutes of browsing, the couple with the floppy hat and burned bald spot brought a railroad lantern to the counter. She looked at the price tag and cringed. *Really? $749 for a rusty lantern? My aunt was a shark.*

She hesitated. Her fingers hovered over the numbers, not sure how she could possibly charge so much for something that likely didn't even work. Then the man with the burned bald spot said, "My great grandfather worked for the Indianapolis Railroad."

"Really?" Jennifer asked.

"Yup. I collect memorabilia from that era. This is a rare piece you've got here. Well . . . that *I've* got here. Museum quality. And it has a blue globe. Fabulous find! It'll look great in my office."

The man's pleased tone and genuine gratitude to be able to buy the lantern staggered Jennifer. He wasn't merely buying the item; he also bought the history listed on the card. And the history obviously felt personal to him because of his great grandfather's connection.

Jennifer entered the numbers into the register, and the till opened up. To Jennifer's horror the till was empty, but the guy pulled out his credit card, which meant he wouldn't need change. The credit card scanner had been turned off, so she had to wait a few extra moments for the system to boot. The check-out method was as antiquated as the items being

sold. Her aunt really should have upgraded to something a
little less cumbersome. But the system finally went live, and
the card scanned through without any trouble.

Jennifer wrapped the lamp in paper before putting it in
a bag—like she'd helped Daisy do with fragile items a
hundred times before. The couple exited the shop with an
aura of excitement over their purchase.

Their emotions were contagious. Jennifer Day had
made her first sale! She felt the temptation to do a victory
dance, but with other customers in the store, it seemed like a
less-than-prudent idea. She scoured through her purse for
any cash so she had some money in the till to make change
with and settled herself in to be in business for the day. She
sold several other items over the next few hours as customers
trailed in and out of the shop—a hobby horse from the Gold
Rush period; a sewing basket that looked straight out of a
Jane Austen movie set and had, in fact, come from that same
time period; a burgundy petticoat that once belonged to one
of the prostitutes who followed the camp of Major General
Joseph Hooker during the Civil War.

She hurried to read the cards with the histories on them
before they left her store forever with the customers, and she
felt a little annoyed that people were buying things before
she'd had the chance to look them all over.

Jennifer couldn't believe the amount of foot traffic, but
with the weather being warm and the sand and surf
beckoning, she supposed she shouldn't have been too
surprised. The hours posted on the door stated that she
closed at six, a thing she was super glad of since she hadn't
eaten anything all day, aside from a fun-size Almond Joy
candy bar that was smooshed at the bottom of her purse.
Smooshed or not, she'd been grateful to eat *something*. The
store still had customers twenty-three minutes after she
should have locked the door, but the last customers were of
the paying variety, so Jennifer smiled and acted

accommodating.

The woman who'd been browsing past closing time finally came up to the counter, dumping several items near the register with an exaggerated sigh. Her hot rod red fingernails had little sparkly decals on them. She looked up at Jennifer with a wide grin but then looked past her for a moment. She asked, "What's with the bottle?"

"Bottle?" Jennifer repeated, her gaze following to where the woman pointed to a small wall shelf behind the counter. The shelf seemed made specifically for the light blue bottle. Jennifer squinted into the thick glass. "There's a note inside it," she said, automatically scanning the general area of the bottle to find the cardstock history of the item.

But there was no card.

Nothing at all existed to explain the bottle and its mysterious note. Even through the thick glass, Jennifer could tell the letter was old. The yellowed paper had a brittle look to it, a fragility that said if anyone were to uncork the bottle and allow oxygen inside, the paper might disintegrate into dust.

A note inside, but no information outside. And no price tag.

"It's kind of perfect," the woman said. "How much is it?"

"It isn't priced," Jennifer murmured, trying to figure out how such an anomaly could exist in this store of agonizing organization and attention to detail. She hated that the shop reminded her of her own apartment. Obsessive organization was a trait she shared with Daisy.

"How much do you want for it?" The woman persisted.

The question startled Jennifer. "How much do *I* want?" She didn't know how to respond. How much was it worth? She'd already proven to herself that she had no idea the value of anything. The idea of putting a price on this item where no price had been previously allocated felt wrong, in spite of the fact that everything in the store belonged to her now; in spite of the fact that she intended to sell everything.

But the bottle, taking up a lone vigil on its shelf behind the counter, felt different from everything else. And for reasons Jennifer couldn't explain, she felt a kinship to this enigmatic item. It was as out of place and forlorn as she felt in the antique store. It had no history card or price tag to claim its value. The transparent bottle still managed to keep its contents hidden. Jennifer could totally relate.

"It's not for sale," Jennifer said finally as she tore her eyes from the bottle and forced herself to pay attention to the customer.

The woman's chin lifted as if she intended on arguing the point, but she must have sensed Jennifer's resolve because she wiggled a shoulder in an apathetic shrug and carried on with the rest of her purchases.

As soon as the woman left the store and Jennifer locked the door, she meticulously walked through the entire shop. She checked each and every item. Everything had a history card—even the creepy little glass doll nestled in frilly bedding inside a miniature perambulator came with a pedigree. The only piece of inventory not labeled and priced was that bottle.

She went back behind the counter and peered at the bottle for a moment before reaching up and removing the heavy glass artifact from its pedestal. Someone had dripped blue sealing wax over the corked top and left the mark of a flower in the wax to fancy it up a bit. Jennifer held the bottle closer to her face as if she could somehow see around the curves in the paper to the inked message that surely existed inside.

An insistent rapping came from the front door, startling Jennifer enough that she nearly dropped the bottle. She tightened her grip over the bottle's neck, as if needing to assure herself that she *hadn't* dropped it, before she placed it back onto the shelf.

With a deep breath, Jennifer went to the door to let the customer know they were closed. She still needed to eat and get her luggage upstairs into the apartment so she could get some rest. And she was tired of selling things she hadn't had time to look over first.

She smiled through the leaded window and said loudly enough to be heard, "I'm sorry, but we're closed."

As soon as the words left her mouth, she regretted them because the man standing on the other side of the door was what her younger cousin would have called *hot* and her mom would have called *handsome*. The only description Jennifer could come up with was her mouth falling open. His blue eyes mirrored the sea, and his dark hair had probably been tamed to one side at the beginning of the day; but now the windblown locks were anything but tame. Maybe she didn't want the store to be closed after all. The man wore a short-sleeved button-up shirt and khaki pants—definitely not beach-combing attire.

He smiled through the window and held up his business card so she could read it.

Seashell Beach Realty
Paul Studly

The card gave a phone number and other information, but all Jennifer saw was the Studly part. *Yes, you are,* she thought. Eddie had made fun of her when she'd originally chosen her realtor from the internet site based solely on the name. She'd done it mostly as a joke, but how was she to have known that the last name of Studly should have been taken so literally?

She realized that Paul Studly still waited patiently with his card in the air; she hurried to unlock the door and allow him access to Daisy's antique shop—*my antique shop, now,* she thought. "Hi," she said as soon as the door was open wide enough to invite him inside. She was startled at first to have to tilt her head back in order to meet his eye; she was tall for a woman and could look most men in the eye. Eddie was her equal in height. "Sorry about that. It's been a busy afternoon, and I . . ." She trailed off, not wanting to admit that in all of the excitement and hustle of helping customers, she'd completely forgotten their appointment. "I needed to count down the register," she said finally.

"No problem at all." He extended his hand. "I'm Paul Studly."

"Yes, you are." She cringed. She'd said it out loud? Those kinds of thoughts were supposed to play *inside* her head. They were not allowed to wander outside where anyone could see them. "It said so on your business card." She took his hand and gave it a firm shake, noting that his hands had calluses, which meant he did more than simply sell properties. A man with calluses was a man who knew how to work. She hoped that the business card comment kept him from focusing too hard on anything else that "yes, you are" might mean.

He didn't look much older than she was, maybe twenty-six or twenty-seven. But he looked more settled—more comfortable in his life choices. And he suddenly seemed so much older. He had chosen a career and was making it work. While she loved music and wanted music to be her career, she didn't feel any closer to her goals than she'd felt the day of her high school graduation, seven years prior. For the first time in her life, she wondered if Daisy had been right about her spinning her wheels in life.

She shifted her shoulders and moved away from her realtor a step. "I need to just count down the register," she repeated and moved behind the counter.

He gave her a sideways glance. "So, you opened for

business?"

"Yeah, people seemed to want to come in, and since I plan on selling everything off anyway . . . why? Was that a bad idea?"

"No. Keeping the business open is a great idea. It increases the value when buyers can see its continued earning potential. It's easier to keep a business thriving than it is to reopen and start over. We discussed this on the phone when you told me you wanted it closed while we worked on getting it sold."

They *had* discussed keeping the store open—well, he'd discussed it, and she had shut him down. But she felt it terribly impolite to bring that detail up now that she agreed with him. "I guess I've changed my mind."

He grinned, which really bothered her because the grin made him go from *studly* to *smugly*.

She cut him a glare. "What are you grinning at?"

"Just nice to see a person who adapts to new circumstances with a level, logical head."

Was he giving her a compliment or being sarcastic? She couldn't tell and so decided to ignore the comment altogether. She pulled out the manual on the credit card reader that she'd seen earlier and flipped through it. She'd done this before—"batching out," as Daisy had called it—but it had been several years, and she couldn't really remember how to make it work. She looked up to see Mr. Studly still staring at her.

"Is it okay if I finish this while you get started on taking pictures?" She nodded to the camera bag on his shoulder.

"Sure. We can start there if you'd like."

She looked back at her papers to indicate that, yes, that *was* what she'd like. Ignoring him and getting the work done so she could finally eat seemed like her best option. But her new realtor was hard to ignore, and not just because he was kind of beautiful. He started reading the cards out loud, and he kept up a running commentary on pretty much everything he saw and read in the store. He gushed about the store in a way that made it seem he was interested in buying it for himself. He took pictures, asked a few questions about the property details—things Jennifer hadn't even thought about, like whether or not she'd be willing to sell inventory at a deep discount if the new owner wanted some of the stock, and if she planned on selling the shelving units as part of the sale price.

"Your asking price is remarkably low," he said. "So I took the liberty of adding fifty eight thousand to it."

Jennifer looked up from her paperwork. "What? Why? I want it to sell quickly."

He gave her his smug look. "Have you even glanced outside your back door? Or seen the view from the upstairs apartment windows?"

She hadn't yet; there'd hardly been time. She had vague memories of those views from her visits, but mostly those were memories she tried to block. She didn't need to answer, since he was already talking again. "Ocean front property in this town is hard to come by. Believe me. If you sell at your original price, people will wonder what's wrong with the place. I admit I wondered before I got here. But after looking around, I can't see any reason for a lower price. Everything seems to be in excellent repair. No one will even blink at the little extra."

Nearly sixty grand didn't sound like a little extra to Jennifer, but she really didn't know how to gauge such things. She could tell someone the price of a saxophone or a Stradivarius violin, but real estate and antiques that weren't musical instruments were foreign to her. That was why she knew she needed a real estate agent.

She finally murmured something that must have

sounded like assent, because he went back to his job.

She frowned at the papers and the adding machine in front of her. They had to be wrong. No way did she sell that much. She added the tickets again. The same number stared back at her. "I made nearly four thousand dollars today." She didn't realize she'd said the words out loud until she caught Mr. Smugly staring at her.

"It's a great location for a business. Are you sure you want to sell it?" he asked.

"Completely certain," she said, though some part of her didn't feel so complete about that certainty after all. The actual real estate was paid for, so she had no monthly mortgage. She'd been given a list of the average monthly expenditures and knew that her raking in four grand would cover those. So even pretending that the day's sales were a fluke, if she had only a couple of those days every month, she'd have a really nice income—especially when she could live rent-free in the apartment located upstairs. The property taxes were steep but not unmanageably so. Paul Studly, the realtor, watched her, his expression amused. "Totally sure," she confirmed. He shrugged and turned down one of the aisles.

"Oh! No way!" His shout made her jump. "You have a real Yoda!" He backed out of that aisle to make sure he had her attention. "Did you know you had an actual Yoda?"

Jennifer smirked. "You are aware that it's impossible to have an *actual* Yoda, since Yoda doesn't exist."

Her realtor waved his hand, as if waving away her logic in spite of only moments before declaring he liked a person who used logic. "Yes. But this is one of the actual puppets used in the actual movies. Did you know you had this?"

"I haven't really had time to look at every—"

Before she realized what he was doing, he had grabbed her hand and was dragging her out from behind the counter.

"You've got to see this. It's movie-making history!"

Dumbfounded by his excitement, she trailed after him, hyper-aware of the fact that a guy who matched his studly name had a decent grip on her hand. All his smugness was gone, replaced by this childlike excitement. She nodded along with him and hoped she showed adequate enthusiasm to the barely waist-high puppet. He finally released her hand and folded his arms over his chest. She felt a little off-balance by the loss of the energy his hand had given her.

Paul's face shifted from one of elation to something else: pensive, wistful, sad. "My dad took me to see this movie when it rereleased in the theaters for some special anniversary," he said. "It was the last thing we did together before he died."

Jennifer froze in the cold shock of such a personal revelation.

Paul Studly had been through a variety of emotions since entering her aunt's antique store. Jennifer had no idea how to take him.

He glanced up, as if realizing his thoughts had been like the card on the side of the Yoda puppet that said: *in a galaxy far, far away.* "I'm sorry. It's been a long day, and I'm always a little off when I go for so long without eating."

"I hear you. I haven't eaten either."

"Would you like to go grab a bite? That is, after I take some pictures of the upstairs apartment and the view?"

She considered his question from all angles. A dark-haired man that looked like he'd been designed instead of simply born like the rest of humanity wanted to take her to dinner. But, he was her realtor, so he likely meant he wanted to kill two birds with one stone by getting food and taking care of the paperwork before the listing went live. On the other hand, he was a little too self-assured for Jennifer's liking. Sure, Eddie was also one of those conceited types, but he was a musician—an artist—not a guy who peddled other people's land for a living. But, his comment about his dad made Paul Studly feel very human to Jennifer in spite of his name and his over-flowing confidence. And humans needed company.

She was one of those humans who needed company, too. She was all alone in a new town and didn't love the idea of going out to dinner by herself. So she smiled and shrugged. "Sure. You probably know where all the best restaurants are around here anyway, right?"

"Right."

And that settled it. She had a date . . . sort of. It wasn't until after she'd followed the realtor through her upstairs apartment that she realized she shouldn't be thinking in terms of dates. She should've been ordering takeout and staying home to sort through her aunt's things.

The upstairs apartment was like a miniature version of the antique shop. Various artifacts lined shelves on her walls and in her bookcases. The bookcases themselves were beautiful—large pieces of art made from a variety of expensive woods.

But more than the antiques and the furniture called out for Jennifer's attention. Incredibly ornate frames hung all over the walls, frames where the wood appeared to have been hand-chiseled by masters. And inside those frames were pictures of . . . "Me?" she whispered.

There were many pictures of her brother and a few of her other cousins too, but it was unmistakable that the person who took up most of the pictorial wall space was Jennifer herself. Many of the pictures were of Jennifer and Daisy together: Daisy's arms wrapped tightly around her young niece's shoulders, the two of them doing duck lips together for the camera, Daisy teaching a toddler Jennifer how to walk.

"Your aunt obviously loved you a great deal. You two must have been very close. I'm so sorry for your loss," Paul said.

Before she could refute his claim, he moved away to get some more shots of the rooms and, by so doing, to give her space.

She didn't love me; she could barely tolerate me, Jennifer wanted to say. But she could find no words underneath the many smiling faces of her younger self staring at her from every wall. If she didn't know better, she would have imagined that perhaps the two people in these pictures were great friends, but she'd barely known Daisy.

And whose fault is that? She wondered.

She wanted to believe it was Daisy's fault but wasn't sure she didn't share in some of the blame. She shook herself, not liking the direction of those thoughts, and went to find her realtor.

"Let's get dinner. I have a lot of work ahead of me tonight," she said. Dinner was a good idea. A meal and conversation would distract her and give her something else to think about that wasn't her aunt or the store or the apartment with all of those pictures that told a different story than the one inside her head.

She was certain he mistook her desire to leave as overwhelming emotion for her *loss,* as he called it, but she couldn't make herself explain. Jennifer pulled at her collar. Was there no oxygen in this apartment? Why couldn't she breathe?

Mr. Studly stopped for one last picture of the sun setting over the ocean through the living room window.

"Please, now," she begged.

He finally allowed her to pull him from the apartment.

Two

Paul watched as Jennifer Day, lucky heir of Daisy Day, locked up her inheritance. He couldn't help but feel sorry for her. She must not feel too lucky if her humorless tone was any indicator. He didn't know why her situation made him instantly think of his own father dying and leaving him the heir to a successful realty company. He felt a sudden need to help her pick up the pieces of everything broken in her life.

"So, where do you want to go?" he asked once she'd checked the lock of the antique store twice to verify its security.

"It's your turf, Mr. Studly. You choose."

"Call me Paul."

She smiled. "But your last name is so much fun; it's hard to resist." She fell silent a second before adding, "Is that really your last name, or is it a marketing ploy to drum up more business?"

"It's the name on my birth certificate, and the name on the birth certificates of all my ancestors. It's just good luck that it helps drum up business as well."

Jennifer laughed, and he felt himself warm to the sound. Paul liked Jennifer's laugh a great deal. In fact, from the moment he'd hung up the phone when she'd called to make the appointment, he'd looked forward to meeting her. It wasn't because of anything specific she'd said to him, but more because of what he'd been allowed to eavesdrop in on. She apparently worked at a music store, and some kid had come in with a broken G string on his viola. She hadn't placed Paul on hold while she handled the dilemma, which had allowed him to listen in on the entire situation. She'd made a side joke about a broken G string being tough for any young man to handle, making the mom laugh and the kid ask why everyone was laughing. She'd been friendly, funny, knowledgeable and, well . . . charming.

He'd chided himself for taking such an instant liking to a stranger on the phone—especially when nothing could really be learned about a person from a single phone call. But they'd talked a few times since then, and each time he'd felt a connection to the voice on the other end of the line. They'd shared a few jokes and interests that made him imagine they shared lots of things in common. He'd felt comfortable enough by the last phone call to suggest she keep her inheritance and move to Seashell Beach.

He had the feeling she'd have strangled him for that suggestion if they'd been face to face. He'd almost given up on the idea of really getting to know her.

But then when he saw her peeking at him through the plantation shutters of her antique store, looking for all the world like she belonged there, his heart had faltered in his chest and his breath hitched in his throat as if all his vital organs had forgotten what they were supposed to be doing. Jennifer Day's clean, fresh-scrubbed look had a timelessness to it that fit perfectly in a store dedicated to timeless treasures.

And he thought of his dad—which made no sense at all. Jennifer didn't look anything like his balding, middle-aged father; but she had a fire in her eyes that reminded Paul of the man he'd loved and lost. And with Jennifer having also recently lost someone, he felt they shared something important.

Paul believed that love at first sight was for teenage girls and middle-aged guys who still lived in their moms' basements and had reached a level of desperation that allowed for such nonsense, but he couldn't deny that his first sighting of Jennifer had definitely sparked something: interest, chemistry, connection.

"Is dinner that complicated?"

"What?" He'd zoned out on her while thinking about her. Classy.

"You're supposed to pick out a restaurant. You know . . . so we don't starve on the street and resort to cannibalism."

"Right. Restaurant. Do you like Chinese? There's a great little café close by that sort of redefines amazing. A friend of mine owns it. And as a bonus, he believes his fortunes cookies are magical. I know. No such thing as magic. But he's a cute, old guy even if he is a little weird. And the food is fabulous."

Jennifer smiled and shrugged. "Maybe a magical fortune cookie isn't the best thing for me. With the craziness of my new life, I don't need any more curveballs like winning a lottery or anything. What are our other options?"

"We have Geppetto's, which has some of the best pizza on the planet, and there's Just North, which has some great molé sauces."

"Just North?"

"It's Mexican food," Paul clarified. "Just North is short

for Just North of South of the Border."

Jennifer nodded her understanding. "How about we try some of that best pizza on the planet?"

"Geppetto's it is." He put a hand on her shoulder so he could steer her in the opposite direction of where they'd been facing and found it quite difficult to remove his hand again. *Get a grip, man, you hardly know her.* But he wanted to know her—had wanted to know her ever since she'd commented on the Beatles being the greatest thing to ever happen to music. Jennifer planned on staying in California until the shop sold, and he couldn't deny that he'd been tempted to raise the price to something beyond reasonable so she had to stay longer than she wanted; but inflating prices simply to see if she was someone worth knowing seemed a little unprofessional. He forced himself to stop being a chump and stuffed his hands in his pockets while they walked up Tangerine Street.

"So, Mr. Studly . . ."

"Paul," he corrected her.

"If you don't want me to call you Studly then you need to change your last name."

"Do you have a no-first-name-basis policy or something?"

"No. I just really like your last name. Anyway, based on the current market, and now that you've seen the property up close and personal, how long do you think it'll take to sell?"

"It depends on a lot of variables, but I believe with it priced well," he gave her a pointed look, "but not so low that people think it's a dump, and with the location being one of the most desirable in the area for businesses, you shouldn't have too much trouble. Probably within the month."

She looked crestfallen by his words. "A whole month?"

She probably had a boyfriend. That would explain her need for a quick exit strategy. Figured. Every time he met someone he might have any interest in, the girl was already attached.

"It'll depend on if you plan on selling as an antique business or just the location. The location alone will sell quickly, but if you want the business to remain intact and the inventory to go with it, the sale will take a bit longer. The fact that it's a profitable business and firmly established are both winning points in your favor."

"So what would you do? Sell it as is, or as just a location?"

Paul considered her question. "Honestly, and this is strictly from a business viewpoint, if I had inherited this shop under your exact circumstances where the mortgage was paid and the business carried no debt, I'd probably keep it, move in, and run it myself."

"I can't do that," she said.

"Why not? Your boyfriend doesn't want to move to California?"

She laughed but not in a way that made him believe she thought he was funny. "I don't have a boyfriend."

"So what's holding you in Oregon?"

She kicked at a pebble that had strayed out of a small garden near the bakery. "I don't know. I guess my life is there."

"Ah, I see. You have a career you really love then."

She laughed again, but, again, not in any way that seemed humored. "Nope . . . don't have one of those either." She sighed and sifted her fingers through her long blonde hair. "I haven't figured out what I want to do with my life yet. And I don't want to get stuck with the antique shop option just because it's convenient and right in front of me."

"I completely understand," he said.

"Do you? Do you really? Because you look pretty right doing what you're doing. Your career fits you."

It was Paul's turn to laugh. "I guess it does. But being in

real estate wasn't my first choice. I actually didn't want any part of being a realtor. I'd planned on being an astronaut or a race car driver or the emperor of Rome."

She bumped his shoulder with hers. "Emperor of Rome? You must have been a terror as a teenager."

He shrugged. "That's the story my mom is determined to stick to."

"So how does one go from Roman Emperor to Studly Realty?"

She peered out at him from under insanely long eyelashes, looking sincerely interested in his past choices. So he answered with honesty. "My dad died. Studly Realty was his business, and he was really good at it. We were always financially taken care of. But he wasn't one of those dads who made a lot of money but never spent time with us kids. He gave us the best of both worlds. He left the business to me because he knew my sisters wouldn't want it. When he died, I was given the chance to be something greater than anything my young mind could imagine. I would get to become like my father."

"Wow." Jennifer's one word came out like a breath, and when she looked at him her eyes were filled with understanding. "I'm sorry about your dad. How old were you?"

"Nineteen. I was home from school that weekend when he asked me to go to the movie with him. He died that night in his sleep. I didn't go back to school but instead stepped into the shoes he'd left by the bedside."

"Do you ever regret it?"

He couldn't keep from smiling. "Nah. Turns out the job for the Roman Emperor isn't even available anymore."

"I thought I heard something about Rome doing layoffs."

He liked that she turned to the joke instead of giving more sympathy. He'd had enough sympathy to last him a

27

lifetime. Most girls he'd dated oozed sympathy until he could see it dripping off of them. He found it refreshing to have someone simply let facts be what they were.

She fell silent and looked into windows of several of the stores and restaurants as they walked. The silence was of the companionable sort—the kind Paul felt no need to fill. That was different too.

"It's kind of a quaint town, isn't it?" she finally asked.

"It's the best."

"Do you actually live in Seashell Beach, or are you from somewhere neighboring?"

"I actually live here, a few streets inland. Nowhere on the planet will you find neighbors as accommodating and friendly as in Seashell Beach."

She squinted up at him in a way that made him want to laugh. "Are you still trying to talk me into running my aunt's shop?"

"I'm only letting you know that there are options, and just because one option seems like the easy way out doesn't necessarily mean it isn't the best way."

She made a *psh* noise. "How many easy ways are the best ways in life?"

"The door."

"What?"

He grinned and put his hand on her arm to stop her from walking since they'd arrived at their location for dinner. "The door," he said, "is always the easy out. And interestingly enough, it's usually the best too. Have you ever tried climbing through a window?" He swept his arm up to indicate they should enter through the particular door they stood in front of.

"Are you making fun of me?" she asked, squinting at him again.

"Not at all. Merely pointing out the options."

She smirked and shook her head. "I so thought you

MESSAGE IN A BOTTLE

were going to say you were pointing out the obvious. I was prepared to slug you." She held up her fist as if to prove the point.

"To be honest, I almost did. But they say a kind answer turneth away wrath." He took her balled-up fist in his hands and smoothed out her fingers. They weren't the smooth hands of the kind of girls he was used to dating. Most girls he dated complained because *his* hands were calloused . . . and *not* that he *was* dating this girl. She was his client. And he knew he wasn't behaving very professionally. But he couldn't help but like this girl with the calloused fingers that, he assumed, came from her guitar.

"Right. Kind." She let out a noise that sounded something between a nervous laugh and a cough. "You're off the hook for wrath this time." She slid her hand out from between his. "Geppeto's . . . seems like it's a good choice."

"Right. It is." He opened the door and allowed her to walk through. They were seated and had their order taken by a waitress who smiled a lot. Once that was all out of the way and they were waiting for their meals, he pulled out the paperwork from his messenger bag. He had to get his act together and behave like an actual real estate agent instead of a high school kid with a crush.

While they waited for their food to arrive, he took her through the other commercial properties that had sold recently in the area and showed her the price ranges, proving to her that she really had been underselling herself. She paid close attention and asked questions that let him know she understood the information he gave. "You have a real eye for detail," he said after they'd been through everything and had the wording for her listing exactly the way they both agreed.

"Nice to know I'm good at something." She twitched her shoulder.

"I happen to know you're good at other things as well."

"Really? That's very . . . *knowing* of you, since you just

met me and all."

Dang, but he liked this girl. She didn't get all coy and ask him to list her good qualities or anything; instead she called him out for making a statement for which she didn't believe he had any back-up evidence.

"It isn't about just meeting you. We've talked several times on the phone, and from that I've discovered that you're well-educated regarding music and a variety of other things, that you don't take crap from anybody, and that you have a way of putting people at ease—which is a good trait for someone who is the new owner of a retail establishment."

Her lip quirked up. "I caught the totally obvious hint at that last one. Is Seashell Beach so desperate for new blood that they're paying you a commission to keep me here or something?"

"That would be great, but I'm doing this as a freebie for the town—like community service. I think you have a lot to offer. And you're in the unique position of having a very lucrative and fulfilling career fall into your lap. Don't get me wrong, you selling the place means I get a commission. I just want to make sure you're happy with your decision. I would be a bad businessman if I allowed you to sell without really thinking it through, because if you didn't end up happy in your arrangement, you certainly wouldn't recommend me to any of your friends. But worse, I would be a bad human. Nothing is more painful than seller's remorse."

"I appreciate your concern. I really do. And I'll think about it."

The pizza showed up, and he smiled over the steaming, pie-shaped perfection. When he'd asked her what she wanted, she hadn't ordered the plain pepperoni or vegetarian that was typical of so many of his dates. She'd suggested the Geppetto's in-house invention: the Monstro. They slathered the herbed crust of the Monstro with alfredo sauce and then smothered the entire pizza with broccoli, mushrooms, garlic, and spinach.

She'd picked the obscure menu item that happened to also be his favorite. He wondered if he should press harder for her to stay.

He was being stupid, he knew. When the place sold, he'd make a nice profit, but he meant it when he talked about buyer's and seller's remorse. He'd seen a lot of people pressured into selling or buying when they really weren't ready or before they had all the facts, and it never did the realtor any favors in the long run due to the loss of that good will.

More than that, Jennifer Day looked like she *fit* in that store.

He knew better than anyone that sales were a feast-or-famine situation, and he had no idea how much the inventory cost or what the utilities added up to, so there was no way to determine actual profit, but he felt certain that Jennifer's aunt knew her business and would have priced with a margin that provided a decent income. Maybe Jennifer wasn't up for the feast-or-famine lifestyle.

"So, tell me about yourself," he said, deciding that if she was really leaving, he'd get to know as much as possible before she left.

Three

Jennifer closed the door to the Antique Shop and locked it. "What was that?" she asked aloud to the Cleopatra puppet. Cleopatra had no answer, and neither did Jennifer. Paul Studly had acted as though they were on a real date, not conducting a business transaction. He'd asked probing questions about her family, her favorite movies, her music. He hadn't spent nearly enough time asking about the property, or discussing the sale, or talking about the venues he planned to use to spread the word about her property.

The most disturbing part of all was that she hadn't realized they weren't talking business until the very end, when he'd dropped her back off at her aunt's shop. She hadn't felt that nervous since the one time Eddie came to her house in the middle of the night after a bad break-up, and, in his distress and confusion, ended up kissing her.

Eddie and she had both agreed the next day that their relationship wasn't meant to go that direction. He'd apologized. She'd apologized—though she wasn't sorry at all and felt nothing but heartbreak over the discovery that he really didn't feel that way about her. She knew if she just kept being his friend, one day he'd realize how important she was to him.

It never occurred to her that the knotted-twisted-tingling-oh-sweet-mercy-is-he-going-to-kiss-me feeling could ever come from anyone besides Eddie.

And then Paul showed up, standing at her door and looking every inch worthy of the last name he'd been blessed with at birth. Paul incited the knotted-twisted-tingling-oh-sweet-mercy-is-he-going-to-kiss-me feeling. And she felt a little horrified with herself, like she'd somehow betrayed Eddie for the mere thought of kissing the realtor, which was stupid because Eddie was making out with girls all the time.

Paul's head had been haloed by the old-fashioned streetlamp in front of her store. When he'd smiled down at her and the sweet-mercy feeling came, she'd dropped her store key. They both reached to retrieve it at the same time, their hands meeting at the metal of the key, which was as antique as the store it helped to lock up.

She'd met his gaze.

Jennifer closed her eyes now and leaned against the door as she relived the sizzling burn in his look. He'd wanted to kiss her too—she was sure of it. She inspected the situation from every angle in her head. They had chemistry—there was no denying that. And more, she felt certain that if they had kissed, it would have been a toe-curling, fiery experience.

"Gah!" she yelled to the store and shoved away from the door. She intended to go upstairs and put her overactive hormones to work cleaning out the apartment. As she moved across the room, her eyes fell on the bottle with its mysterious message. She detoured so she could walk behind the counter and get a better look.

"Wouldn't it be great if there was life advice inside?" She reached up, her fingers grazing the cool glass. "What's your story?"

The mystery of the bottle intrigued her, much like working the store had invigorated her, much like spending time with Paul Studly awakened her.

Mixed-up emotions battled for space inside her head. She wanted to get back to Eddie, her apartment, and her band. Her boss had only allowed a two-week grace period of absence, and she would be in trouble with her job if she didn't make it home before her time was up.

This morning, her only thoughts had been of selling the place.

Tonight, in the dim light coming from the streetlight outside the windows, her resolve faltered. She saw no point in denying that she'd liked working in the store, selling things to people who were excited to receive those things. It really did feel like so much more than selling old junk; she sold the memories that went with each item, the history on the card, the time lost but found again to the person making the purchase. And she'd turned a profit. A *good* profit.

At the music store, she only made fifteen dollars an hour. Her boss believed her to be horrifically overpaid and threatened to cut her salary all the time. And for being a dinky retail store, she supposed she did receive wages that surpassed the norm. But she had the music degree, and when her boss hired her, he'd been impressed enough to offer higher wages.

It would take nearly two months of working to bring in the kind of money she'd seen in only one day of the antique store. And she knew there were inventory costs and other bills, but those were things she didn't have to worry about quite yet. The store came to her fully stocked. It was pretty much all profit.

And then there was this man to consider—a real, live,

breathing man who looked at her, not past her, or over her, or around her.

"Do you think I've wasted time chasing Eddie?" she asked the bottle. But it remained as mute as Cleopatra had.

Jennifer took a deep breath. "I'm wasting time talking to antiques is what I'm wasting my time doing. You keep your secrets, little bottle, and be glad you don't have a nosy aunt confusing you enough to talk to inanimate objects."

She headed toward the back stairs, wishing she could stop thinking about the store, about the way Paul had looked at her, about the way Eddie never did . . .

When she entered the apartment and faced the many pictures Daisy had of her on the walls, she wondered if maybe talking to the creepy stuff downstairs wouldn't be her better option.

"Your aunt must love you very much," Paul had said.

He'd talked more about his dad during dinner, about taking over a business from someone he respected and loved so much. His pain still felt raw as he'd spoken. Jennifer worried that the connection he felt to her might only be because he viewed their circumstances as the same.

But their circumstances weren't the same at all.

Daisy had meddled in Jennifer's life. Daisy had hated listening to Jennifer play the guitar and called the instrument a tool of the devil. Daisy scolded, lectured, and involved her opinion where it absolutely wasn't welcome. She'd called Jennifer cheeky when Jennifer informed her that unsolicited advice was never appreciated.

Jennifer heaved a deep breath and let her gaze trail over the walls of the living room. There were five pictures of Jennifer with Daisy in that room alone. And from her visit earlier, she knew there were many more throughout the apartment.

What she didn't know was *why.* Why would Daisy have all these pictures? The feeling of suffocation settled over her again. How was she supposed to stay in this place with all this stuff that disproved her best-loved opinions of her aunt? She did the only thing she could think to do. It was habit, really, that led her to pulling her phone out of her pocket and pressing the phone icon next to Eddie's name.

He didn't answer, which irritated her, since he never went anywhere. The hour was a little late simply because she'd lost track of time with Paul, but not so late that he'd be asleep. Eddie was a night-owl. She hit end when his voicemail answered, but before she could stuff her phone back into her pocket, she thought about Misti coming over to "practice." Jennifer suddenly wondered what exactly they were practicing. She pressed her finger on the phone icon again and listened to the rings.

On the third ring, he answered with a, "Wassup, my flower?"

She was surprised that he actually answered and, at first, could think of nothing to say. Finally she said, "Do you remember those times when my aunt came to visit me?"

"Yup."

"Do you think she liked me?"

"I dunno. I didn't pay attention to anything much beyond you not liking her."

Jennifer frowned, not thinking much of that answer at all. He didn't remember Daisy not liking her but only remembered her not liking Daisy. "What if I was wrong about her?"

"So what if you were? She's dead. It's not like it matters."

"Eddie!"

"What?"

"That's a horrible thing to say!"

He laughed, which made Jennifer want to reach through the phone and punch his shoulder. "She always lectured you, tried to tell you what to do, and interfered with your life choices. You can't tell me you care what that crazy lady thought of you."

"Right. There's that." But as Jennifer looked around the room at the pictures, she didn't think it was as true as it used to be. What if Daisy hadn't been interfering; what if she'd meant to be helping?

"So how did practice go?" she asked, changing the subject.

"Practice?"

"Yeah. With Misti."

"Oh. Right. Misti."

The way he said it led Jennifer to believe that there hadn't been any music practicing going on, unless one counted the siren song of seduction. And for the millionth time in her life with Eddie, she felt the flare-up of jealousy, of never being good enough, of always being a backup plan, but never the *actual* plan. So she changed the subject again. "I had a great night."

He seemed relieved to follow the new topic of conversation, anything that led away from him having to discuss his time with Misti. "Oh yeah? What'd you do?"

"I went on a date. Turns out Paul Studly is everything his name promised. He took me to the most quaint little Italian restaurant. Then we walked the boardwalk back to my place. I'm kind of hoping the store takes a little longer to sell." She didn't know where the words had come from, just that she wanted him to feel even the smallest sting of jealousy in comparison to what he put her through all the time.

A byproduct of her trying to make Eddie jealous, she found herself capable of sorting through the tumult of feelings she'd had in regard to Paul and discovered that, yes, she did want to stay a little longer if he was always going to be so attentive and interesting to talk to.

She'd liked Paul, genuinely liked him. And maybe . . . no, no maybes. She was in the market to sell her business and her apartment, not in the market for a man. She'd spent a long time trying to get Eddie's attention, and she couldn't allow those years to be wasted.

"You can't date your realtor. There's gotta be some kind of law that doesn't allow them to fraternize with their clients." He seemed irritated by the idea. Good. She was irritated with his "practice" time with Misti. Now they were even, or at least closer to even, because she doubted Eddie felt any real jealousy.

"There aren't any laws about dating your realtor," she said.

He didn't respond for a few beats before saying, "Well, there ought to be. How do you know he isn't just after your inheritance?"

Now she was irritated for reasons she didn't want to examine too closely. Had Eddie *really* implied that Paul couldn't possibly like her for her, but only for her inheritance? "Paul is not after my money. He's amassed his own fortune. He owns his own business and carries no debt." Paul had informed her that the best way for businesses to *stay* in business is to manage their debt intelligently. He'd given her all kinds of information as if schooling her in the fine art of entrepreneurism, as if he wanted to make sure she knew how to run a business successfully, as if he planned on her staying.

"Nice. So you're into him because he's hot and rich. How shallow does that make you?"

She pulled the phone way from her ear long enough to glare at it. "After all these years of being my friend, you really think that I could ever behave like that? You know what? I don't even know why I called you. Goodbye, Eddie. Tell Misti I'm sorry if I interrupted her *practice*."

She threw as much scorn as she could into the word "practice" and jabbed her finger at the icon that ended the call. "Moron!" she yelled to the phone before hurling it at the couch.

Paul would never call her shallow. Paul would never ditch her for another girl and then act all wounded when she went out with someone else. Paul would be her true friend, he would—

Jennifer straightened. One date, that wasn't technically a date, and she was making assumptions about the guy? How did she know what he was really like? A few hours wasn't enough time to know anything about a person.

Except she felt like she knew more about Paul from those few hours than she did about Eddie after years of trying to figure him out.

Jennifer sighed, closed her eyes, and put all thoughts of Paul, with his quiet kindness and his smoldering gaze, aside. She also put aside all thoughts of Eddie and the silky richness of his voice when he sang, the pure poetry of the words he put to music that made her whole body shiver, and the way she kind of hated him at the moment. She moved to the wall closest to her and took down one of the pictures. She had work to do.

But in spite of her best intentions, she thought a lot about Eddie. And to her surprise, she thought even more about Paul.

Four

"You've met someone," Alison said.

Paul readjusted the Bluetooth in his ear as he surveyed the beach house in the town just north of Seashell Beach. "What?" he couldn't keep the guilty squeak of surprise out of his voice. His secretary knew him too well, and there was simply no hiding anything from her, but that didn't stop him from trying. "Why would you say that?"

"You were humming in between telling me dimensions. It's like you forgot I was on the phone. What's her name?"

He sighed and gave in. "Jennifer."

Alison groaned. "This Jennifer doesn't happen to have the last name of Day, does she?"

He squirmed under the scrutiny of her question. "It might."

"Paul, dating your client is a terrible idea."

"Why?"

She made a *tsk* noise. "Because it means you aren't thinking about what's best for the transaction; you're thinking what's best for you."

"You say that like it's a bad thing. When was the last time I thought about what was best for me?"

She didn't answer, but only because she didn't know the answer. No one knew. Not even *he* knew.

"Exactly," he said. "So isn't it about time?"

She waited a long time before responding. Since he needed to walk off the property to make sure the fencing didn't have any issues, he let her take her time. The client who wanted to buy a beach-front property refused to have his time wasted by people who didn't build adequate fences. He refused to look at anything until Paul had personally checked it out first.

"I guess it is about time," she said finally. "So are you going to ask Miss Day out before the property sells or after?"

"If the property sells, she's planning on heading right back to Oregon." He spied a hole cut in the fence with tin snips. It was likely the work of some local teens using the point to gain access to a private beach. He'd have to let the owner know and let his client know that maybe this wasn't the best property after all. Even if the hole was fixed, the teens would just find a way to reopen the access point.

His secretary made a noise Paul didn't recognize. "Don't sabotage a sale just to keep a girl around."

He thought about that advice. "But what if keeping the girl around is what I want?"

Alison actually laughed at that. "Well in that case . . . want me to buy some mice to let loose on her property?"

He laughed too. "I'll keep you posted if it'll be necessary."

"Okay. And if the mice don't work, we can always try an ant infestation, or we could spray paint the walls with gang-related symbols and tell prospective buyers that, for whatever reason, the gangs have declared this property their turf."

Paul laughed even harder. "You deserve a raise."

"Duly noted. I'll make sure to put a reminder to make it happen in your calendar."

"Goodbye, Alison."

When she hung up, he was still smiling. Before he went to any kind of extremes of sabotaging the sale, he needed to make certain that his emotions were real. That meant he needed to spend more time with the girl. Paul eagerly finished up his work for the client who was fussy about fences so he could ask Jennifer Day out on a proper date. And he'd be certain to clarify the detail of it being a real date to her to make sure she understood his intentions. He'd too often been involved in mixed signals and wrong signals. He didn't want bad communication to get in the way of something that felt promising.

He called her cell phone several times, but it went straight to voicemail on each occasion, making him wonder if she'd forgotten to charge her phone or if she'd turned it off on purpose because she didn't want to be bothered.

Either way, he'd have to go see her in person.

He didn't mind that idea at all.

Five

Jennifer turned her phone off when she realized Eddie wouldn't be calling to apologize. Apologies weren't his style. They never had been. But it still hurt her feelings to look at her phone screen and see nothing. No missed calls, no waiting messages.

Eddie was a tool.

And in order to stop obsessing over what that tool thought or did, she turned her phone off. It made it easier to focus on all the work waiting for her.

She'd had no idea how hard it would be to clear out Daisy's apartment—the clothes, the books, the spices kept in the pantry, all served as different pieces to the complicated puzzle that made up her aunt. And the more pieces she snapped into place, the more she found herself respecting Daisy for the woman she'd been and the life she'd lived. Jennifer even grew to almost like her aunt.

It was the journal she'd found somewhere around two

in the morning that solidified Jennifer's regret that she never took the time to get to know the woman hiding underneath the floppy hats. The journal began during Daisy's college days. They began with a boy named Gregg.

Gregg, according to nineteen-year-old Daisy, was a tall, blond, blue-eyed pillar of perfection. He was the TA for the beginning guitar class Daisy had signed up for. He put in a lot of overtime work helping Daisy learn the instrument, but Daisy spent more time studying him than she did studying notes and strings. She fell hard into the abyss called love.

In the meantime, Daisy mentioned a lot about some other guy named Kade. She called him her best friend. He seemed to be present in a daily sort of way. She complained that he was a Jiminy Cricket sometimes; complained that he wasn't adventurous enough other times. She complained that Kade didn't understand her love of music. She complained that Kade spent a lot of time complaining about all the time she spent with Gregg. "I can relate, Kade," she said, thinking about Eddie.

Jennifer was still up at six in the morning reading the journal. She stretched from where she'd cuddled up on Daisy's couch with Daisy's afghan before she closed the book Daisy had written.

She rubbed her hand down her face. "I'm sorry, Aunt Daisy. I didn't know," Jennifer said to the apartment. And there was so much she really hadn't known. She hadn't known that Daisy had a fiery spirit or that she'd loved music so much—especially since she always treated Jennifer's music as if it was the devil's own lyrics. But most of all, what Jennifer hadn't known was that her aunt deserved her love.

Jennifer stayed up all night with the artifacts and writings of her aunt, yet she didn't feel exhausted like she knew she probably ought to. Jennifer stood from the couch and wandered to Daisy's kitchen to see what she could forage together as a meal. She felt a strange intimacy with her aunt

MESSAGE IN A BOTTLE

as she opened cupboards and the fridge. This was all food Daisy had purchased with the intention of eating. Most of the fridge contents needed to be thrown out since they'd all spoiled under the abandonment of the person who'd bought them; but the eggs still looked okay—okay enough for Jennifer to dare scramble them up. And she found bacon in the freezer.

She thought a lot about her aunt as she used her things, ate her food, lived in her world. She decided she'd definitely keep the antique store opened and operating until the sale went through—in honor of the woman whose friendship Jennifer suddenly missed very much. "I wish I'd known," she murmured several times as she prepared and ate her meal, as she tidied up so the place looked respectable to prospective buyers, as she readied herself to open the antique store, as she unlocked the door for the day's business.

She kept her phone in her pocket, though she still kept it off, but half-way through the day, it occurred to her that maybe Paul would try to reach her regarding the sale of the store. She turned the phone back on immediately and checked her messages to make sure she hadn't missed anything from Paul.

She had.

According to her phone, she'd missed four calls from him, and she had one message asking her if she wanted to go to dinner again. The way he phrased the question made his request sound official—like a date. Warmth shivered through her as she considered the idea of another dinner with Paul.

Warmth and dread.

She'd never really considered dating anyone aside from Eddie. He'd been her goal since high school. He was the best friend she followed around in hopes that one day he would see her for who she was; that one day he would love her the way she loved him. Eddie's talent had been what captured her. His voice made her entire soul quake; it stirred up emotions in her she hadn't known existed until that first time she heard him sing. And the reaction never changed. All these years later, she still felt that stirring of her soul, that sifting of her consciousness.

His lyrics had the same haunting effect as his voice. He wrote songs about politics, government, change. He wrote words that mattered—words that would alter the world if the world would only listen.

She'd turned away a lot of dates waiting for Eddie to really see her; how could she go with Paul? Would it be a betrayal? But she couldn't deny that she wanted to go with Paul—the man who looked at her, not past her.

It was as she considered the implications of spending time with Paul in a decidedly social environment versus business that her phone rang in her hand. She pressed the answer icon, thinking the call had to be from Paul even as her brain finally registered that the name on the phone said Eddie.

Her emotions tangled inside her. It wasn't Paul. Eddie called back? Eddie never called back. "Hello?"

"Jenn, my flower, how are you?"

"I . . . I'm okay?" She hadn't meant it to sound like a question, but she couldn't figure out his reason for calling, and she burned a little with the guilt she felt over considering going to dinner with Paul.

"Good. I'm glad you're doing good. Hey, listen, I just wanted to say I was sorry about last night."

She pressed her palm to her forehead. Eddie called to say he was sorry? What did that mean for her? "Really?"

"Yeah. I know you aren't shallow, and you aren't stupid either. You wouldn't let someone take advantage of you—especially when you've only just met him and don't know anything about him."

Eddie was right. She wasn't stupid. She heard the real

message under his words. He wasn't telling her he believed she wouldn't let anyone take advantage of her; he was telling her that Paul was trying to take advantage of her and that she should be suspicious.

She felt disappointment that he'd only called to give her a lecture, that he didn't feel genuinely sorry. "Yes, well . . ." she said, "Paul isn't like that. He doesn't have to take advantage of anyone, because he's already successful on his own. But he is a great help in matters of business. I think under his tutelage, I could really be great at running my aunt's shop."

"What are you talking about? You don't want to run it. You want to sell it and come back. That was the plan. Face it. Conquer it. Come home. That's always been the plan."

Always. He made it sound like they'd been working on this for their whole lives and not just the two weeks since her aunt's passing. "I might want to run it. I opened the store for business yesterday, and I liked running things. There's a lot more satisfaction in operating my own business than there is in working for the music store."

"No. No, Jennifer. You don't want to run it. You've never wanted anything to do with your aunt."

Jennifer straightened one of the tags on a set of metal soldiers on the counter and grunted at Eddie's manic insistence that he knew what she wanted. "I might. Look, customers are coming in, and I want to help them, so we can't talk right now."

"Fine. Call me tonight when you close your aunt's store." He emphasized the words *aunt's store*.

Which just made her angry. "I won't be able to call tonight. I have a date with Paul. Maybe tomorrow."

She hung up as she heard him say, "Wait, Jenn—"

There was a certain level of satisfaction to her actions. She'd been hanging on to Eddie for so long that to hang *up* on him instead brought relief, an ability to stand straighter without that weight of unrequited love on her shoulders.

She called Paul, but his phone went straight to voicemail, and she felt too insecure to leave a message; she hung up. What would she say to him anyway?

She decided to put Eddie and Paul out of her mind for the rest of the day as she helped customers. She loved when people showed up and found an item that spoke to their souls to the point they couldn't leave the store without buying it. Her aunt had known what she was doing when she purchased her inventory.

As Jennifer's second day of shop-keeping wore on, she grew to love it more and more. She loved the histories printed on the cards and found that she'd even grown a sort of fondness for the life-size Cleopatra. Jennifer no longer feared the wooden fingers wrapping around her throat and closing off her breathing. In just two days, she found comfort in the items that had frightened her as a kid when she'd come to work with Daisy.

When there were no customers, she worked hard to become acquainted with her merchandise so she could be more helpful when people came in with specific requests. Maybe it was just because of the tourist season and the warm weather, but the second day open was equal to the business of the first day.

"I could really make a decent living here," she murmured to herself. It was late afternoon, and Jennifer's stomach grumbled over its neglected state. The store had finally emptied itself of shoppers—probably because they were all hungry too—and Jennifer decided she'd close for a minute and try one of the restaurants within the general radius of her store and then come right back with her food. She could eat in the backroom until she heard the bells jingling on the door.

She wondered if that was how Daisy used to handle being in the store all day with no breaks. Or maybe Daisy hired someone. Or maybe Daisy was simply superhuman and never needed to eat.

But superhuman people didn't die before their nieces had a chance to get to know them . . . before their nieces had a chance to say sorry.

As she reached to turn the lock so she could sneak out the back to go get food, the door opened.

"I'm sorry, but we're closing," she informed the man.

"You can't be closing," he said, his hazel eyes narrowing. "It isn't six yet. Daisy would rather drink a bottle of poison than close early. Where is she anyway?" He looked around in an attempt to find the missing owner. He was tall, with dark hair and nice eyes. *What is it with the good-looking men in this town?*

"Daisy isn't here." Jennifer wasn't sure how to handle this new situation of someone actually knowing Daisy. She should've seen it coming. Daisy might have been buried in the family plot in Oregon, but her life had been here. This was her neighborhood. The woman lived in the upstairs apartment and worked in the shop. She likely knew everyone on the street—probably everyone in all of Seashell Beach. How many times would Jennifer have to share the news that Daisy had died?

"Is she at an estate sale?" The man didn't wait for Jennifer to answer before he turned and started to pace. "I hate it when she beats me to those things. So who died?"

Jennifer startled, her throat felt like it might be closing off. "Excuse me?"

"Who died? Mrs. Perkins up on Galfrey? I heard her health was failing. Blast! I hate to think she got Perkins' estate before I had a chance to pick it over."

"*She* did." Jennifer finally spit the words out.

The man gave Jennifer a long, sorrowful look. "She really did?" He must have really liked Daisy for him to be taking her death so hard. "I can't believe I missed out! I was so looking forward to it!"

Jennifer took a step back, horrified by his declaration. So maybe he didn't like her aunt that much after all. "Excuse me?"

He stopped his ranting long enough to give Jennifer a look of confusion. "Did I say something wrong?"

"I didn't exactly get along with Daisy, but I don't think it's in very good taste to say you were excited to see her die." She couldn't believe she was defending Daisy. So many things had changed in the course of only two days.

It was his turn to take a step back. "*Daisy's* dead?"

"Yes. Wait. Who were you talking about?

"Mrs. Perkins—and don't get me wrong. I'm not glad to see Mrs. Perkins die either. I don't actually know her. I just know her estate was quite valuable. I was only talking business."

"Oh." Jennifer looked at her hands and felt confused and overwhelmed.

The man spoke again, his voice considerably softer and carrying the mournful note of someone genuinely sorry. "I didn't know about Daisy. I'm so sorry for your loss. She was a good friend to me."

Jennifer nodded.

"I'd ask if you were her daughter, but since Daisy didn't have kids . . . ?"

"I'm her niece," Jennifer confirmed.

"I'm Henry Lancaster. Daisy and I work—*worked*—together a lot. We're in the same sort of business. We buy estate furniture and sell what we find."

Jennifer felt a little dubious of his explanation. "So you buy things cheap from dead people and their mourning kids so you can sell it for a profit?" He made the business that had been growing on her sound pretty base and inhuman. Maybe she'd get rid of the thing after all . . .

To her surprise, Henry chuckled. "Wow. That makes us sound like sharks when you put it that way. No, it isn't like that. I mean it sort of is, but not in a bad way. We buy things from estates where the children or heirs don't want to deal with the hassle of researching the value on individual items. Sometimes we handle the liquidations as well, if they don't want to hold a public estate sale. Some people just want to collect their share and move on with their own lives— especially those who are not-so-grieving. Your aunt and I understand the value of the items left behind and facilitate the transactions that allow the people who desperately desire those items to obtain them. We connect people with the past."

She liked that he'd put it that way and offered him a smile. "That's exactly how I feel when I sell items to customers in my store." She felt surprise at her own words. She'd just called it *her* store. Paul's suggestions must really be rubbing off on her. "I like that every item has a story."

"Daisy was a stickler for stories. She never let any item enter her store without finding out where it had come from and what it had been through. Which brings me to why I'm here," he continued. "Daisy mentioned an antique show coming to Seashell Beach. Since I was in the neighborhood, I thought I'd stop by and get the information. You wouldn't happen to know anything about it, would you?"

Jennifer shook her head.

"Well then, maybe I'll get the information and let *you* know about it."

They talked awhile longer about the business until finally Henry handed over his card and told her to call if she was interested in learning the ropes. She tucked the card under the till and felt torn between the idea of making the business work and walking away.

She thought a lot about her conversation with Henry. She'd basically accused him of taking advantage of the people left behind, but his defense had been an inadvertent attack on her. He called some of those people left behind with their inheritances the *not-so-grieving*—the ones wanting to collect money from their inheritances so they could get on with their lives.

Wasn't that what she was? A not-so-grieving heir who just wanted to collect without being forced to look at the real value of the legacy left to her?

Her stomach tightened with her new self-awareness. She had received a great gift. She hadn't asked for it but had received it anyway. And what had she done with it? Complained, whined, moaned, belittled, and cut down the person who had apparently been so much more than Jennifer imagined. Jennifer was the very person she'd criticized her aunt and Henry of being. She swallowed the guilt.

Being someone and staying someone aren't the same thing. She gave a self-depreciative laugh. That saying came from Aunt Daisy's. Daisy had been filled with little moral quips like that.

Jennifer reached up and let her fingertips hover over the glass bottle. She thought she'd known everything about her aunt, but it turned out Daisy was like the bottle too, seemingly transparent on the outside but keeping her true self furled up in an unreadable note of secrets.

I could stay, Jennifer thought. Staying would allow her to fully realize the value of what she'd been given. If she decided to sell it later, at least she would have given her aunt a chance—the chance she'd never given while Daisy was alive. Paul would help her and this Henry guy, too. She could make a life here in this new community and unlock the secrets of Daisy Day. She liked the idea of the stories and decided if she stayed, she'd never let anything in her store that didn't have a history.

Customers came in, forcing Jennifer to turn her attention to the present and not the myriad possibilities of the future in front of her. While she busied herself with helping a young couple find a vintage engagement ring with which to make their relationship permanent, Paul walked in. He tossed her a knowing smile as she handed off a white gold ring with a half-carat miner's-cut diamond to the young woman and then parroted information from the history card.

"It's perfect," the girl cooed and leaned into her fiancé.

The price tag made the young man swallow hard and gently suggest they try a jewelry store instead. The girl's expression fell, and she slowly tugged the ring back over her knuckle to hand off to Jennifer. But Jennifer shrugged and made a *tsking* sound instead of taking the ring back.

The girl paused. "What?"

"I've just always believed that when you start out a relationship that's meant to be timeless, it seems to mean so much more when you use something that's already stood the test of time to represent that relationship."

Which was all the encouragement the girl needed. Her young man warmed up after several minutes as the girl made comparisons to the life they would live together that would be as strong as the lives of the people who had given and received the ring before them. They would marry, like the young shoemaker mentioned on the history card married the daughter of a prominent banker. They would live together in harmony in spite of all the outside forces that would work against them. And they would make sacrifices for each other—the way the young shoemaker made such sacrifices to buy the woman he loved the perfect wedding ring.

Jennifer placed the ring in a velvet box, then wrapped the box up in gauzy paper and tied the package into a neat little square with a bow of lace.

The girl gushed and sighed and acted as though her

fiancé had bought her the world. Jennifer smiled because she felt that, in a way, he had.

"You're scary good at this," Paul said after the couple left. He approached her, maybe to shake her hand or something professional like that, but with the sale being so huge, and her excitement over pairing together the couple with the ring, she forgot herself and wrapped her arms around his neck and squeezed tightly.

For the barest of seconds, he seemed too surprised to respond, but that moment passed quickly and his arms tightened around her in a way that made Jennifer feel like she hadn't made a mistake in spontaneously hugging him. When she pulled away, she only moved far enough to look into Paul's eyes. She wanted to discern what his feelings were because she knew her feelings at that moment were anything but professional.

Their faces were close, his breath warm on her cheek. He chewed some sort of minty gum. Her heart rate quickened as their breathing tangled into each other. He smiled and stepped away, leaving her feeling dizzy.

"Sorry," she said. "That was just kind of . . ."

"Exhilarating?"

"Yes."

"A good sale always is. And *that*, my lady, was a good sale."

She smiled, feeling a surge of pride that she never felt at the music store, that she honestly never felt anywhere except with her own music when the chords came out sounding exactly as she'd intended them to sound.

"So, you got my message I'm assuming?" he asked. "Because you called but didn't leave a message back. My mom says it's arrogance, but I say it's confidence. I am assuming that you are very happy to have dinner with me tonight and that you've spent the whole day excited to see me." He grinned wide, but in his face there was also a question, an uncertainty that belied his arrogance or confidence. He was afraid she'd say no.

Her cheeks warmed with the realization that she'd called him but not dared to leave a message. Of course he'd seen the missed call. It humbled and excited her to realize she could make him feel such insecurity. "Yes, I called. The store was . . . busy. I should have left a message for you. Sorry."

"Sorry?" His insecurity transformed into something else; something like pain registered on his face.

"No, I mean. I'm sorry I didn't leave a message. And I've been looking forward to spending time with you all day." She took her turn to flash her biggest and brightest smile.

He visibly relaxed, his shoulders loosening. "That's very good to hear. You ready to close up?"

She nodded, and he locked the door and helped her straighten the shelves while she counted down the till. Then he led her out onto the street.

"I confess I want to show off my town a bit," he said after offering her his arm. The last person to offer her an arm to hold onto was Mike Higgins. Mike had taken her to senior prom. She believed he might have actually liked her, might have been interested enough to get to know her better. But she'd spent the majority of the dance seeking out Eddie's tall, lanky silhouette back-dropped against the low lights. That was the first time during their friendship that Eddie had asked a girl out on a real date—a girl who wasn't Jennifer. She'd accepted Mike's invitation to the dance because she believed staying home alone while Eddie went on a date would be worse.

She'd been wrong.

Watching Eddie dance and laugh and nuzzle his date's neck had been the worst torture she'd ever known. She didn't date much after that. Dating never felt fair to the person taking her out. How could she expect someone to pay for her movie ticket or dinner and pretend to make small-talk conversation when the entire time her only thoughts were of the one boy who never asked her out?

As she wrapped her hand around Paul's arm, she felt something new, a stirring of excitement, a desire to know more about the person who walked by her side, a need to be close to him.

"And this is where you'll find the best cupcakes and pastries on the planet. Seriously. I make a habit of becoming acquainted with all bakeries, and none of them come close to our bakery." Paul pointed to the store to their right. Jennifer planned on just peeking in the window, but he stopped so they could go in.

He bought a lemon blueberry cupcake for her and an apple crisp for him from Delilah's Desserts. Figuring out how to eat the confection proved to be a task since the thing was nearly as big as her face and done up so beautifully that it seemed like a crime against humanity to eat such artwork.

With her first bite, she almost committed to stay permanently in Seashell Beach for the rest of her life. Lemon custard and real blueberries burst into her mouth. Jennifer never considered herself a cupcake fan, but she was now converted. "I think I just died," she said after swallowing the first bite.

He cocked his head to the side for her to explain herself.

She rolled her eyes with pleasure. "That was heavenly."

Paul laughed. They walked the boardwalk all the way to the end, and since it was the weekend, street musicians, chalk artists, and a guy who made bubbles big enough to hold a person inside them were all out collecting coins from tourists entertained well enough to part with their money.

"So tell me about yourself," Paul said, taking a final bite of his own cupcake.

"There's not much to tell. I grew up in Oregon; I have one brother and two parents. We're pretty typical. I majored in music—much to the dismay and disapproval of pretty much everyone I know, and now I work a job that only mostly meets the bills because it turns out my parents were right: there really aren't any jobs for my major unless one plans on teaching in junior high schools."

Paul gave her a look she couldn't read. "I take it teaching wasn't on the menu?"

"I considered it. But ultimately, I didn't want to teach music. I wanted to *be* a musician."

"Just guitar?"

She shrugged. "I also play the piano and the saxophone."

"Strings *and* wind? Is that hard?"

"No harder than someone speaking Russian, Chinese, and Turkish."

Paul nodded. "Turkish is easy. I learned that one when I was fourteen."

"Really?"

"No. But I have an excellent Pig Latin accent."

Jennifer laughed, unable to think of anywhere on Earth where she'd rather be, or any person she'd rather be with. Paul felt comfortable, like a nice pair of flats after an entire day of being stuck in high heels.

"So why the saxophone?" he asked.

Her face warmed as she thought of the one person she did *not* want to be thinking about. "A guy once told me he thought it was the sexiest instrument ever created and that he imagined girls who played it would be the best kissers on the planet."

Paul considered her answer for several long moments before tossing his cupcake wrapper into a nearby trash bin. "So is he right?"

"Right about what?"

"Are sax players the best kissers ever?"

Her face heated up even further, if such a thing was

possible. "I don't know," she answered. "I haven't ever kissed any."

Paul laughed, "I'm not talking about who you've kissed. The guy never confirmed or denied his own rumor after you learned an instrument for him?"

She blew out a long breath and muttered, "He never figured out I was even alive."

Paul went silent for a second before he said in a low voice, "Obviously, that guy was blind and stupid." And then he put an arm over her shoulder and gave a squeeze—just like that—an arm over her shoulder, as if such a thing was easy, as if their new friendship had moved into that kind of intimacy already.

And maybe it had, because his arm felt natural around her; it felt safe. His taller frame allowed his arm to settle nicely in a way that neither of them were hindered in walking like she'd always felt when Eddie tried to put his arm around her when they walked.

But Eddie never meant the arm thing to be something intimate. He treated her like he'd treat one of his buddies, like a kid sister, like someone he never intended to kiss or to love. She leaned into Paul a little, liking this very different kind of attention.

Paul gave another squeeze. "I personally always thought the piano was the sexiest instrument, but then I've never kissed a saxophone player, so maybe I've been wrong about that all my life."

Did he mean he wanted to try kissing a saxophone player? Her heart rate went into double time, making her feel as though she'd been sprinting down Tangerine Street rather than casually strolling. She loved the piano too . . . all her studies had been for the piano until the day Eddie mentioned his band needed a guitar player.

"The piano is a beautiful instrument," she agreed.

"But not sexy?" He peeked at her from the corner of his

eye and gave a teasing smile that melted her insides into puddles.

"It is definitely an instrument of passion." Did he know what it did to her when he smiled like that?

"But it's not your favorite instrument," he guessed. "I can tell by your hesitation. I'm assuming the guitar is your favorite?"

"It's been the one to occupy most of my days over the last few years." She didn't add that it was because of the same guy who had insisted that saxophone players were great kissers.

"I'd be interested in hearing you play."

"Which one?"

"All of them . . . as long as you promise it takes a long time."

She smiled. "Are you flirting with me?"

"I certainly hope so."

Before she could process his honesty, he'd stopped and swept up his arm to indicate the restaurant. "I told my friend Cái about you. He insisted we have dinner with him tonight at the Fortune Café. Are you okay with Chinese?"

"I'm okay with any kind of food I didn't have to make."

He held open the door for her, and she led the way into the restaurant.

They were seated by a younger woman who said, "Paul! You did show up! Cái will be so glad to see you. He'll want to serve you himself."

The older Asian man in question appeared with a notepad in one hand and his other hand smoothing back his feathery white hair. "I didn't think you were coming," Cái said, his voice holding a tone of reproof.

"We were exploring the town a little," Paul said.

Cái blew a raspberry. "You mean you had dessert first." Cái pointed at Paul's face, which went immediately red as he snapped up his cloth napkin and dabbed it at his cheek where a bit of apple filling gave away the truth.

Cái gave a knowing grin and turned his attention to Jennifer. "So I hear you're my new neighbor."

Jennifer fumbled a second before answering. "Temporary neighbor. I'm actually selling the antique store, which is why I'm hanging out with a realtor."

Cái nodded, his eyes sympathetic. "That is too bad to hear. Daisy wanted to keep her store in her family. She'd hoped you would love it like she loved it. She'd hoped it would give you happiness like it gave her happiness."

What could be said to that? Jennifer's mouth worked as she tried to form some kind of answer. This man had known Daisy, had known Daisy's intentions, and now knew Jennifer's intentions were to throw Daisy's gift away.

"Not everyone's meant to own a business, Cái," Paul said. "You know that."

Jennifer felt intense gratitude at Paul's interruption.

Cái dipped his head to show his understanding and mentioned something about giving them more time to look at the menu, but before he could walk away, Jennifer said, "I think I understand her better . . . my aunt, I mean. And I *am* considering my options with the business. I just . . . wanted you to know that."

Cái smiled warmly, the deep lines in his face folding up around his eyes. "Make sure you eat a cookie before you leave. There's always good advice in my cookies."

Paul grinned at Cái's retreating back and whispered, "Told you he thinks he has magical cookies."

Jennifer laughed and focused her attention on the menu.

Dinner conversation had nothing to do with the antique store. Paul told her about growing up in Southern California and confessed to having never once been surfing in spite of the fact that he lived right next to the ocean.

"That's like living in Colorado and never skiing. Even *I've* been surfing, and I didn't grow up here," she told him.

"You've been surfing?" he asked.

"Yep. And I'm pretty good at it. Daisy took me." She felt a pang in her chest. *Daisy had taken her.* How had she never noticed that so much of her life had roads leading back to Daisy? "Maybe I'll teach you sometime," she added, trying to shake off her guilt. "You know, Cái shouldn't get too excited about having me for a neighbor. You wouldn't believe the awful things I did to my neighbors back home."

He smirked at her. "I don't really see you as the type to do awful things."

"Well, okay. I'm usually not that type, but we were in a feud of sorts with our next-door neighbors because the dad ran over my brother's new puppy on purpose."

"On purpose?"

"Yeah, the guy was a total loser. He complained because Wags dug holes under the fence to try to escape. One day, when Wags managed to get out so he could follow my brother to school, the neighbor saw him and backed up faster to hit him. We declared war after that."

"Wait. You named your dog Wags?"

She smirked at Paul. "We were little. I was ten. My brother was only six. It was his dog, and he named it. The point is that we are vengeful neighbors."

Paul laughed out loud at that. "I'm sorry. I know I should be giving your tale—no pun intended to the dog named Wags—more sobriety, being that the dog died and everything, but how vengeful can a six- and ten-year-old get?"

She gave an innocent shrug. "In the heat of summer, we put a dead fish under his car seat so it would rot and stink up his entire car."

He laughed again. "Okay. Remind me to never get you or your brother mad."

She grunted. "As mad as my brother is at me, the chances of him ever coming to California and you meeting him are impossibly thin."

"Why would he be mad at you?"

So Jennifer explained the will and how Tony had always sent cards to Aunt Daisy, had always been the one to draw her pictures and to make the phone calls Jennifer had never found the time to make. Then she explained how Tony had been left with a meager inheritance and how furious he'd been by his aunt's dismissal.

Paul listened and swirled the ice in his glass a moment before asking, "So you got the inheritance he wanted and that you wanted nothing to do with. That makes for some fun family drama."

"Right. Super good times. Things would've been better if she'd left the business to Tony. He's the solid one. I'm the . . ."

"What? You're the what?"

"The mess."

He gave her a half smile, the kind that made her heart skip beats. "You're in good company since you're talking to the guy who got caught with cupcake on his face. I wouldn't worry about your brother. He'll come around. After all, how many big sisters are willing to terrorize their neighbors for their baby brothers?"

She smiled back. "I just wish it wasn't all so complicated."

"Have you ever considered offering to let your brother buy the store?"

She frowned. "No. I didn't think he'd want it that way."

Paul shrugged, took a drink, then put his glass down. "You could at least invite him down here to help you sort through her things. Maybe there's something in your aunt's apartment that has special meaning to him and would mean a lot for him to receive."

The idea had merit. Involving Tony in the packing up process might go a long ways toward reconciliation. Or it might tick him off even further. She would have to take a little longer in considering asking Tony to help her . . . maybe call her mom for a second opinion.

When her parents left her to handle her inheritance on her own, it made her feel like she was hovering on the edge of a black hole. She felt the pull of her task's enormity and had no one to help her navigate her way out again—at least not until Paul showed up.

It occurred to her that perhaps her parents' lack of intrusion meant they'd taken her brother's side. She wouldn't blame them if that was the case. She was on his side too. "I don't blame him for being angry with me," she said after a moment of pushing food around her plate.

"I doubt he's angry."

She gave up on her food, not that dinner didn't taste great, but because she'd already filled up on the cupcake, and because thinking about her family made her stomach clench. "He's acting exactly like the greedy, grubby cousins who've made it very clear that they're angry. He has to be mad too. Why else isn't he talking to me?"

"Maybe his feelings are hurt alongside the fact that he's grieving over a loss he didn't see coming. He obviously cared about your aunt. Why else would he take the time to call her all the time before she died?" Paul put his fork down as well, and leaned on the elbows he'd propped up on the table. "Grieving turns perfectly rational, normal people into emotional lunatics. It took a long time for my family to figure out how to work without my dad."

"But you work now?"

Paul grinned. "Like a Swiss clock." He grinned even wider. "Okay. Not all the time. Sometimes we still have our quirks and issues, but all families do, right?"

"Right. So . . . your sisters . . . are they older or younger?"

"Both. I have one on each side."

"Does it ever bother them that you inherited the business and not them?"

"Not at first. It bothered Renee after the shock of losing our dad wore off. She felt like somehow she'd been left out of the decision-making process. She felt like she didn't get a say."

"What did you do?"

"The same thing I'm telling you to do. I offered to share it with her, offered to let her work for the company or go through stuff. She changed her mind about the whole deal after a couple weeks of hustling business. It just wasn't her thing. I still pay Mom a monthly percentage and will do so until she dies. Now, Renee and Amy are glad to know Mom is taken care of and that they won't ever have to worry over her finances."

"What do they do now?"

He talked about his sisters, the colleges they attended and the careers they now held. His older sister, Amy, had announced her engagement recently and turned their mother's head toward the idea of all her children marrying and providing grandchildren. They laughed over stories of him growing up with a house full of girls, with only his father to even things out a little. After dinner, he walked her home, his arm over her shoulder again, the laughter and good conversation continuing right to the last step up to her door.

She turned to face him, feeling the charge of energy between them intensify. "Thank you . . . for a wonderful evening," she said. "I didn't come to California expecting to find friendship. You were a delightful surprise."

The way he tilted his head to the side and the way his eyes seemed to search over her made her heart feel like it was skipping beats and beating too hard all at once. She didn't notice him move or shift, but somehow the distance closed until they were nearly touching. His eyes stayed riveted on hers. "The surprise has been all mine," he said. "I can't remember the last time I've laughed so much." He looked like he might say more but instead smiled softly.

A silence charged with all that crackling energy Jennifer thought just might kill her settled between them. "You know . . . you've almost convinced me to stay," Jennifer finally confessed.

"Really? What would it take to push you over the edge?" he asked.

"I don't know. I really like you, Paul." Honesty. Had she ever given such naked honesty to anyone before?

"I really like you too, Jennifer."

The words washed over her in the warmth of his breath, his lips suddenly so much closer. How did he keep moving forward without her noticing? Or had she been the one to close the distance?

If she were to shift in the slightest, her lips would be pressed against his. As she was in the midst of deciding to make that shift, her phone rang from inside her bag. She stepped back, confused by the distraction of the violin rendition of "Radioactive."

She tugged her phone from where it glowed in her purse and glanced at the screen. Some part of her hoped that after all the conversations she'd had about her brother and parents, maybe her family had decided to call. She frowned. "Eddie." She hadn't meant to say his name out loud.

"I thought you said you didn't have a boyfriend."

She looked up from the screen. "I don't."

Paul peered through the shadows cast by the streetlight and squinted as if trying to see her more clearly. "No. You don't. But you do have a guy you took sax lessons for. A guy whose call you seem eager to take." Was that hurt in his voice?

She stuffed her phone back into her purse and shook her head. "Yes. No. I mean, yes, the sax lessons were for him. But no, I'm not eager to take his call. I was hoping this was from my family. We spent so much time talking about them that I really miss them. I was hoping that they were calling."

Several seconds ticked by as Paul adjusted to this information. Then he smiled, and Jennifer felt like she could breathe again. "I think I understand." He took a step back, and her heart sank. If he was moving away from her then he couldn't possibly understand. She'd been planning on kissing him goodnight. And she still wanted to.

"Do you want to come inside for a minute for a drink?" She caught herself from physically cringing at the cliché of her words. How transparent did such an invitation make her?

His eyes spoke a kindness—a genuine understanding of something she didn't understand yet. "Maybe tomorrow night?"

"It's a date," she said, hoping he understood her meaning. She wanted it to be a date—wanted to see him again.

"Then I'll come by tomorrow night . . . if that's okay."

She considered closing the gap between them and kissing him anyway except he moved farther away so she bobbed her head up and down in agreement and turned to let herself into the shop. She fumbled with the key in the lock, knowing he waited to verify she made it inside safely. Relief flooded her when the lock finally clicked, proving she was not entirely incompetent. She turned back to Paul, who looked seriously good under the warm glow of the streetlight. "I'll see you tomorrow then?" she confirmed.

"I wouldn't miss it."

"Good."

She wouldn't miss it either. Not for anything.

Six

She punched her finger on the delete button to rid herself of Eddie's message without even listening to it. Not only did Eddie refuse to kiss her, he ruined all her chances of ever being kissed by anyone else. Jennifer stared at the phone in her hand and frowned as she wandered up the stairs to Aunt Daisy's apartment.

Once she changed into yoga pants and an old Fender T-shirt, she picked the phone up again and hit the call button for her brother's phone number.

She nearly dropped the phone in surprise when he actually answered. "Hey, Tony."

"Hey."

She looked out the window to the space where the black ocean felt like a hole in the world. "How are you?"

"Good."

Great. Monosyllables. Her favorite. He only resorted to monosyllables when he felt hurt. Paul had been right. Tony wasn't angry. He was sad.

She felt incredible guilt over her inheritance, which might account for why she wanted so badly to get rid of it—to sell it and not have to inspect her guilt too closely.

"So I've been thinking . . ." She decided to jump in with both feet. Forget asking for advice from her parents. Tony had been her buddy from the moment her parents brought him home from the hospital. She wanted to fix their relationship. "What if I paid for a plane ticket and you came down here to stay with me."

"I have to work."

Well, at least he'd moved past one syllable. Progress. "I know. But I also know you have vacation time coming. It would be nice to have you here. There's so much I think you'd want to see and be a part of. I want you to be able to gather things that are important to you."

"Why?"

And back to monosyllables. "Because you're my friend. Because she's your aunt too. Because there are things here that are special to you and that I know you want, but I don't know what those things are, and the last thing I want is to sell something or give it away or, worse, *throw* it away when it might be something you want. Come. You don't even have to talk to me if you don't want to. Don't come for me. Come for you."

"Me?" He grunted. "Why?"

"Because you deserve to know how much Daisy loved you. She has pictures of you all over her apartment and drawings you made when you were a kid tacked to her fridge. You deserve to see that."

Tony didn't say anything for a long time. Jennifer listened to the waves she could not see as they broke upon the sand. "Okay." The word came out as if it had torn his vocal cords on the way past. "But I'm driving. I don't need you to buy me a plane ticket."

Her chest tightened with his declaration of not needing her. She needed him, and it ached to not have the feeling reciprocated. "Okay." She almost added that his driving would be a good thing since it would save them from having to ship stuff back home, but she feared offending him and so left it at *okay*.

They hung up, and she found she felt better than she had since before Aunt Daisy died. Hopefully she'd feel better still once Tony showed up.

Seven

Jennifer was glad that the afternoon proved easier than the morning. She sighed deeply as she watched a young woman speaking quietly with an older man as the two of them stared at the vintage typewriter in the window. The store continued to do well, providing evidence that the first day's sales had been more than a simple fluke of good weather. Paul told her the sales would fluctuate—feast or famine—but she hadn't seen any signs of famine yet. She sighed deeply and thought about Paul.

She went to sleep thinking about Paul. And she woke up thinking about him still. The fact that he'd given her the courage to bandage her relationship with her brother raised Paul to hero status in her eyes. In a very real way, he'd saved her. Jennifer had spent pretty much the entire morning and a good part of the early afternoon fantasizing about kissing Paul when he came to get her that night. No more waiting. It was time to move forward with her life, and that meant letting other people in.

The bells on the door jingled, and she turned away from where she'd been staring at her bottle. But it wasn't a new customer.

"Tony!" She ran around the counter and nearly knocked him over in her rush to hug him. If he'd decided to hate her and to keep his visit all business, his resolve must have melted at her fierce embrace because, after a moment, he hugged her back.

When she finally pulled back enough to take in his disheveled clothes and mussed-up hair, she stated the obvious. "You drove all night?"

"I haven't been sleeping very well lately anyway. It gave me something to do other than stare at my ceiling."

"I'm glad you're here." She hugged him again before he could mention anything about *not* being glad to be there. "You have no idea how much I've missed you."

He made a noise like he'd intended on saying something but let the noise end on a strangled, unfinished note. He gently pulled free from Jennifer's grasp. "So . . . any buyers?" His voice carried the hurt, but more, now that Jennifer could view him fully, she *saw* the pain in the hunch of his shoulders, in the crease between his brow, in the tightening of his lips.

"No," she said. "Not yet. I . . . I'm not . . ." She almost told him about her second thoughts and her crazy idea of moving to California and running the place on her own but didn't want to commit to something without really knowing for herself that she wanted it. Besides, what if he wanted to buy the store? He'd never tell her he did if he thought she wanted it. That's the kind of relationship they had.

"Let me show you around," she said as she tugged his hand forward. She showed him the store, the backroom where the extra stock was dwindling and would soon either need to be replaced, or the business sold. When the man and woman came to the front, Jennifer realized the typewriter still sat in the window.

Jennifer had seen the girl staring at the typewriter with evident longing, and she felt fairly certain that the man wanted to buy it but for whatever reason, they approached the counter empty-handed.

Tony stepped back to allow Jennifer to work. Jennifer greeted them and asked if they had any questions.

"No," the woman said, casting a long look back toward the window.

"Just let me buy it," the man said. "You know you want it."

"It's okay to let me be independent, Dad. That isn't a necessity. It's a want. Not the same thing at all."

"But I'm the dad. It's my job to buy you things you don't need."

The woman laughed but shook her head and said she wasn't about to let him buy the typewriter.

"Before you go, you should at least get the entire story." Jennifer smiled.

"Oh, I read the card," the woman said.

"The whole story didn't fit on the card, so only the famous information went on display. You want to hear the rest?"

When they nodded that they did, Jennifer told about how the Royal Standard typewriter, like the card indicated, had once belonged to **David McCullough**, the author behind *1776*. "But more than a famous person having used it to write famous books, this particular typewriter had been found by a young father digging through the trash bin to try to find anything of value that he might sell to support and feed his family. He found the machine in the dump behind their house and took it inside to clean it up and sell it, but once his little daughter saw it all fixed up and looked at it

72

with such desire, he couldn't bear to part her from it. So he let her have it. Her name was Dezi Irene Jones. She didn't grow up to write the great American novel, but she wrote mysteries for *Good Housekeeping* and really found that expressing herself through writing gave her happiness. She upgraded to a more modern machine when she was older and donated her typewriter to a secondhand store. When her father died, she attributed everything she was in life to the day he let a silly little girl keep a machine. Isn't that sweet?"

The father didn't reply but instead turned, marched to the window, and brought back the typewriter. "No arguments," he said to his daughter. "You type out your books on this if you want or even just keep it in a corner, and whenever you look at it, you'll know you have a dad who believes in you."

Jennifer almost wanted to protest, to say she only wanted them to have the story and wasn't trying to solidify the sale or anything, but one look at the father's face told her that he didn't want any arguments from her either.

She gave them a discount and waited for them to leave before she placed a back-in-fifteen-minutes sign in the window. Tony's expression was unreadable when she turned her attention back to him. "You know," he said, "maybe you do belong here. That's exactly how Daisy would have handled that situation. Daisy always said that the story makes the item."

"And the person," she whispered, finishing Daisy's favorite quote. Her cheeks burned with the compliment and the compassion in Tony's voice. His words spoke forgiveness. She gave him a quick hug before leading him upstairs to get settled.

She'd taken care to put the pictures she'd pulled down back up where they'd been. She wanted Tony to see the full effect and didn't think it would mean the same if he saw the photos sitting in a box. The pictures didn't affect him the way they had her. He didn't feel surprised or guilt-ridden at seeing them. Instead he got all teary-eyed and then blamed his tears on exhaustion from the long drive. He touched one of the photos where he and Jennifer had been small kids digging on the beach with an enormous lump they'd called a sand castle in between them.

"The place feels different without her in it, doesn't it?" he said.

It did feel different. The antique shop didn't scare Jennifer like when she'd been younger, but the place felt more haunted than ever before—in a sad way, not a scary way.

She allowed Tony time alone while she returned to tend the store. The busy afternoon left her exhausted but exhilarated. Henry, the antique dealer popped in for a visit and invited her to an estate sale so he could show her the ropes.

Jennifer had sketched a glance to her surroundings. With Tony in town to help, she would be able to break away from the store and check out this new side to being a business owner. She agreed before she could change her mind.

She spent the rest of the day rethinking her life, her plans, her goals. Paul called, and she almost didn't answer, afraid maybe he'd found a buyer or something. She finally clicked the phone icon and said, "Hello?"

It was worse than him finding a buyer. "Hey, I just wanted to say I'm so sorry, but a client is pretty insistent I meet him tonight rather than in the morning like scheduled. I won't be able to come by. I'm so sorry."

"It's okay." Lies. Her heart sank into her stomach at the thought of not seeing him. "Maybe later?" She hoped she didn't sound desperate.

He sighed, which didn't bolster her confidence any. "Actually, I have to be out of town for several days. Don't worry about the sale. I'll make sure someone is available to show the business off to any perspective buyers."

She wanted to tell him to forget it, to take the business off the market, but couldn't make herself commit to the words, so she stayed silent until he apologized several times more and hung up.

I should stay, she thought. Not just could, but *should.* She loved Seashell Beach. She loved waking up to the sound of the ocean and spending her day with happy, vacationing people who were searching her shelves for some piece that connected the past to their present. She loved Paul smiling at her—not that he was the reason to stay, but that he made for a nice side benefit.

A benefit she wasn't going to be seeing for several days.

Eight

Several days turned into two weeks. Paul texted her numerous times a day with funny quips on life in general and with questions about her life in particular. She answered his *hotdogs or hamburgers* question with *Lucky Charms cereal*, and he answered her *dogs or cats* question with *iguana*. She hoped he laughed as much as she did and found herself learning more about him from his evasive answers than she might have otherwise.

In the meantime, she called her boss in Oregon and let him know she needed more time off. He argued and blustered but relented when she informed him she'd just quit if he said no. Her brother had really taken to working in the store. Sales remained steady, enough to pay him a decent wage while he worked; enough that she desperately needed the new inventory Henry helped her acquire at the estate sale.

She'd acclimated to being a retailer much better than she liked to admit and was glad Tony also obtained an extended leave of absence from his work due to the family emergency of running his dead aunt's business. Jennifer and Tony switched off shifts. She worked mornings so Tony didn't have to get up early and so she could walk along the beach and watch the sun sink into its watery bed at night.

It was just before her morning shift that Jennifer startled at a knock on the store door. She peeked out the plantation shutters and hoped to see Paul on the other side. It was Henry. She'd spent enough time with him to have really learned the ropes of the business but also enough to get to know him. He wasn't her type as far as guys went—too put-together-handsome—but she couldn't deny her gratitude for his friendship. "You didn't even bring me my favorite bagel," she said after letting him in.

After a bit of banter, he held up two tickets to a concert for Imagine Dragons. She tried to keep her face passive. He did know they were just friends, didn't he? She peeked into the envelope, thrilled with the tickets but worried about him maybe asking for a date, and made a half-hearted suggestion that they go together.

He held out his hands and shook his head, letting her know both tickets were hers since he had things to do with his mom. Good. No weirdness could develop from a gift where he wasn't expecting a date from it.

He then asked if he could hide his mom's birthday present—a 1926 Singer 15-30 Tiffany Treadle sewing machine—at her store. So he wasn't giving her tickets to be nice. He'd given them as a storage fee. She laughed at that.

She sized him up after he'd explained the machine's significance. "I'd love to store it here, but you need to bring me its story."

Henry looked slightly alarmed at the inference of her

displaying his mom's present. "Can't you keep it in your back room?"

"Ha," she said. "I'm not going to let a piece like that sit in my shop without being seen. That's sacrilegious to me, you know, goes against my newfound values." She'd really come to love the stories. She'd decided to never let anything come into the shop without a story attached. The past and present being connected by stories filled her with a purpose she never thought possible. And for as long as she ran the store, she'd keep running it the way her aunt would have.

Henry finally agreed to her terms and left the antique shop with a sulk to his step. She laughed at that too.

Later that night, Paul surprised her by making an appearance at closing. She wanted to throw her arms around him but felt the distance of time tugging at her enough to be excited without blowing her excitement out of proportion. Tony showed up from the back room. "Who's this?"

Paul stiffened nearly as much as Tony did but relaxed immediately when she said, "This is Paul, the realtor and my friend. Paul, this is my brother, Tony."

Paul reached out to shake Tony's hand, but Tony acted like he didn't see it as he went to lock the door so they could count down the till and reconcile the day's receipts. Paul took the slight in stride and said, "I got that new game, Water Wars, today. I was wondering if you wanted to play it with me later."

Jennifer shot him a look that said she absolutely did not want to play and caught the look on Paul's face. She also caught how Tony's head bobbed up with interest. "I don't know, maybe," she said.

"Are you kidding?" Tony said. "Maybe? Water Wars is the hottest game to hit the market, and you only *maybe* want to play? Are we even related?"

And just like that, Paul and Tony were friends, talking

about gaming and movies and things Jennifer knew nothing about.

Tony mentioned loving Mexican food, and suddenly they were all three on their way out the door to Just North. Jennifer had hoped to go out just the two of them but was grateful Paul included Tony, allowed him to know he was valued and important. Jennifer felt like an observer watching as Paul ordered his meal, spoke kindly to the waitress, winked at a little girl who'd been peeking at them from over the booth seats, and picked up a napkin dropped by the little girl's mom as she scooted out of the booth. And with each interaction that had nothing to do with her, she felt more certain.

She needed to stay in California.

The live band in the restaurant played across a variety of genres, from alternative punk-pop to country to actual Mexican music that gave atmosphere to the place. "She's really good," Tony said of the lead singer. When they went on break, the lead singer approached their table. "Hey, Paul."

"Hey, Maggie."

"You said you were dating a guitarist." Maggie gave Jennifer a pointed look.

Jennifer choked on her drink. He was telling people about her?

Paul grinned. "I am, as a matter of fact."

Maggie stepped back and swept her hand in the direction of the small stage. "Awesome. Wanna jam with us?"

"I, I don't think—"

But Maggie crossed her arms and gave a smile that said she wasn't the sort of woman a person argued with.

Jennifer scooted her chair back and followed Maggie to the stage. They consulted songs for a while, agreed on a few, and Jennifer took a guitar and slung the strap over her shoulder. For the first time since high school, Jennifer was playing music for a real, live, human audience. The notes and rhythm swelled inside her. She tossed a smile of gratitude at Paul, who had coordinated a moment in her life she didn't think would ever come.

She performed her music on a stage.

When Maggie finally gave Jennifer permission to step down, she did so to the sound of applause and cheers from the crowded restaurant. She walked straight to her table, pulled Paul up, and gave him a hug. The crowd cheered even more loudly, and several called out for him to kiss the guitarist. Jennifer felt heat in her face, and the two of them shared an awkward laugh and an intense look that said they both had every intention of making good on the crowd's request as soon as they got each other alone. Jennifer would've done it right there, but it had been a long time since she'd been kissed, and she wasn't about to break that dry spell with an audience.

By the end of the night, Jennifer worried she might not be able to get a kiss in after all, since it seemed Tony had no intentions of giving them time alone together. But as they entered Boardwalk Antiques, Tony stretched, declared himself exhausted, and slipped upstairs from the shop without another word.

Jennifer puffed out her cheeks and said, "That went better than I'd hoped."

Paul gave her a sideways glance, an invitation to explain what she meant.

"Tony actually likes you."

Paul leaned against the counter. "And that surprises you why?"

She joined him at the counter and scooted close enough that their arms were touching. "You're the guy helping to sell his favorite aunt's life. I'm not just surprised he likes you; I'm surprised he hasn't thrown a punch at you."

He didn't laugh the way Jennifer had expected. Instead

his brow creased. "I've been meaning to talk to you about that—"

"I've been meaning to talk to you too. You go first, though," she said.

He sucked in a ragged breath and drummed his fingers along her counter before saying, "I have two buyers aggressively interested in viewing the business. Both are energetic when it comes to acquiring your property. They've almost started a bidding war over the phone and via email, and they haven't even seen the place yet. I wouldn't have put them off—even with me being out of town—but this all came to a head today. I told them I would have to check your schedule first."

Jennifer stepped away from the counter and from Paul and felt the world swirl out of focus a little. "Buyers? Already?"

He nodded.

She didn't respond, not sure what to say. It had been a few weeks, so she knew the word *already* should have been wrong. She should have been irritated that it took this long. Instead, she was horrified to see it all happening so fast. With a restless energy, she wandered around the counter and looked up at her bottle. "I was just getting used to the place."

"You don't have to sell it," he said quickly. "You don't even have to show it if you don't want to. You can take it off the market any time you want." He joined her behind the counter.

Jennifer reached up and let her fingertips graze over the bottle. "It doesn't have a story."

"What?" He looked from her to the bottle, confusion clear on his face.

"The bottle. It's the only thing in this entire shop that doesn't come with a pedigree of ownership."

"Maybe that information is on the note inside." He stepped closer to the bottle. His tall frame allowed him to peer into it without having to get up on tiptoe.

"It's sealed with wax." She paused. "There are so many secrets in this place. Maybe staying a while and figuring them out is—" She turned to face Paul and found that he'd moved closer to her, close enough to let her know he was thinking the same thing she'd been thinking all day.

"Figure out?" he leaned in, meeting her in the middle and waiting for her to close the distance.

The bells on her door jingled, making them both startle and jump. She turned, breathing hard with the adrenaline of the near-kiss and the shock of the noise, feeling furious she'd forgotten to lock the front door. "I'm sorry, we're closed—"

But the man glancing up at the bells with a smirk on his face wasn't a late-night customer.

Eddie had come to California.

Nine

"What are you doing here?" She felt dizzy and breathless seeing him in so surreal an environment. Eddie belonged in a smoky nightclub in Oregon. He belonged in her apartment living room. He belonged in a life that wasn't California, that wasn't Boardwalk Antiques.

"I missed my song." Eddie moved toward her, his arms open, expecting her to fall into them for the embrace he always gave so casually and she always received with so much hope.

She backed up farther behind the counter, as if using it as a shield to protect her. But protect her from what? This was *Eddie*. Why did she suddenly feel like she'd been put on high alert?

"Your song?"

"I have no song without you, so I followed you." He tilted his head and smiled wider. "Surprise!" He rounded the counter, brushed past Paul, and left her nowhere to go, no other choice but to accept his arms around her.

Her eyes met Paul's over Eddie's shoulder. "I'm sorry," she mouthed. Paul's wide eyes expressed the confusion tangling inside her. She pulled away from Eddie and headed to the middle of the shop in a rush to remove herself from the claustrophobic presence of two very different men.

The way they both stood behind the counter sizing each other up made her wish she could leave, ditch out the back door, and go for a walk on the beach until they'd both gone.

Eddie finally cast his gaze away from Paul as if deciding Paul's importance to be nonexistent. "So how's the garage sale going?" Eddie asked.

She grunted, feeling all her exasperation building. "Don't be a jackwagon, Eddie. It's an antique store."

"Right. Okay. So, how's the expensive garage sale going?" He grinned and seemed to be waiting for everyone to laugh at his joke.

No one laughed.

"She called it an antique store. It's good manners to do the same." Paul levelled an irritated look in Eddie's direction.

Eddie didn't bother to look at Paul as he addressed Jennifer. "So who's this?"

When Jennifer made the awkward introduction, Eddie relaxed. "Right, you're just the realtor. So how's it going? Any takers?"

Jennifer tried to unravel the knots of confusion wrestling in her stomach. Eddie had come to California for her. What did that mean? Why now? "Two prospective buyers are coming to view the place. It looks promising," she found herself saying, wondering why she wanted to make sure Eddie knew that plans were moving forward in spite of her almost-decision to stay.

"Good. It feels like you've been gone forever. It's time to come home."

Paul blinked as if trying to understand where this guy had come from.

Jennifer looked back and forth between the two of them. "I . . . I might want to stay."

Eddie was shaking his head before she even finished. He slid a rapier from the scabbard hanging on the sidewall nearest the cash register and held it aloft as if making a royal decree. "No, you don't."

"I should go," Paul said, obviously uncomfortable with the tension and conversation. He stiffly inclined his head at Eddie and then did something that shocked Jennifer almost as much as Eddie's presence. Paul reached over and pulled Jennifer to him, holding her in an embrace that felt warm and inviting and making her realize just how much she'd been cheated out of, *again*. Eddie had stolen her kiss with Paul *again*.

"You belong here in this store and in this life, and you looked great on that stage," Paul whispered in her ear, his lips brushing her earlobe and sending shivers coursing through her. Paul slid his face alongside hers before leaving a warm, lingering kiss on her cheek and then turning and striding from the store without another glance back.

As the bells settled, Eddie swung the rapier to point it at the door. "What was that all about? Who does that guy think he is?"

"That's Paul. He's my friend."

"I don't like him. He's no friend of yours."

Jennifer pressed her palms into her temples. "You not liking him has nothing to do with how I feel. I like him a lot. He's definitely my friend."

Eddie gaped at her before pacing in tight circles, all the while swishing the rapier across the air in agitated little swipes. "You've been gone almost a month. You hung up on me the last time I called. You're acting weird. You need to come home, because this place is changing you."

"What do I have at home?" She wondered if this would be the moment, the moment he said she had *him* at home, that he was there waiting for her and loving her.

"You don't belong here. This isn't gonna get you your dream. No one will ever see you on stage playing your guitar here. You need me."

"I *need* you?" She crossed her arms, imitating Maggie, the woman who actually took her onstage, and hoped her glare equaled her anger.

"You need the band," he amended.

"I'll have you know that just tonight I played on stage at a restaurant—something you told me I wasn't ready for all those times you got gigs but didn't invite me. And I'll have you know, I was great. No, not great. I was amazing. How is any of that me needing you?"

His mouth worked as he tried to find an answer. "We had a deal. Face it; conquer it; come home. You were supposed to come home!" At the last, he swung the rapier up high in the air, the metal tip clanking against the glass bottle.

The bottle wobbled, toppled, and shattered against the floor. Bits of blue glass sprayed out, pelting Jennifer's arms as she held them out, as if she could pull all the pieces together by sheer force of will. Her eyes burned with hot tears even before she registered the depth of her horror at the one item in the store she'd declared as hers lying in ruins. No words made it past the breath caught in her throat as she stood, mouth agape.

Eddie dropped the rapier with a clatter and held up his hands as if to prove they were empty. "I'll pay for that," he said, bending down to pick up the worn paper furled among the glass.

Jennifer couldn't find her voice enough to stop him from handling the bottle's note, couldn't demand that he put it down and stop assuming he could pay for something she felt held a value higher than anything monetary. Paying for it didn't fix it.

Eddie wiped at his nose. "Hey, it's like a real message in a bottle. Cute."

She wanted to tell him to stop. But he was already reading. "Dear Daisy." He glanced up. "Hey! That's the aunt you hate!" He looked down to keep reading. "I've been waiting. And waiting. And WAITING for you to realize that I'm still here. I know you love your music. I know it's important to you, and I will always support you in that. What I don't understand is why you think us being together will get in the way. You don't have to climb this mountain alone. I'm willing to take it step by step with you. I guess what I'm saying is that I am done waiting. I love you, and I want to be with you. I'll be at our bench on the Tangerine Street boardwalk. I have a surprise for you there. The surprise isn't an engagement ring, because you know I bought that months ago. That ring and I will be waiting. If you show up and put the ring on, I'll know what your answer is. If you don't show up . . . well . . . I guess I'll know that answer too. I love you Daisy. Forever. Love, Kade."

Eddie grinned over the piece of paper. "Guess your aunt wasn't such a homeless after all, huh? She had a secret boyfriend."

His interpretation of the letter made Jennifer more certain of her feelings than anything else could have. She swallowed hard and closed her eyes to prevent any traitorous leaking. Aunt Daisy had been loved. The man who loved her waited for her until he couldn't wait any longer. And that was where Jennifer now stood. She had waited for Eddie, chased him and the dream of him for a long time. Daisy had left her this—Jennifer felt sure of it. More than just the store and the apartment and everything, Daisy had left Jennifer this letter. A message in a bottle reaching into the future to help Jennifer find solid ground. "Why are you here, Eddie?"

"I missed you." He straightened as if completely confident in how that statement would affect her. He leaned in, his lips close to hers in a way she'd imagined for years.

Instead of closing the distance, she pulled back, put her palm against his chest to stop him from advancing, and let one word settle between them. "Why?"

He frowned, tapping his fingers against the side of his jeans in a need to find his rhythm. "I dunno. I'm just used to you, you know. It's weird with you gone."

She scrunched her eyes, as if closing them tighter would change his words. "You're used to me?" She opened them again and pinned him to the spot with her gaze. "Okay. Here's another question. Did Misti spend the night?"

He stumbled back in the wake of the question. "What does that have to do with—"

"No. You're right. It doesn't have anything to do with anything." She glanced around. "It's just this place, you know? This store filled with things from the past, things that were lost—like this letter." She moved toward him, her hand stretching out and pulling the letter from Eddie's fingers.

He frowned at her. "You're not making sense."

She looked down at the words scrawled in faded blue ink. "But that's what this store is: an eternal lost and found. The past gets lost as people die off, like this letter, and the rememberers forget, but each of the pieces in this store holds information about that past ensuring that even when it *feels* lost, it's still findable."

Eddie nodded and intercepted the conversation. "Right. Found, like I missed you while you were gone and then came here to find you."

Jennifer shook her head. "No." She laughed, feeling relieved and incredulous standing among the broken glass and pieced-together life. He joined her in the laugh, though she could tell he didn't get the joke. "This isn't about you. Not this time. This is about me." She smiled and found her

88

eyes were burning again, but not in anger. "*I found me.*"

Eddie moved forward to take her hands in his as if to take control of the situation, to lead her to some other conclusion than the one that hovered over the both of them. The glass crunched under his shoes.

"You should go," she said.

"But I came to be with you—to take you home."

Instead of letting him lead the conversation, she tugged on his hand and led him back to the door. "I know, and I appreciate that, but I am home. There's a great hotel down the road. You can stay there, my treat. But you can't stay with me."

He dropped her hand. "Fine. Whatever." He turned on a heel, grinding glass into the wood grain of the floor, crossed the room, and threw the door open, making the bells clang in agitation.

"Be brave, soldier," she said to his retreat. The door slammed.

Ten

P aul felt like a stalker as he patrolled the sand on the other side of Tangerine Street. He wanted to stay at the antique store, hold his ground, and evict the interloper. But Jennifer had gone from all but saying she didn't want to sell the store to telling this moron that she had two buyers coming to check the place out. She called the buyers *promising*.

"Broken promise," Paul said to the night sea air. He'd been on the other end of that sizzling energy too many times to deny something worked between them. He and Jennifer had definite chemistry. But it was more than chemistry. It was her excitement in operating her business, her way of laughing and being delighted by everything around her, her determination to chase dreams and to allow others to chase theirs. And if he hadn't already been falling for her, the guitar would have been enough to make him ask for her number and then call her every minute until she answered.

Her music was soulful and, at the same time, optimistic. When she'd closed her eyes and let her fingers pick over the strings, he'd known he could never be happy without her.

"So what am I doing out here?" he asked himself. He straightened, determined to go in and make a stand against this guy who looked like he was still living in high school. He strode back to the boardwalk.

Eleven

She hadn't been able to move from the epicenter of broken blue glass. It was a lot to take in. From performing on stage at Just North to coming home and seeing the heat in Paul's eyes to Eddie coming and Eddie going, and discovering her own bravery in all of it. She needed to call Paul, to apologize and hope he understood; but even if he didn't, she was still staying, not for him, but for her.

She blinked in surprise when the very person occupying her thoughts tugged open her front door, the bells getting another opportunity to work that night. He halted at seeing her there, standing alone in a pool of blue glass. "Your bottle," he said.

She shrugged. "Turns out it had a genie in it."

Paul cast a quick glance around, clearly verifying that they were alone. "A genie, huh?" He moved into the store, letting the door shut firmly at his back. His hand went behind him and fumbled with the lock. No more visitors tonight.

She took a step toward him, the glass crunching underneath her feet. "I think my store is haunted."

"You saw a sheet rattling chains recently?" He took a step forward as well.

"It's Aunt Daisy—well, not her exactly, but there are ghosts in the things she left behind." Her hand trembled as she moved closer and held up the letter. "She's everywhere here," Jennifer continued. "I just hate to think she's left me new opportunities and then forced to watch as I screw them up."

He took two more steps. "What are you screwing up?"

She took three. "I let you leave."

He closed the distance, his hands rough and warm and cradling her face. He leaned in until they were almost touching and said, "But I came back." His lower lip brushed hers.

She responded by pressing her lips to his until they were lost in a fusing of heat and new promises.

When they broke apart, Paul grinned. "If this is how hauntings go, I hope your aunt never leaves."

She laughed, dusted his lips with her own, and whispered, "By the way, since I'm not putting the store up for adoption any longer, you're fired."

He laughed too. "I've been hoping you'd fire me."

They celebrated his newfound unemployment with another kiss, and somewhere in the store, maybe from atop the counter or leaning against the Cleopatra puppet, Jennifer knew Aunt Daisy was watching from under the brim of her floppy hat. Watching and smiling.

Part Two

Solving for X

One

A bbie tried not to look in the window of Boardwalk Antiques when she passed it; she really did. Her cozy beach house was becoming cozier by the day with all the treasures she stuffed into it. Abbie turned to shake her fist at the antiques store window and Jennifer, the proprietor behind it, she with her impeccable taste and her *stories*.

But the second Abbie saw the window display, her fist froze in the middle of its fake angry shake, and it wasn't until she caught her reflection that she dropped it. She rushed to the window and leaned as closely as she could to peer at the toy soldiers inside. Four vintage World War II army privates in their olive green uniforms, each in a different pose as they prepared for the enemy.

She straightened and shoved the door open, tinkling the tiny brass bell over the door. She wished she could make it her personal sound effect to precede her everywhere she went. People would hear the cheerful ringing, and, ta-da! Abbie would appear.

"How did you know?" she asked Jennifer, the store owner, who glanced up in confusion. Abbie waited a beat for her to catch up. She had to do that often for people. It puzzled her. It's not like she wasn't speaking English.

Jennifer blinked. "How did I know what?"

"How did you know about the soldiers? The ones in the window. They weren't there yesterday."

Jennifer shrugged. "I've had those young men for a few weeks. Today felt like the day to put them out."

Abbie narrowed her eyes. "It's because you knew I would be walking by, isn't it?"

Jennifer looked like she was trying not to laugh. That was another expression Abbie was really used to from people. "You realize that the whole point of a window display is to make people want to buy what they see inside it, yes?"

"Yes," Abbie conceded. "But why does everything in your window have to be something *I* want to buy? Can't you put stuff in there that other people will want?"

Jennifer leaned forward, her expression serious. "It's not my fault we're both blessed with amazing taste."

"Wavelengths," Abbie grumbled.

"Ours are the same," Jennifer agreed.

Abbie eyed the soldiers, then the five beautiful clocks in the case behind Jennifer's head. The ormolu, she decided. That's which one she would tell time off of today. She had four hours until her big presentation, and she should go home and center herself so she would be ready to deliver it. But . . . the soldiers. She had zero belief in coincidence. Therefore, they must have been meant for her to find.

She made one last attempt to resist the universe. "Can I see them?" she asked. Maybe they would be good imitations. Or even better, bad imitations. Or in terrible condition.

97

Except that Jennifer Day wouldn't let anything less than the best into her store. She could hardly wait to get the soldiers' story. That was half the fun of buying things from Jennifer. Maybe more than half.

"I'll get them from the window for you," Jennifer said. As she rounded the corner, another tinkle sounded, and a tourist walked in. Abbie eyed his pressed khakis and red tie. No, not a tourist. This guy was on a corporate retreat, and he still didn't understand that the "business casual" dress code meant he could lose the noose. They saw his type almost every weekend. His precision haircut probably cost more than her sandals. With his dark hair and light eyes, he'd be kind of hot if he didn't have the hard-set features of someone who had forgotten how to laugh.

He glanced around the shop until he spotted Jennifer reaching into the window for the soldiers. "I'll take those, please," he said, striding over to her. He stopped and crossed his arms across his chest, watching her like he was her supervisor. Jennifer offered him a patient smile and turned back to the window to retrieve another soldier.

"No," Abbie said.

The guy didn't look her way, just watched with a raised eyebrow as Jennifer removed the last soldier. He acted like he already owned them. No, like he owned the whole store.

"Excuse me," Abbie called louder, and her tone didn't match the polite words at all. He spared her a glance and she said, "No." Again.

His other eyebrow flew up. "Are you talking to me?"

"Yes."

"I have no idea what you're saying no to."

"You said you'll take those soldiers, and I said no," she repeated and said all the words slowly, like when she read for the toddlers at Wonderland Books. "I'm already buying them. That's why she's getting them out of the window."

"Sorry about that," Jennifer said to the man. "You just

missed these, but I keep a great collection of vintage toys. Feel free to wander around and see if anything else catches your eye."

He frowned, his eyebrows now scrunched together in a squiggle. "No, thank you. I need those soldiers. No disrespect to your customer at the register, but I'd be glad to offer you more."

Of course he could, entitled corporate jackass. Abbie limited herself to a patient, "You can't do that."

"Of course I can," he said, following Jennifer back to the counter. "It's called business. And it's good business for her."

Abbie had to acknowledge she might have earned his condescending tone by using her storytime voice on him. But it didn't change the fact that he was wrong, and Abbie held the trump card here.

"False. I win. You don't need to wrap them up for me, Jennifer."

But Jennifer was leaning on the counter, her chin in her hand, waiting to see what happened next.

"Jennifer," the man said, his voice warm for the first time. *Fake charm*, Abbie noted. "I'm Holden. And I need these soldiers. What can I do to get them from you?"

"Nothing," Abbie answered. "Because she's already selling them to me. I told you, I win."

The irritation crept back into his expression. "What does that even mean?"

"You said it's good business for her to sell them to you for more, but in fact it isn't. You're negotiating without all the facts."

"The facts are simple: we both want the same item. That creates a scarcity, and now Jennifer has increased demand. We can, and should, expect the price to go up. It's simple economics. Double?" he asked Jennifer.

Abbie walked the three steps to cover the distance between herself and this Holden person, stopped and snapped her fingers in front of his face. He jerked his head back. "What are you doing?"

"Getting your attention. People do it to me all the time. You're overlooking that you're a one-time sale and I'm a valuable repeat customer. Jennifer makes way more bank on me over the long haul than she will off of you, so it's smarter to keep me happy. I repeat: I win." A split second of shame at her snottiness flashed through her until he glanced down at his watch, annoyance written all over his face. Clear message: this is a waste of my time. *You* are a waste of my time. Abbie didn't feel in the least bad now, although Jennifer's mouth had fallen open.

"Jennifer should decide what she wants to do," Holden said.

Abbie smiled. Definitely let Jennifer decide. She could buy her soldiers and get out of here.

"Three times the asking," Holden said, interrupting her thoughts.

"You can't do that!" Abbie yelped. "Regardless of who was here first, or of why you need them, do you really think you can peel enough bills from your money clip to get what you want?"

His gaze was cool. Not angry, but controlled. He packed a thousand watts of confidence into it, confidence that he would get his way because he always did. That truth rolled off of him like a stench, but it was the moment when his expression slid to a "spare me from unreasonable women" look that she lost it.

She'd gotten that look far too many times from far too many uptight business executives who worried more about having their neckties straight and their spartan apartments in immaculate order than in really living. Okay, she'd gotten that look far too many times from three specific uptight business executives, but they'd made her an expert in interpreting that expression, and it was painted all over this Holden guy's face.

He smoothed his tie and cleared his throat. "I think I can get what I want with more money because it's common sense."

It was the slight emphasis he put on the last two words that got her. That was a phrase she hated: *common sense*. People flung it at her in conjunction with questions like, "Do you have any?" and "Where is yours?" He may as well have waved a red flag in her face. But he didn't. He just smoothed the red tie down one more time, and that did it.

Abbie plucked a pair of scissors from the pen holder on Jennifer's counter, and he flinched.

She studied him, allowing pity to show on her face. "Did I scare you?"

"You've got to be kidding me. You think I'm scared of someone dressed like a cupcake?"

"I'm not—" Abbie started to argue before she looked down and realized that her solid white skirt, pink top, and yellow beret could, to certain practically minded people, make her look like a candle-topped cupcake.

Abbie picked up the end of the red tie. She didn't move fast, but he froze as she cut right through the middle of it, severing the stupid little embroidered man on his horse from the rest. The only sound was Jennifer's gasp at the first snip. Abbie tucked the scissors back into the cup and watched him.

It was a full minute before he said anything, and in the final ten seconds she almost felt bad until his sneering "common sense" inflection echoed through her head and she got over it.

"What the hell?" he finally managed, staring down at his tie. *Half* a tie.

"Isn't this what business negotiations are all about?" she

asked, her voice icy. "Flexing metaphorical muscles and proving who wants something more?"

"Bad business negotiations are." He fingered the sheared-off end, confusion on his face. "Are you a crazy person? You're a crazy person, right?"

"No. I'm trying to save you from yourself. You're very entitled. Your money makes you that way, but you can rise above it." She dug into her purse and pulled out five twenties. "Here. You can go replace your tie. But you shouldn't. Seashell Beach isn't a tie kind of place. Buy yourself a shirt that no self-respecting guy would wear with a tie. Wear it. Try to bond with our little town. It's great."

He grimaced as he whipped the remainder of his tie from around his neck. "I think it isn't great. It's the opposite of that. What is that? This town . . ." He seemed at a loss for words.

"This town is a burr in your expensive dress socks, irritating you more the longer you deal with it?" she offered.

"Yes."

"I'm good with words." The familiar satisfaction of finding the right word settled in her chest, an inner sunshine that faded the second she realized what she'd said. "That's only the right analogy for what you're thinking," she clarified. "It's the absolute wrong analogy for Seashell Beach. So what I'm saying is that your thinking is wrong even if I can explain it well. Also, people who can't relax at the beach are deeply troubled."

He looked at her again, this time his eyebrows perfectly straight, eyelids the tiniest bit lowered. Boredom. Fascinating how many moods he'd communicated with those brows inside of ten minutes. They were well-groomed, which Abbie couldn't decide if she wanted to respect or mock, but they still had a life of their own. It gave her an idea for a story . . .

". . . Story," Jennifer finished, and Abbie realized she'd missed everything Jennifer had just said. Jennifer propped her chin back on her hand, her gaze expectant, like she was waiting for a show to start.

"What?" Abbie and Holden said. Holden looked dumbfounded. Abbie must have missed something good.

"I said I'll sell these for their marked price, but only to whoever tells me the best story about why you want them," Jennifer repeated.

Abbie's story was unbeatable, and she relaxed, but Holden didn't look any more enlightened.

Jennifer smiled at him. "I don't sell anything in here that doesn't have some story about its origins, something that makes its history come alive. These soldiers have a great little story, so it seems only fair to sell it to whomever tells the best story to win them." The cuckoo clock behind her emitted a series of clicks and chirps. "It's eleven. I'm going to take an early lunch. Why don't you both come back in an hour, I'll hear your stories out, and we'll figure out who gets the soldiers."

Abbie nodded and bounced one of her corkscrew curls right over her eye. She shoved it out of the way and grinned at Holden. "See you in an hour, but it would probably be more efficient for you to get on with the rest of your day, because you can't beat my story. And you definitely seem like one of those guys who loves efficiency, so that's a total win for you."

"Why are you saying efficiency like it's a bad word?" he asked, but he held up his hand as soon as he said it. "No, forget I asked. I'll be back in an hour," he told Jennifer. Without another glance at Abbie, he left, his quick, determined stride all wrong for walking down a street a stone's throw from the ocean.

Two

Holden barreled down the sidewalk for several yards before he noticed the attention his pace was attracting. He slowed down, and the stares drifted away, back toward the ocean dotted with boat sails.

He knew he was supposed to look out at those boat sails and feel peaceful or something. Or wish he were on them. That's what the CEO had dragged the executive team down here for—to change their physical environment so it would "change their work environment." Which would be great if it needed changing, but it didn't. They were in the middle of a new phone launch, and the goal was Apple Omniscience—to be everywhere, and to dominate the news cycles like the whisper of a new iPhone release did. But they weren't Apple, and that meant they didn't just have to have the best product —they had to have the best product by far.

And they did. What they did *not* have was the media saturation they needed. They needed the kind of buzz that would bring industry tastemakers like *Wired* to their door, begging to put them on the cover. Without that, the phone launch would be a pop and a fizzle, not the seismic shift they needed to change the face of the communications industry forever.

These weren't small ambitions. Holden couldn't have people with narrow vision on the team. And David Macklin, CEO, disliked Holden's approach to motivating them so much that he'd used words like "burnout" in conjunction with "ocean retreat" to explain why Holden and his entire team had to lose three valuable days to bond over this bogus touchy-feely Hallmark card motivational stuff instead of pushing even harder on the phone launch.

They'd gotten in late last night after a four-hour drive down from Silicon Valley on a luxury bus. Those two words did not belong in one sentence, but it wasn't a Greyhound, so whatever. He'd managed to use most of the drive time to focus his team on brainstorming ideas for product positioning, but they'd gotten kind of irritable toward the end. He'd dropped it, but he'd climbed off the bus more wound-up than when he'd gotten on it, thanks to losing that final hour, plus the next three days, for work.

Well, for work with his team. They could bond. He'd strategize on his own while they drew self-actualization portraits or whatever ridiculous class he'd seen on the schedule this morning that had sent him back to his hotel room and laptop. He'd only come out for coffee, but the Boardwalk Antiques window display had hijacked that plan.

He didn't need a lot of material things. He'd moved around too much as an army brat to get too attached to things he'd have to leave behind. But the need, the pure bolt of wanting that shot through him when he'd spotted those soldiers in the window, had made his hands shake when he'd pushed open the door.

Holden pulled the prototype Apex from his pocket, the gun-metal gray gleaming in the bright coastal sun. The phone was so close to being perfect. It would definitely be the best thing on the market. Instead of thinking of ways to prove it, he had to burn seventy-two hours listening to people talk about their feelings. His dad would definitely not respect that.

He put the phone away. Sometimes he wished he could go back to the days when it was just him and ten other people trying to get DBR Tech off the ground. He missed the high stakes of talking to venture capitalists and having to be the guy with the idea out of thousands of competing ideas that got the nod and the money. Holden had excelled in those battles, a warrior who took no prisoners, because they were fights that mattered.

Yet another store window caught his eye, more children's stuff, but it wasn't a good thing this time. It was some bookstore display of the most ridiculous pink covers he'd ever seen. They appeared to be about a white cat, dressed like a tulle factory had vomited on her, who went on adventures. He shook his head and moved on. Wasn't the upcoming generation supposed to be raised on gender-neutral stories that didn't encourage damaging stereotypes like all girls liked cats and pink and frivolity? Who was out there producing books about girls who wrote kick-butt computer code or engineered kick-butt robots? That's what he would want his niece to read.

This whole town was backwards. He couldn't wait to leave. 'I was here first' was not a valid reason for her to get the soldiers. But if he was going to have to go back to the hotel and engage in ridiculous team-building activities, then he'd fortify himself with some hardcore business wheeling and dealing, just for old times' sake. The woman from the antiques store popped into his mind's eye. Did she seriously not realize that she looked like she'd walked off a bakery shelf? Zero surprise that she didn't have the first idea of how business actually worked.

Even with the owner's absurd "story" condition, he was determined to get what he wanted. The slight spike of adrenaline at the prospect of a contest felt better than caffeine. Holden would take his challenges where he could get them, and right now that meant winning the soldiers. He needed that connection to his childhood and simplicity, unlike he'd needed anything in a long time.

He ducked into the next café and ordered a coffee that tasted better than he wanted to admit for something that came out of Seashell Beach. He found himself a patio table, then executed a search on his Apex for "stories + tin soldiers."

Tell the truth, a whisper through his brain said. But he wouldn't. The owner hadn't specified a true story, and he wasn't about to lay his lonely childhood bare for two strange women, especially not when one of them was a cupcake, not even for a cupcake with a tiny waist and ridiculous curls. He didn't even get into that stuff with people he knew well. It wasn't a big deal. He'd survived it and become a successful adult who was still on speaking terms with his father. It was way more than most people had, and not one part of him, besides that stupid whisper, wanted to lay out some sob story that didn't matter anymore.

He needed a far more interesting story than the truth, and on the fifth page of search results, he found it. A link to a book review popped up for some blog called Retro Reads. The cover in the image showed a boy around eight years old saluting a Barclay tin soldier under the title *Private Dan Saves the Day*. The book had been published in 1952, the decade of America Is Awesome, when there was nothing wrong with building an entire children's story around a soldier. It was definitely not the vapid tutu-kitty brand of stories selling now.

He read through the reviewer's summary of Private Dan's heroics. Yeah, this was the key to winning the toy soldiers. He'd add a few of his own details, and Abbie Cupcake was doomed.

He sat back and grinned, noticing the ocean breeze for the first time that morning. Must be what victory smelled like.

Three

bbie spent the hour going over her notes for her presentation that afternoon. Work always focused her, usually to the exclusion of everything else, but she remembered to set an alarm on her phone so she wouldn't get so lost that she forgot to show up at Boardwalk Antiques again. She forgot to show up a lot of places.

She would reward herself with a treat from Delilah's Desserts in honor of winning over a guy who called her a cupcake. In fact, she'd choose the most indulgent cupcake Delilah made, something with cream cheese frosting *and* sprinkles *and* chocolate shavings, and if Delilah made one with all that plus some sort of ganache-stuffed center, even better. She could almost taste it. There was no way the guy's story could beat hers.

When her alarm went off, she tucked her notebook into her tote, a bright bag quilted from pieces of fabric printed with birds that she could not love more. The store bell announced her arrival, and Holden looked up from the counter, where he was studying the soldiers Jennifer had set out.

Huh. He was better looking without the tie. Well, hotter in a general sense. She didn't know what her type was, exactly, but he was definitely the opposite of it. But other girls might find him hot. Until he talked to them like they were morons, anyway.

He nodded toward the soldiers. "Let the battle begin."

Jennifer waited for Abbie to reach the counter. "Since Holden got here first, we'll let him start."

Holden picked up the solider standing at attention with his rifle by his side. The soldier looked almost alive, like he was ready to spring into action at the first sound of a snapped twig while he stood watch. Holden started to say something and paused to clear his throat, the sound her dad made whenever he was trying to talk but feeling sentimental.

"When I was little, maybe seven or eight, I went to spend the summer on my grandfather's farm. He was a World War II vet, the Sixth Infantry Division serving in the Pacific. My grandmother was really proud of his service, and she thought her only grandson should know about the kind of man his grandfather was, even though Granddad never talked about what he did. But she decorated the room I always stayed in with an army theme that she thought would be perfect for a little boy.

"My favorite part was the toys. It was the coolest collection ever, and I got to play with all of it, a bookshelf full of bombers and tanks. And toy soldiers. A whole set of them just like these guys. She'd sewed the blanket on my bed to look like the terrain of the Pacific Theater so I could re-enact battles on it."

He picked up the soldier standing at attention. "I never really liked this one when I was little because he looked like he wasn't doing anything, just standing there for boring guard duty. But then one night my grandmother came running in from the barn, her face all white. You read that in books, you know? That someone's face goes white? But you don't realize how scary it is until you see it with your own eyes."

"What happened?" Jennifer said. Her voice was library quiet, like she didn't want to derail the story.

Abbie couldn't wait to hear either, but she bet their reasons were very, very different.

"There was a bad summer storm that night, massive thunder and everything. They'd been in the barn doing an evening milking, and a cow got all skittish at a thunderclap and kicked Granddad in the head. He was conscious, but barely, and my grandma had gotten him into the cab of their truck. She wanted to take me with them, but it was raining pretty hard, and she couldn't put me in the truck bed in that kind of weather. She told me I would be safe in the house. The storm had knocked out the electricity and the phones, but she promised she would figure out how to send someone over to stay with me, or she would come get me and take me back to the hospital the first second she could."

The rhythm of Abbie's heart changed, skipping a beat, then pounding faster to make up for it. Unbelievable.

Holden set the soldier down and brushed the top of its head. The gesture was so tender, and a strangled sound escaped Abbie even though she tried to stop it. Holden smiled at her. "It was a hard night. Grandma left me with their emergency electric lantern, but it made too many shadows downstairs, so I went up to my room to wait. The soldiers were on the floor because I'd been playing with them, and when I sat down to pick them up, I just had this thought about how good soldiers march on no matter what. I tried to make them win the battle I'd been staging earlier, but suddenly it seemed stupid to play about life and death when those might be the real stakes for my grandpa. It's funny how something inside you understands that, even when you're a kid."

This time it was Jennifer who made a sound, a soft, sympathetic sound. Abbie didn't think Jennifer realized she'd even done it, but the slight upturn in Holden's mouth showed that he'd heard, and he knew that his story was getting to her.

What a punk.

"Instead of playing war, I picked this guy up, and suddenly his job seemed so important, to watch over everyone, to be alert and ready. It made me want to be a good soldier too, so I put him in my shirt pocket and imagined what he would order me to do. I went downstairs and cleaned the kitchen, and the shadows weren't so scary since I had this guy watching over me. I straightened every single thing I could find and even got brave enough to go out on the porch and sweep off the mud Grandma tracked in when she'd rushed from the barn. She loved her house to be clean, and I could be the soldier to get it there."

He gave a tiny salute to the guard soldier on the counter. "He got me through that night. My uncle drove over late from the next county to get me, and in the morning we found out everything was going to be okay. But seeing these guys in your window, all I could think about was how good it would feel to have them in my office, keeping an eye on things for me." His smile invited them to laugh at him.

Jennifer did, hers soft and appreciative.

Abbie laughed too. It was not appreciative, but Holden and Jennifer didn't seem to notice. He was too busy watching Jennifer wipe a single happy tear from her cheek.

Abbie was going to kill him.

"Thanks for sharing that," Jennifer told him. "Stories *matter*. So much. Are you ready to tell yours, Abbie?"

Abbie didn't answer. Instead she dug into her tote and pulled out a checkbook.

"What's that for?" Holden asked, like she'd pulled out a parrot.

"I gave you all my cash, but Jennifer knows I'm good for the check."

"You can't buy it until Jennifer chooses the best story."

"Holden, is it?" Abbie asked, looking him dead in the eye. He nodded. "I could tell the worst story in the world right now and these would still end up with me. You want to know why?"

"Definitely."

"Me too," Jennifer said, her tone confused. "That was a great story."

"Sure it was, if you don't know that Holden here is a lying liar."

"Excuse me?" he said, his face darkening like one of the storm clouds he'd conjured with his words.

"My grandmother wrote *Private Dan Saves the Day* in 1952. She used to make up bedtime stories for my uncle Dan about soldiers exactly like this that he kept in his room."

Color darkened the top of Holden's cheekbones, and she grinned. She really hoped that was humiliation. She turned to Jennifer. "It was her first book and a huge children's bestseller in 1952. It even got turned into a comic book series for a while. It was about a boy whose father gets injured on their farm, and so his brother has to drive him to the hospital and leaves little Billy, not little Holden, behind to keep an eye on the house. But really, Private Dan here," she said, patting the soldier like Holden had, "keeps an eye on little Billy through the scary night, helping him do brave things, until morning comes and Billy finds out that all was well. Other than that, his details were pretty good."

She smirked at him and almost felt badly about it. She wasn't really a smirker, but never had someone deserved it like this guy did. "You should have stuck with a widowed father."

113

"Just seemed over-the-top sentimental," he said, his voice flat.

Jennifer sighed and named the total with tax for Abbie before fixing Holden with a measuring stare. "The true stories are always the best ones."

The red on his cheeks deepened, and Abbie relented. "I happen to love that story. It's the main reason I do what I do. I just grew up kind of in love with the idea that stories can give kids courage in rough situations. And even though I've read and heard that one a thousand times, you did a pretty decent job with it. Did you read it when you were a kid too?"

"I read a summary on a blog. Good win," he said. "Enjoy it." He nodded to them both and walked out. They watched the door close behind him, the tinkle extra loud.

"Sorry," Abbie said. "You were kind of loving that, I could tell. Would it make you feel better if I brought in a first edition of the real story for you?"

"I'd love to see it." Jennifer finished tucking the last soldier into a gift box and tied it off with twine. "I'm glad they're going to you. It's almost like you're getting a piece of your family history back."

Abbie didn't want to ruin Jennifer's happiness for her by telling her that at least half of the sweetness of owning the soldiers was the satisfaction of beating Holden the Jerk to get them. But she didn't feel too guilty—the soldiers in her tote would be proud of her for winning the fight fairly. She hugged the purse tighter to her side and left the store with a wave to Jennifer followed by a fist pump when she was out of sight. She had a couple of hours to figure out where these could go in her little house before she had to head out again and change the world. Or at least a couple of lives. Okay, minds. She'd settle for changing a couple of minds at the retreat this afternoon.

Four

Holden headed back down the boardwalk again, his hands in his pockets, deep in thought. He looked like the dozens of other people out for a casual stroll, enjoying the boats in full sail out on the water. His colleagues were probably drawing metaphors from them about smooth sailing or sailing through life. There couldn't be a more inaccurate symbol for him right that second. He needed sailboats out there with no wind in their sails. Then it would be about right.

Yes, he'd totally lifted that story, but his true story was lame. And boring. Besides, the owner hadn't asked for true— just good. Why of all people did he have the bad luck to tell it to the granddaughter of the author? What a stupid, stupid coincidence.

Whatever. Time to shake it off and get back to his hotel room to do the work that mattered. He pulled his phone from his pocket to check the time. It vibrated in his hand,

and for a split second it was like it was laughing at him; but the display lit up with Dave Macklin's name, and Holden answered the call. "Hey, Dave."

"I don't care where you are, because no answer you give me is going to be a good one," Dave barked. "You know why? Because it's not here, eating with your teammates, or doing much of anything with your teammates at all today. And that's the whole point of this."

His tone startled Holden. Dave was one of the most even-tempered men he knew despite the CEO's high-energy approach to business. "Sorry, I was just using the down time to work on some Apex strategies."

"It's not down time." The words clearly came through gritted teeth. "You are the main reason we're doing this retreat. You're too good to lose, but you're burning your team out. You need to recalibrate as a team so you all have the same vision for where you're going next."

Holden wondered if he should burn incense and pass a peace pipe after they all found that vision together around a nighttime beach bonfire. He said nothing but rolled his eyes. It was juvenile and made him feel ten times better.

"You need to be at the first session after lunch, or I'm transitioning you off of this project for everyone's mental health."

"But—"

"Most especially *yours*," Dave said in a tone as commanding as any Holden had ever heard from his major general father. "If I have to save you from yourself, then I'll do it. Be there after lunch."

Fine. The beauty of the Apex was it could be a complete office for him even while he sat in some Tony Robbins-lite pep rally.

"And leave your phone behind," Dave ordered. "You're not just showing up, you're going to be *present*. In the moment. Pick the motivational fridge magnet that makes you happiest, but I want you all there, not just your carcass, you got it?"

"Got it," Holden said. Dave didn't even say goodbye.

He did, however, give Holden a marginally pleased nod an hour later when he walked down the hall for the first afternoon session. Holden mustered a smile. *See, Dave? I'm enjoying this so much this fake smile is going to break my face.*

He glanced at his program to see what the next session was. "Storyboarding: Writing Your Success Story." It was scheduled for three hours. Seriously?

Dave passed him on the way to the snack table. "Good to see you, Holden. Appreciate the effort with your wardrobe too."

Holden glanced down to his open shirt collar. He'd been forced to ditch his Ralph Lauren tie in a boardwalk garbage can. He glanced around at his colleagues. Everyone was in knits and shorts. He felt over and underdressed at the same time, which was unsettling. Still, he'd probably get Dave further off of his back if he dressed down more for tomorrow—assuming he could find a shirt without surfboards or hibiscus flowers in this place. Man, he hated this town.

There were still ten minutes to go before the session started, so he wandered after Dave and snagged a chocolate chip cookie off one of the snack platters. It was still warm, and when he bit into it, it tasted purely homemade. That took him right back to his childhood, before his mom got sick. A warm chocolate chip cookie reminded him of her hugs.

He followed his group into the session room, feeling like he needed to give Seashell Beach, or at least the Mariposa Hotel, some major points back for the cookie. He popped the last bite into his mouth and scanned the room for a seat. That's when he spotted the presenter readying a series of easels and oversized paper pads. It was her—the cupcake.

He stopped dead, and the hotel staffer behind him crashed into him. Holden gasped as the six pitchers of ice water the waiter carried splashed down his back. The gasp caused him to inhale the cookie instead of swallowing it, and that made him choke. But it was the look of sympathy and amusement on Abbie Cupcake's face that sent him straight over the edge.

"You all right, man?" That from the staffer. "I'm so sorry, sir."

Holden waved him away, too mad to say anything. He wasn't mad at the waiter. It was Holden who'd stopped short. But he was mad nonetheless, mainly at Abbie's trying not-to-laugh face. Murmurs from his coworkers reached him through the blood pounding in his head. They thrust handkerchiefs and tissues at him to help with the mess. *That* was how you were supposed to act when someone got two gallons of ice water down their back. You were not supposed to hold back a laugh, especially not when the victim was a guy you'd already humiliated twice in one day.

Someone handed him a bottle of water, and he drank enough to clear the cookie out of his throat. And that was sad too, because no warm chocolate chip cookie should ever be washed down with water. "Are you all right?" his launch manager, Sarah, asked.

"Fine," Holden said. He caught Dave's eye. "I'd better change. I'll be back."

Dave nodded. Holden managed a tight smile at the hotel employee who'd soaked him and walked casually back toward his room when every cell in him wanted to stomp away. But stomping was really ineffective when your shoes made a squishing sound with every step.

He passed the hotel gift boutique and made a quick detour inside, hoping that at least one thing would go his way today. Luckily, it sold golf clothes for the nearby course, and he picked up a blue golf shirt, plain, no flowers or palm trees, and some tan shorts. At the last minute he threw in a pair of flip-flops—sandals? He couldn't decide which name was worse. But the only footwear he'd brought with him where his now-soaked wingtips and a pair of beat up running shoes that would look ridiculous with anything but his running shorts.

He hurried to his room and changed in five minutes flat. He didn't want Abbie Cupcake thinking he'd retreated. He slid the flip-flops on and grunted with annoyance when they felt every bit as comfortable as his two-hundred-dollar shoes. He wanted to hate them. But he couldn't help but appreciate how well they allowed his soaked feet to dry.

He returned to the conference side of the hotel. The door to the storyboarding session made a loud click when he opened it, and he'd never felt as stupid as he did walking up to the only open seat, a spot his product development manager, Dustin, had saved him at his team's table near the front of the room. At least four mouths at that table dropped open slightly, and he could feel the lame heat across the tops of his cheekbones again. Abbie didn't help at all when she quit speaking completely. Fine. He'd play it off. He stopped in the middle of the aisle, held his hands out to his side, and did a slow turn. The room burst into laughter with a few claps thrown in.

"You seen the boss anywhere?" Sarah called out. "Button-down-shirt-and-tie guy, wouldn't know how to put on flip-flops with a YouTube tutorial?"

That really set the room off. Holden sighed. "Apex team retreat lesson one: there's stuff you don't know about me. Surprise. I own more than wingtips and Oxfords."

"You should probably pull the price tag off of that shirt," one of the women on the marketing team called. That set off another round of laughs. Holden grinned as he reached behind him to pull the tag off. He slid his hands in his pockets and did his best to saunter to his seat. He eased into it and nodded at Cupcake.

Except she wasn't looking like a cupcake now. The bright skirt, shirt and beret were gone. Her hair was still a wild mop of curls, but she'd changed into a dress, still bright, this time blue. It had a collar and tied around the middle. It looked like dresses he'd seen women in his office wear a million times, but on Abbie Cupc—er, Abbie, it looked different. Partly it was her untamed hair, looping and flouncing away from her head, like a shorter, blonder version of that one Disney character his niece, Hailey, liked so much—the redhead Scottish one. The women in the office all had well-behaved hair. But mostly it was the revelation that the cupcake had an incredible body her poofy skirt this morning hadn't even hinted at. Wow.

He tore his eyes from her and surveyed the rest of the display she'd put up so she wouldn't catch him staring. He'd missed her introduction, but her visual aids filled in all the blanks. Each easel now had a book poster on it, covers that looked all too familiar, all with the author name "Abbie Lake" under the title. There, dead center, sat the cover he'd spotted in the bookstore window earlier showing a cat in an absurdist rendering of a tutu. It was a tutu on crack. And mushrooms. Hailey would probably love it.

But Hailey was also obsessed with princesses who had corkscrew curls and no hairbrushes, which showed a clear lack of strategic thinking. He wanted to walk up and tuck the one curl that had fallen into Abbie's eyes twice already behind her ear. It was annoying. There were things to help that. Like hair gel. Or spray. Or . . . bobby pins? Most likely. The curl fell again. He winced.

Abbie blinked, once, shook her head, blinked twice more, and cleared her throat. "As I was saying, the point of stories is to capture the imagination. There are a million stories out in the children's book market about cats."

"So why did Miss Leona Kitty here win the Caldecott? And why does she stay at the top of the New York Times bestseller list?"

Good question.

"Because I think her story is every girl's story. And my job here today is to help you understand the very important stories that you need to tell so the Apex is literally the top of every list too."

Stories. Great. Because that had worked out so well for him today so far.

Five

Holden the Suit had been interesting to look at once, maybe twice, in a summing-you-up-as-an-artist kind of way. Holden in a shirt as blue as his eyes, with ridiculously hot legs shown off by his shorts—too neatly pressed, but points for not being chinos—was . . . The phrase "ridiculously hot" came to mind. Again.

It wasn't until he'd grimaced at her that Abbie even realized she'd been staring, but she snapped right out of it and got back on track, which she was proud of. It was hard to think in here because the whole place had smelled like chocolate chip cookies the second Holden opened the door. It was only the aroma from the snacks still out in the hall, but for a split second, she'd thought it was him. Someone should make a cologne that smelled like that. It would enslave all women forever.

She'd suspected he might be here, but she was sorry to be right. She taught these seminars about six times a year, and only for the companies whose vision she really believed in. She couldn't teach people to be passionate about something if they had no vision. But if theirs had merely grown fuzzy, or if they were having too many visions at once, she helped them focus. And in every case, the power of storytelling worked. Words mattered that much.

Those results had corporate event managers begging her to come in and teach her process, but she was choosy. Interesting that Holden worked for DBR Tech. It stood for Dream Big Revolution Technologies, something she could totally get behind. She wouldn't have guessed such an uptight guy would work in such a freewheeling corporate climate.

"Every story is about a quest," she said, picking up where she left off before he appeared. "Someone wants something, and they get it or they don't. That's what a story boils down to. The goal here today is for everyone to have clarity around DBR Tech's quest. Then we work backwards to figure out how each of you, as a character in this story, moves the narrative along."

She pointed to the cover for *Miss Leona Dances Flamenco*. "I already told you the secret that every aspiring writer is dying to know: the key to writing a smash hit is telling a story that everyone recognizes as their own. They become so sucked into it that every part of them is yearning for your main character to succeed. So your goal is no less than that, people. You need to write the narrative that will make the whole world pull for DBR Tech. Let's look to my friend Miss Leona for lessons."

She pulled off the cover and revealed the first page of the story, taking the group through Miss Leona's adventure, hiding a grin at the halfway point when she saw the magic begin. It was always the same—when she first started telling her favorite kitty's story, she got, at best, some polite, indulgent smiles. *How cute. A children's story.* Generally, she got what Holden was giving her, a glazed-over look, like she was robbing him of his time.

But right around the time the bold Miss Leona gets herself trapped in the pet store overnight, the first look of concern would appear. That was the moment she knew she had them—they were invested in Miss Leona's success, just like millions of little girls around the country. By the end of the story, every face in the room would be grinning at her.

And when she looked up from reading the final page, they were—on all but one face. Holden sat with his arms crossed, his stupid eyebrow up. Super easy to read again. It stated as loudly as a yell, "I'm not impressed." Actually, based on the boredom etched into every line of his face, his eyebrow was probably saying something way ruder.

No one had ever failed to fall under Miss Leona's spell before. *You love the unpredictable,* she reminded herself. And she smiled. Challenge accepted. She'd get him. He was doomed.

"Miss Leona wanted to dance Flamenco with Joaquin Cortés more than anything," she summarized for the group.

"Who wouldn't?" a woman called. "He's dead sexy."

"Focus," Abbie said with a grin. "How did Miss Leona make it happen?"

The group called out answers for a while, and she nodded, validating their participation.

"She worked hard."

"She persisted."

"She thought outside the box."

Yes, yes, and yes. But they weren't all the way there yet.

A guy with a name tag reading "David" spoke, his voice quieter than the others but somehow cutting through their answers. "She got everyone she met up with to invest in her goal."

YES. "A million awesome points to you, David. And how did she do that, Holden?" It irritated her the same way out-of-towners did when they descended on the beach and cranked their music from their portable iPod docks, forcing everyone within a fifty-yard radius to listen whether they wanted to or not. She didn't like being subjected to his mood.

"I'm guessing she made them a part of her story."

"Exactly," she said, smiling at him. "It's amazing what a story can do for you."

The dull red flush appeared on his cheekbones again. Every time that happened it made his eyes look bluer, but that's not what sent a tingle of satisfaction dancing down her spine. Nope. That was purely about putting him back in his place like he was trying so hard to do to her.

"We need to define the story goal here. What is the plan?" She moved to another easel, scribbling answers as fast as people called them out, grouping similar answers together, dividing them into the measurable and the intangibles. She'd run this workshop so many times that it was second nature to her, but she loved the satisfaction of seeing the surprise on their faces as they saw their answers take a clear shape in front of them. That didn't get old.

She'd formed a tree out of words, the trunk made up of the core principles she could hear coming out of the group, the branches made up of the products DBR Tech made; and then, lastly, she drew a single, plump red fruit hanging from one of the branches.

She pointed to it, a sharp tap of her marker. "This is the prize, ladies and gentleman. What is it that every other part of this tree is working to produce?"

"The Apex," one of them called out. "Everything is about the Apex right now."

Abbie shook her head and tapped one of the larger branches extending from the trunk. "No, this one is the Apex. What is the fruit?"

125

"World domination," David said, and everyone laughed, but he wasn't joking.

"Better," she said. "Almost there, in fact. But that doesn't feel exactly right. Who else?"

A long silence fell, and the only sound was the soft rustle of fabric as people shifted in their seats. That didn't bother Abbie. The silence would produce the answer. It always did.

Holden spoke. "Not world domination. Changing the world."

Abbie closed her eyes for a moment to consider this, to see if it resonated. It did, and she sighed. Of course it would have to come from Holden. She opened her eyes and nodded. "Yes. That's the one that feels right. The goal is to change the world. We can file what happens after that under happily ever after. We don't get to see that part of the story too often, but let's talk about it right now. What does a world changed by the Apex look like?"

More answers flew, and she drew each one as a seed coming from the red fruit. Holden's table especially poured on the answers: the Apex and its planned partner tablet, the Pinnacle, would gain market share with users, and DBR Tech would be able to get it, free of charge, into the hands of people who could use it most: nonprofit organizations, urban schools with punishing budget deficits, community centers. Not long after that they could go worldwide helping to power small businesses in developing nations and revolutionize family economies on a global scale.

The energy around these answers was different, a higher frequency, and focused. She smiled out at the room again, excited for them as they let their thoughts flow. All of them except for two. David sat quietly, but his eyes darted from speaker to speaker, weighing their words. And Holden. He was not engaged. His eyebrow rose and fell a few times, but his face stayed otherwise bored. So bored.

When the group's answers began to slide toward tangential chatter, Abbie reined them in. "You guys are nailing this." Corporate types responded to praise. They couldn't help themselves, the overachievers. "But I want to remind you that this is a process that works, and has worked for a dozen companies before you, when you give yourself over to it. So stay open, and let the magic happen. You're sharing an incredible vision of your happily ever after."

A woman her mother's age sitting next to Holden jerked her thumb at her stone-faced boss. "It's this guy's vision. He dreamed it and made us believe it. That's where the company name came from."

It was a powerful compliment, but Holden's expression didn't change by so much as a twitch. Abbie fought to keep her smile from growing brittle. How could he be the guy with such a profound vision *and* the worst attitude she'd ever seen in one of these sessions?

She pulled herself together. "Now that we've got the story goal, we need to work backwards and discuss who is going to get us there. It's time to talk about the characters. We'll use animals since I draw those better than I do people. We need to start with our chief animal. He's not always the main character, but it's usually his decree that sets things in motion. Let's do fish." That would lend itself to bright colors, and that always made her happy. "We'll make the big guy the orca whale. Who's the big guy?"

"Dave!" said at least a half dozen voices.

"Dave it is." She turned to start the orca, but Holden interrupted her.

"Maybe something besides fish. Fish are pretty dumb when you think about it. They're not exactly great strategic planners."

"Fine," she said. "Birds then." Still plenty of bright colors she could work with.

"Birds as in birdbrains?"

127

"Nooo," she said. And if Holden had known her at all, he would have recognized that the drawn-out sound of that word meant trouble was brewing for him. "More like hawks and eagles."

"But that's so predatory," he said, his voice calm. But since everyone was facing her as he spoke, only she could see the glint in his eye that said he was messing with her.

She took a deep breath. The energy was shifting back toward him, but it was changing to a more frenetic, spiky energy, and quickly. These people were used to listening to him. "We'll go with a jungle theme. Clearly Dave is the tiger, setting out on this quest with the goal of changing the world." She turned to sketch out the tiger and recapture the group's attention.

Dave interrupted this time. "I wouldn't say that's quite right. It's Holden on the quest here, so I guess he's the tiger."

Abbie straightened. Nope. Not a tiger. "That's not it, exactly. Holden's not a tiger, but I know exactly how to draw him." She whipped back around to the drawing pad and sketched out an ape, a giant, gray ape with a sour mouth. She heard the good-natured jokes they threw Holden's way, but it wasn't until she added the wildly exaggerated eyebrows onto her ape and stepped back that the picture drew full-blown laughter.

"How did you do that?" A middle-aged woman asked through her laughter. "It looks exactly like a gorilla but exactly like Holden at the same time."

Even Dave was grinning. Holden, not so much. He wore the same sour expression as the gorilla, but when one of his co-workers pointed from his mouth to the gorilla's mouth and burst into laughter again, Holden forced his into a smile.

Well, he probably thought he was smiling. If she drew him now it would be as a gorilla baring its teeth. When the laughter kept coming, his smile tightened, and weirdly, Abbie felt the same tightening in her chest. Was that . . .

guilt? She tried to push it aside. Holden had without question earned his caricature, but the forced smile on his face made it all seem less funny. She spun back to the drawing pad, eager to get past this and redeem herself. And she could only do that if she redeemed him.

Her marker spun out a tiger, benevolent but watchful. "Meet Dave." That earned claps of approval, and from there she characterized each part of the Apex team as a different animal. The marketing team became a macaw; the product development team became capuchin monkeys, clever little tool users that they were. And so it went. As soon as she could, she directed each team to work at their tables to develop the frame for their part of the story, sketching out a plot of how they fit in. Holden stayed quiet through all of it. She was beginning to feel like a Bad Human.

She'd told the group she wasn't good at drawing humans, but that wasn't true. She was an exceptionally gifted caricaturist, but she hated that her art tended to betray character flaws that her subjects didn't want to see. And, in most cases, weren't ready to see. So she'd given up caricature years ago and switched to animals. But making Holden into an ape had made him way too easy for her to mock. And now he was dealing with the emotional aftermath of having his entire department laugh at him and his communicative eyebrows. She'd made it okay for them to ridicule him.

When had she become a bully?

Inside, a sick feeling grew. How could she write *Miss Leona Beats the Bully* and then turn around and do this? She moved from table to table, supervising the progress of their stories. Her job would be to pull it all together and facilitate a discussion that would allow the group to write a happy ending where the gorilla got the fruit.

She'd gone to every table but Holden's, and she couldn't put it off any longer. She swallowed and walked over, standing so she wouldn't have to look directly at him. "How's

129

your story coming?" she asked the table. She expected them to defer to him, but he said nothing, so a woman named Sarah explained the narrative they had come up with. They'd decided that Holden would be trying to shuttle a human child, a la Tarzan, through the jungle to get the baby to the fruit tree that would provide all the nutrients the human would need to grow big and strong like his new ape family.

"It just kinda made sense for the story since the goal is to give people everywhere this technology as a lifeline to the outside world," the woman said. The rest of the group voiced their agreement, but Holden fidgeted as the story continued. When the gorilla fought off attackers and rescued a baby capuchin, he crossed and re-crossed his legs. Three times. By the time the ape banished a giant anaconda (apparently Apple Inc.), Holden rose and excused himself with a mumbled apology.

The rest of the group was wrapped up in the story, trying to decide what the climax would be, so no one said anything about his disappearance, but Abbie's chest tightened even more. She, too, excused herself to no one in particular and slipped out to the hallway, wondering where to even look for Holden or what to say when she found him.

She didn't get a chance to figure it out because he was standing right there, picking up another chocolate chip cookie from the snack table. Once again, Abbie decided that the combination of Holden and that cookie scent was, at a minimum, intoxicating.

When he fixed her with his blue eyes, she upgraded that to lethal, until she remembered what a pain he'd been until the ape thing. She still owed him an apology but there was zero danger she'd be falling under any Holden/cookie spell.

"You okay?" she asked.

"Sure. Just bored. Needed to stretch for a minute."

Ouch. Nice to hear he had such a high opinion of her presentation skills.

"It's not you," he added, and she wondered if she'd winced. "It's all of this. I know Dave thinks dragging us here for three days and doing stuff like this is important, but I think being in the office and actually working on the Apex rollout is important."

He made "stuff like this" sound like a dirty phrase. It was crystal clear to Abbie in that short explanation why exactly Dave had "dragged" everyone down here, especially Holden.

"Sorry you're bored." That sounded snotty and defensive. She drew a cleansing breath, counted to five, and tried again. "And sorry I drew that ape. That wasn't cool. I have a temper. Or so I hear."

His hand crept up to pat his chest for a second like he was checking for the tie that used to be there. "Right. Don't worry about it. It was a good ape."

She felt the need to make a better apology, something more than "I'm sorry," so she tried for a compliment that it pained her to pay. "It seems like it's a great ape, if what that table in there says is true. They're big fans of that ape."

That won a small smile from him. "Maybe. But they kept trying to send him into patches of stinging nettle. Does that even grow in the jungle?"

Abbie laughed. "Maybe the nettle is a metaphor for setbacks."

"Nope. Pretty sure they just want the ape in the nettle."

Abbie didn't know what to say to that, and she wasn't one to talk just to talk. Maybe he was a bit of a jerk, but she'd seen with her own eyes that he'd had a rough day, one she had contributed to, and it was barely after lunch time. So she bit back a joke about how much he *nettled* people.

"I've taught a dozen or so of these storyboarding classes, and I've learned how to read a room full of you corporate types. In my expert opinion, they may want to see you in the nettles a little bit, but I've seen it when they want

131

to shove the guy into a pit of crocodiles, and that room doesn't," she said, pointing behind them. "And that should count for something. Probably." Maybe it didn't with this guy. But if it had bothered him enough to seek solace in a chocolate chip cookie, maybe it would matter.

"You came out here to make me feel better?" A laugh hid in his question.

"The guy who got his tie cut off by a clearly crazy person, lost out on a business deal to said crazy person, had fourteen million gallons of ice water dumped down his back, and then got thrown into the nettles—repeatedly—by his subordinates? Yeah. Seemed like you could use a pep talk." And before she could stop herself—why could she NEVER stop herself?—she leaned over and swatted him on the butt.

He jumped about a foot, and she grinned at him. "Go, team!" *That's what the sports guys did. Right?* Oh please, let her have gotten that right.

Holden opened his mouth. He closed it. He opened it again. He closed it again. He opened it a third time and said, "Yay?"

And Abbie burst into laughter. "Well done. Now go get yourself out of the nettles."

Holden slid his hands in his pockets and walked past her, which stretched his shorts across his backside. It kinda made Abbie wish she'd taken the full split second to appreciate the smack more when she did it.

He stopped and turned, and she hoped she'd looked up quickly enough. "You have not been the same person in the three times I've run into you now," he said.

"Should I be? That doesn't sound fun."

"But you've been three totally different people. I kind of want to know which one is really you."

"All of them. Most people are a lot of things."

"People play different roles, yeah. Sure. But before lunch

you were like a cross between my stepmom's little Maltese and my loony aunt Heidi, then after lunch you were like the guy on *To Catch a Predator* except that I'm not a perv, and now you're like Cheryl Sandberg crossed with Beatrix Potter."

Why did he sound so puzzled by that? Although to be fair, he wouldn't be the first person she'd confused just by existing. She shrugged. "There's nothing wrong with being any of those things."

"Nope. But there's nothing norm—um, common about being all of those things between lunch and dinner."

"If you say so."

"I can't wait to see who you are next."

She couldn't tell if he was setting her up for a mean joke about multiple personality disorder or if he was genuinely curious. She hated that she'd learned to be guarded enough to even wonder, but life, and ex-boyfriends who didn't know when to take off their ties, had taught her to be wary.

"We won't have to cross paths again after this afternoon, so I guess it'll stay a mystery. Race you to the table," she added, hustling to beat him to the conference room door.

"Wait. I don't like unsolved mysteries. Go to dinner with me, and let me see what else I can figure out."

She froze with her hand on the door and glanced back at him, finding exactly what she expected to see: a look of total confusion on his face, like he wasn't sure who had opened his mouth and invited her to dinner with his voice.

It was happening again. And it had ended badly all three times before: hotshot business guy is attracted to his polar opposite, a cute, artsy children's book author who lives her life by impulse. That, and by a carefully regulated system of cell phone reminder alarms so she could function kind of like a grownup.

She'd learned to say no to the Holdens who drifted through Seashell Beach. No, Holdens didn't drift. Holdens strode through Seashell Beach, purposefully, with no intention of stopping for longer than their weekend golf trip or corporate retreat.

And while it should have been easier to say no to Holden, even with his Pacific blue eyes and caramel hair, she still at least said it. "I don't think so, but thanks."

"I know, I've been a jerk. Does it help that I'm sorry?"

She shook her head, but before she could speak he sweetened the deal. "I deserved to have my tie cut off. And you didn't need to pay me for it. So how about we take the money and use it for dinner and broker some kind of peace treaty?"

He was making it even harder with his genuineness and his . . . his . . . *smiles.* But Abbie didn't want to be his mystery. She made sense to herself, and it only exhausted her when the suits in her past had tried to understand her. Generally, understanding her meant slowly trying to change her into someone else. And it didn't matter that Holden wasn't in a suit now; his bones were probably tattooed "Hugo Boss."

So she shook her head and crossed the last few feet to the door to check on the progress inside. She turned to offer him one last "no hard feelings" smile and caught an expression she didn't expect on his face: real disappointment. Could she really pile a rejection on top of everything else she'd done to him today?

She let go of the handle. She did owe him a date. But he was asking out her corporate trainer alter ego because he thought he understood that version of her. What he would get at dinner would be pure, unfiltered Abbie, the straight up real thing. Let's see how he handled her then. "I changed my mind. I'll go with you, but I pick the place."

His shoulders relaxed. "Cool."

"Meet me on the corner of Tangerine and Beach at seven. No tie."

He grinned. "No tie."

"All right. Let's go get you out of the nettles."

Six

Holden should be more bothered that Abbie didn't add up. He was a numbers guy, an engineering guy, a make-it-all-work-in-the-most-efficient-way-possible guy. But it had quit bothering him after about twenty minutes of watching her in action when he'd walked into her class. Everything about her in that session spoke volumes about her talent and passion. In fact, his niece was getting a Miss Leona book every year for her birthday. Abbie had converted him in a half hour flat.

But beyond that, there was an almost scary intelligence in the way she was able to take storytelling principles, meld them with the corporate-speak, and lead an entire room to produce a cohesive vision—something he hadn't realized had gotten lost along the way. By the end of the session, his team had quit throwing him into the nettles and had him scaling the tree for the fruit, but he'd insisted the ape couldn't have it unless he carried the macaw up the tree on one shoulder and a couple of monkeys on the other.

After Abbie drew the final scene with the ape back on the ground, holding the fruit out to his jungle friends to share, the entire room burst into applause. Even Holden had sat there grinning. Abbie was crazy good with a marker. And more. She was good with people. She'd processed information very, very quickly and conceptualized it in an imaginative way. It fascinated him. He'd asked her to dinner on a rare whim, but he looked more and more forward to it as the afternoon wore on. When the session broke, he caught her eye and mouthed "Seven." Her return nod made him feel way better than a simple nod should. It was as good as the chocolate chip cookies.

And so what? The Apex had been his sole focus for over a year, and if Dave was going to make him stay down here for two more days, then he might as well take full advantage. Of the situation. Not Abbie. Because that would be a jerk move.

If Abbie was into a mutually beneficial flirtation, well, that was something else. He grinned all the way through the hotel lobby and almost got on the elevator before he realized he'd need to make another stop at the hotel boutique. It was the kind of compromise a guy made when his date hated ties, and as he lifted a black linen shirt off the rack and enjoyed the sensation of an unstarched fabric, he thought maybe she had a point.

By 7:05, Holden stood on the corner of Tangerine and Beach, staring out at the pinkening sky. He didn't really take the time to look out of his office window in Cupertino at this time of day often enough. But he'd had five solid minutes of uninterrupted sunset-staring now, and he was beginning to feel pretty dumb. By 7:08, he was too distracted by his watch to appreciate the sunset anymore. Had Abbie forgotten? Changed her mind?

By 7:12 he was halfway down the block back toward the hotel when he heard a bicycle bell and his name being

137

shouted. He turned to see Abbie on a beach cruiser, the retro-looking bikes people rode up and down the coast highway. She was a fuchsia blur as she coasted to a stop next to him, already in the middle of a sentence.

"Sorry! I forgot to set my alarm. Well, no I set it to remind me to eat, but then I left my phone in my bike basket when I went down to the tidepools. Low tide is awesome. It's at five tomorrow. Ish. Five-ish. I believe in -ish, you know? I'm late way less often when we're dealing with -ish time. Anyway, there was this amazing little hermit crab who was fighting this way-bigger hermit crab, and it seemed like it went on forever, and I was like, 'I could watch this all night,' and then this voice that pipes up every now and then to save me was like, 'Nope, you're meeting Holden,' and I ran back to my bike and saw that it was already seven, so I pedaled like crazy. Which is not really what beach cruisers are built for. It's hard work making a bike that heavy move that fast. I think I'm going to have He-Man calf muscles by tomorrow."

She climbed off her bike as she babbled and leaned it against her while she smiled up at him. "Anyway, I was wondering if, on account of the exceptional effort I put into turning this station wagon into a drag racer," she patted the bike, "we could maybe pretend we were supposed to be on -ish time all along, and I'm not really being incredibly rude right now by showing up—" she squinted at her phone display—"let's not talk about how late."

He could only laugh. Her mad dash had flung her curls in a million directions, and those, on top of the bright sundress she'd put on, and her exertion-flushed cheeks, did him in. "Yeah, we're on -ish time. So what's the plan?"

Her eyes shone. "It's a surprise. Let's go up Tangerine. I'll park my bike, and then I'll lead you to food."

When her bike was handled and she joined him on the sidewalk, his stomach grumbled, and he winced.

"I'm really gifted in nonverbal communication cues," she said. "Your stomach just asked if food is soon, and the answer is yes." She stopped in front of a bakery with a sign marking it "Closed" and pushed the door open, releasing the scent of butter and warm sugar. "Welcome to Delilah's Desserts."

"But it's closed."

She grinned at him. "I know Delilah. For me, she's only ever closed-ish. Besides, this is the perfect place to start. You don't seem like the dessert first kind of guy. You probably eat your vegetables first at every meal."

"Why does it sound like you accused me of cheating on my taxes? I do eat them first. So do a lot of people."

"You're right. The entire population of Boring, USA eats their veggies first. You probably even like them."

"You're very judgmental," he said, smiling in spite of himself. "Yes, I like vegetables."

"Say veggies."

"I just did."

"No, you said vegetables. Say *veggies.*"

He sighed. "Veggies." He felt stupid.

"Good job." She patted his arm. "Using a cutesy name for serious food is a positive sign that you might be able to handle dessert first."

"I could honestly eat anything right now." He followed her into the store, where the warmth was a nice contrast to the cool breeze sweeping up Tangerine Street. "What are we having?" He was looking down at her, or he would have seen the answer.

"Cupcakes, of course," she said.

He looked at the case and laughed. It was full of all kinds of color, sugar crystals, elaborate swirls lined up in tempting rows behind the glass. "I know I'm probably supposed to be embarrassed or apologize, but I can't lie. The cupcake comparison was right on."

"If you mean the frothy tops hide a rich and textured interior, then I'll give it to you."

"Yes, that's what I meant," he said, his face straight.

A door from the back swished open, and a pretty brunette stepped out with a streak of frosting across her cheek.

"Hey, Delilah," Abbie said with a subtle swiping motion at her own cheek.

Delilah flushed and tried to wipe away the frosting with the back of her wrist, but that only left a trail of flour behind. "Did I get it?"

"Um, kind of?" Abbie said.

Delilah sighed. "Never mind. If I feed you, will you go away? I'm working on a new flavor."

"Yes," Abbie said. "You know I'd hate to mess with your art."

Delilah smiled at that. "Sorry. I'm just on to something, I think." Her gaze wandered back toward the kitchen before she blinked and focused on her after hours guests. "What can I get for you?"

"Cupcakes," Abbie and Holden said together.

"I want chocolate-chocolate chip with peanut butter frosting, please," Abbie said.

Delilah was reaching for that flavor before Abbie had even spoken. "And for you?" she asked Holden.

He rubbed his jaw. "I'm going to need whichever cupcake has the swirliest frosting on top of the most richly textured flavors you've got."

"O-kay," Delilah said as Abbie laughed. "That would probably be the Mocha Marble. Cream cheese frosting on top of a mocha vanilla marbled cake, stuffed with a chocolate ganache."

"Sounds about right. Could you make it extra complicated?" he asked. "Sprinkle some unusual savory spice on top or something? I really want to get this right."

"Ignore him," Abbie told Delilah, delivering a light punch to his arm. "Your normal Mocha Marble will be great."

"Normal? I don't think so—" Holden started before Abbie cut him off by catching his sleeve and tugging him toward a table.

"All right, you've made your point. You're committed to this apology. You're prepared to see me as more than my outward appearance and admit that I have complex layers. You acknowledge that someone can unironically wear a beret. Did I miss anything?"

Delilah appeared and set a cupcake in front of each of them before retreating back to her kitchen.

Holden sampled his cupcake. His eyes widened, and he'd be damned if a series of flavors didn't unfold and flood his tongue with that single bite. "You missed that I really like cupcakes. A lot," he added around a second bite. When the dessert was gone, and it was gone far too fast, he wiped the crumbs from his hands and eyed her across the table. "I'm going to fill up on cupcakes. We may never get to actual dinner."

"Slow your roll, homie," she said, her tone lazy. That made him snort, and she grinned again. "One cupcake. And then we try the next taste adventure."

He shook his empty cupcake wrapper. "Bring it."

Abbie walked to the counter and called into the back. "We're taking off, Delilah. Fabulous, as usual."

Delilah popped her head out, now with flour streaks in her hair. "Thanks for stopping in," she said and disappeared again.

Abbie led the way out of the shop. "Delilah and I are like soul sisters. We both have a deep spiritual appreciation for cream cheese, and she gets as lost in her cupcake experiments as I do in my stories."

"I need something more interesting to get lost in than a cell phone."

"I don't know," Abbie said, her voice thoughtful. "This Apex thing you guys are making sounds like it's totally worth getting lost in. Your coworkers definitely think so. It's obvious they see the vision you have for that technology."

"Maybe," he said, but he couldn't fight another smile. That had been a completely unexpected surprise—to realize how invested his people still were in the Apex despite all of Dave's burnout warnings.

"Definitely," she corrected. "Remember, I'm kind of an expert in objective corporate observation."

"There you go, being a mystery again. One second you're immersed in cupcake-eating, and the next you're this totally incisive business analyst."

"It only seems like a mystery to you because you probably have the insane notion that you have to be one thing. You don't. Nobody does."

"But how can you be so many things? Someone who runs on -ish time and gets lost in tidepools *and* someone who can wrangle a roomful of MBA-fueled egos?"

"I don't think about it that hard, you know? I just am whatever I want to be. Look," she said, and her whole face brightened. "I changed my mind about dinner. We're going there instead." She pointed at a candy shop. Candy's Shop, specifically, the sign said. "You see how easy it is? I can start the evening intending on Indian food and detour to candy just like that."

"We're having candy for dinner?"

"Think of it as sugar tapas," she said, picking up her pace like she was ET on the trail of Reese's Pieces.

"Tapas is real food. Candy isn't."

"Sure it is. The exact same processes in my body are involved. I consume it, enzymes digest it for me, and all the systems in this here bone house work together to metabolize it and distribute it to my cells for energy."

"Bone house?"

"Words, Holden. I play with words all day long. You should try it. It's fun. Sugar tapas and bone houses are way cooler than taffy and bodies. Candy!" she called as she pushed open the door to the shop.

"Are you demanding it or stating the obvious?" he asked.

She laughed. "Candy!" she called again.

"Abbie!" a voice called back. "Got new taffy today: mashed potato."

Holden's stomach lurched.

A person followed the voice out, a tiny person with pink hair who was now blowing a bubble.

"This is Candy."

Okay . . . seemed a little far to take the branding, but whatever.

Candy read his expression easily. "It's really my name. I mean, ask the priest at St. Joe's and he'll tell you he baptized me as Candace Marie, but I've always been Candy, so what was I going to do really, except this?" She swept her arm to encompass the shop, every surface of it crammed with bulk bins or barrels or tubs. "Try whatever you like, but I'm guessing you're an import guy," she said, pointing to a corner that was all brown, with glass cases full of fudges and truffles and foil-wrapped bon bons.

Abbie jumped in. "Oh no, we're definitely doing taffy."

Please don't let that be someone's stripper name. But there was no human named Taffy in Candy's Candy Shop, just an entire floor-to-ceiling section of taffy in more colors than he bet Abbie's illustrator mind could come up with. There was even a machine pulling taffy behind glass right in front of them.

"I'm putting together your next course for you, but feel

free to wander," Abbie told him. She darted away, scanning the bins and plucking out pieces. He checked out the nearest wall. Cotton Candy. Green Apple. Root Beer. That one sounded good. He moved farther down. Pina Colada. Passion Fruit. Mai Tai. Exotic, but nothing he couldn't handle. Whiskey? Bacon? Corn? Wait, corn-flavored taffy? He could do popcorn maybe, but he had a feeling this was the cob kind.

Abbie was back. "Hold out your hand. Dinner is served."

He obeyed, and she named the pieces she set in his palm. "Fried chicken and waffles, bacon, maple syrup, and orange juice, which, to warn you, is more sour than regular orange taffy."

He looked from her to his hand and back. "No."

She shrugged. "Still playing with your idea of meals and order. Dessert first and now breakfast for dinner, one of my favorites," she said with a nod at the abomination of taffy he held.

"No." He tried to give it back.

She put her hands behind her back. "Yes. It's good for you. It'll stretch you."

"It'll stretch out my stomach maybe, in a bad way."

"You're a lightweight. We need to toughen you up. Follow me."

She stepped ahead of him, ready to zip over to a different part of the store, but an impulse he couldn't understand or control overtook him as he reached out and tangled his fingers with hers. He didn't know why he did it, but he loved the soft slide of her skin against his.

She stared down at their hands, then back to him. Her eyes held a question, but she didn't pull away.

He smiled. "I'm hanging on to you so I don't get lost."

She nodded and pulled him toward the next nook, and something about the way he fell into step behind her, so easily, so ready for whatever ridiculous thing she threw at him next, forced him to wonder if he meant she was helping him find his way in a metaphorical sense too.

Seashell Beach and metaphors, man. What was it with this place?

But he didn't let go of Abbie's hand. He was too curious about where she would take him next.

Seven

Abbie didn't know what to think about the fingers twined through hers. *So don't think,* the irresponsible part of herself said. It was a hard voice to ignore since it was always the loudest one. *Just feel.*

But "just feeling" when it had come to cute, hard-driving businessmen never worked. Not in the end, anyway. She didn't let go, though. His hand surprised her. It wasn't as soft as she thought it would be. Calluses on his palm rasped against hers and raised the hairs at the nape of her neck, a delicious sensation she hadn't felt since her week-long flirtation with a ridiculously cute visiting travel writer the previous summer.

She fought a shiver and navigated them around candy barrels toward a nook that looked like Dr. Seuss had exploded in it, full of blinding neon and cartoonish candy wrappers. It was here she let go, pretending she needed to scrub her hand through her hair to think while she located what she was looking for. Really, she couldn't think with the constant tingle of his skin against hers. Holding his hand under the pretense of playing his guide was much different than standing there, holding hands for no reason at all.

"We'll do the crash course in toughening you up, you and your stomach," she said, searching the bins.

"Are you looking for Mentos and Diet Coke, maybe? Because if so, I won't fall for it."

"Nope. And what I'm about to prescribe for you is even Mythbuster tested and guaranteed not to do anything to you." She reached out to a shelf and pulled down three black envelopes about the size and shape of seed packets. "This should do it."

"Pop Rocks?" He looked resigned more than resistant. *Good. Progress.*

"Yes. Let's get this all rung up." She pointed toward the cash register and swept her arm toward him in a go-ahead gesture. There would be no hand-flirting this time.

The teenager at the register totaled everything up. "Eight forty-two," he said.

Holden dug out his wallet, but Abbie waved his money away. "I've got this. Your money is no good here."

"I'll take it," the teenager said.

Holden laughed and set a five dollar tip on the counter for the candy shop employee, separate from the money Abbie paid. "Nice hustle, kid. Here's an even better tip: never be afraid of asking for what you want. You might not get it, but if you don't ask at all the answer is always no."

He took the white paper bag from the grinning cashier, and Abbie led them back to the sidewalk. "Sorry again about the tie and being irrational earlier or whatever. I hope that bag of sugar is enough to bribe your forgiveness."

"It's a start, but talk to me again after I've tried the mashed potato taffy."

"You'll have to let me know what you think."

147

THE BOARDWALK ANTIQUES SHOP

He studied her, his eyebrows drawing slightly together and furrowing his forehead. "Why are you saying that like you won't be right here watching me try not to make dorky faces while I eat it?"

"Because I won't. I have to go. I have work to do. But my conscience is clear. You've got food and a great view." She nodded toward the ocean and the sky painted with cotton candy poofs of orange and pink.

"You have to work at eight at night?"

Abbie smiled at the disbelief in his tone. "Artists don't really work on a nine to five. Not unless we have bosses with no concept of what it means to employ a creative type. But I'm my boss, and so I do work as it comes to me. And right now I feel like working. So enjoy Seashell Beach. I don't know if I'll be out of my studio much before you leave, but if I don't see you again, good luck with changing the world. That's my favorite story I've ever drawn at one of those trainings. I hope it works out for you."

She waved and turned to walk away, her heart pounding as if she'd taken off in a sprint. It was too tempting to stay and slip her hand into his again, to walk down the coast highway laughing as he worked his way through his taffy "breakfast."

"Hey," he called, his voice soft enough to blend with the waves. But since every atom in her had been straining toward him, she heard him. She stopped and glanced back at him. "Yeah?"

"I'm only here until Tuesday. I want to see you again."

She walked back and planted her hands on her hips, staring him straight in the eye. "Why? We've had more bad interactions than good ones."

"I think those are at least tied now," he argued.

"Even if they are, it's a bad idea."

"Feels like the best idea I've had in a while."

He said it with no swagger, and she dropped her hands

148

from her hips and took another step toward him. "It's a bad idea because you're only here until Tuesday and then you're gone, so what's the point?"

"Fun?" He said it like it was a new vocabulary word. "I need more fun, I think. A few hours with you in that hotel room this afternoon, and suddenly I was seeing things totally differently." He heard how it sounded even as he said it and winced while Abbie laughed in spite of herself. "I meant the hotel conference room. And I meant that I was seeing the Apex launch differently."

"I know," she said on a giggle. "But thanks for clarifying." It was the pink along his cheekbones that kept her from pulling herself together faster. Somehow when he did that, she could imagine a young Holden like the one he'd invented in his toy soldier story. She'd crafted enough stories, and studied even more stories crafted by others, to know there had been truth in his version of *Private Dan Saves the Day*.

She took another step away from him. "But I always have fun. What would be in it for me, really?"

This time he took a step toward her. "What do you want?

She hesitated and closed the gap between them, reaching up to set her hand on his arm. His skin was warm against hers, and the muscles in his forearm tensed, coiled for action. She should have taken that as a cue to snatch her hand away and walk off. But instead she rubbed his arm ever so slightly, a gentle back and forth. "I'm not going to spend time with you because you are too good-looking and warm and your hair is too nice and your smile is too crooked in the best way."

That smile peeked out at her, and he leaned toward her, like she'd reeled him in, and maybe she had. But she stepped back again. They'd been doing a poorly counted cha-cha for the last five minutes. "I've been down this road. From where you're standing, you can't see the dead end sign, but I know it's there. I've run into it a few times."

"What if I promise not to ask you to marry me?"

"What? Who's talking about marriage?"

"No one. That's my point. But in a single afternoon you shifted a key piece of the way I see a project that has been my life for six years. I wonder what would happen if I spent even more time with you. And I guess what I have to offer you is a true story. Of why I wanted the soldiers," he added when her eyebrow flew up.

Now that was tempting. She'd never collected antiques until Jennifer Day and her irresistible stories came along. And it was the stories Abbie saw when she looked out over the pieces tucked into every corner in her house.

But she took another step back, and then another, wondering how many it would take before it lessened his pull. "Sorry," she said, reaching up to rub her forehead. "But as hardheaded as I am, it still really hurts when I run into the dead end sign." She dropped her hand to wave goodbye before she turned and walked away. There would be no dancing back to him this time. She caught a flash of hurt in his eyes as she turned. He probably didn't offer up that story very often. Or maybe at all. Guilt twisted her gut, but she only sped up her getaway. The intensity of how much she wanted to hear his story scared her.

She couldn't get lost in someone else again. Maybe this was karma or something, and she would be stuck repeating the same mistake until she learned from it. *I am learning this time,* she promised the universe or whoever noted such things. *I'm stronger, better, and smarter than this. No more dead ends.*

An hour later, she was in her studio and should have been well into the illustration for a story about a sparrow she'd been drafting in her head. Instead, the gorilla from the afternoon session had come out of her drawing pencil. She'd tried to make him into a cranky old man of the forest. But whatever she did with this gorilla, his eyes were still nice, almost smiling.

And now she had to acknowledge a lesson she'd learned forever ago: she couldn't fight the story. She could only tell it. So she'd let the gorilla do his thing for a couple of pages. He was on alert after hearing a noise in the forest, every muscle standing at attention, eyebrows drawn straight as he prepared for whatever was coming.

She kind of wanted to know what it was too, but instead of drawing the next sketch to find out, she threw her pencil down. A gorilla was all wrong for Holden, anyway. If she were really going to represent him as an animal, he was more like a German shepherd. Lean build, proud head, intelligent eyes.

And there was something else. Some dog breeds had laughter built right into their faces, like they were ready for the next joke or caper. Retrievers were like that. German shepherds were definitely not. Holden didn't have a sadness about him, exactly, but she wondered what had led him to see the world so analytically, to be so wound up that he spent his first day in a seaside town marching down the boardwalk in a tie.

She shoved away from her desk before she decided to do a series of dog sketches. This was so stupid. She didn't need to get into a character study of Holden Suit-Man now or ever. She rummaged through her supply cabinet for the finger paints she kept on hand for her nieces and nephews. It wasn't until she'd smeared every dumb gorilla sketch with abstract streaks of primary colors that she felt better. She needed to remember to be four years old more often. It was way more fun than twenty-seven.

Her phone rang at too early o'clock the next morning, but the display said it was in fact a few minutes after ten. Abbie blinked twice, sat up, and answered. "'Lo?"

"Did I wake you up?" It was Gentry, the owner at Wonderland Books.

Abbie cleared the sleep out of her throat. "Yes."

"Good," he said. "You're due at story time in five minutes."

"Dang it! It's the third Saturday today, isn't it?"

"It is," Gentry agreed, sounding more exasperated than angry that she'd nearly stood him up. Again. "I'll distract the kids until you get here, but you'll get here soon, right?"

"Right," she said, planting her feet on the furry rug beside her bed. "Be there in a bit." She pulled out her favorite cutoffs and a halter top made from a vintage café curtain printed with steaming cups of coffee, the faded fabric perfectly soft against her skin. She'd never gotten over the idea of drinking something made out of beans, which she hated, but she loved the retro feel of the design against the super soft fabric. It was a fun shirt, and it would let her soak up the sun as she pedaled down to the bookstore. Besides, the kids loved it when she wore unusual prints.

September was the month smart people came to the beach. It was as warm as July, with a fraction of the crowds. She stopped at her front door to slide on flip-flops, but when she couldn't find any, she gave up and climbed on her bike barefooted, happy to let her toes stretch in the morning sun. The kids wouldn't mind that, either.

The fifteen-minute ride landed her at Wonderland Books wide awake and apologetic when she saw how many kids were waiting for her. Over a dozen. *Sorry,* she mouthed to Gentry, who waved away her apology and finished reading a story about a foul-smelling pigeon.

He set the book aside and stood up, clasping his hands behind his back and squaring off his stance like he was a soldier. He cleared his throat and in a baritone so deep it made several of the kids laugh he announced, "Ladies and gentlemen, we now present the one, the only, the fantastic Abbie Lake to read to you the newest story about Miss Leona's adventures."

The kids cheered, and Abbie walked to the front and slid into the empty story reader's seat. This was one of her very favorite things to do, and she was glad Gentry had woken her up to do it. There was no audience she'd rather read for than the crowd of excited little faces staring up at her from the floor of Wonderland Books.

Thirty minutes and three stories later, the restless wiggles started, and when she closed the cover on one of her favorite Mo Willems books, she smiled at her listeners. "That's it for story time today. Why don't you each go grab your mom or dad and go show them your favorite book in Wonderland."

The kids scrambled to their feet and scattered toward the grownups browsing in the store. She handed the books she'd read back to Gentry, when someone behind her called her name.

"Abbie."

The sound of it, the rich timbre, sent a tiny shiver down her spine, and she curled her bare toes into the Persian rug that often became Aladdin's magic carpet during story time. "Holden," she said, turning to face him as the front door closed behind him and he stood smiling at her, his hand behind his back. Man, he looked good in black shorts and a heather-purple T-shirt, the kind her cat, Artemis, would steal and knead for its softness. But so help her, if he was hiding flowers she would march right past him to find a different adventure as far from Holden as she could get on her bike. Two of her dead ends had started with flowers.

Wait, no. She *wanted* him to have flowers so she could write him off once and for all, confident that he was the

153

cliché—that they would be the cliché together that she'd assumed they would be all along. *Oh, and* please *let them be roses. Red ones.* He'd be dead to her, easy as that. "What brings you in here?" she asked, wishing she wasn't so curious to know.

A sheepish look crossed his face, and it was adorable. "I heard you last night. I did. But I'm not a quitter. So when I saw the poster in the window this morning saying you'd be reading in here, I thought I'd take a shot at changing your mind."

How was she supposed to resist that? But she had to. And it half made her angry that he was putting her in the position of having to reject him again. She wanted to be a nice person. A nice, unattached person. Or at least unattached to someone with whom she had no future other than an eventually emotionally exhausting relationship. Just the thought wrung a sigh out of her. "You know, for two seconds last night, I thought I maybe got it wrong about you. I had assumed that you were another corporate calculator-head who was more interested in profit-loss statements than anything. And that would make you the type to just charge in and take what you want by any means necessary. You know, like making up a story to win a contest.

"Then yesterday you're all, 'I have this noble vision,' and your people were all, 'Holden is the best. He can even take a joke. Good old Gorilla Holden.' And then you charm me into meeting up with you, and you almost charmed me into sticking around last night."

She rubbed her hands over her face, mostly to give her a chance to hide from his searching eyes, eyes that measured and analyzed her as she spoke. She didn't like the feeling. He was good. Too good, in fact, showing up with flowers and expecting her to throw the common sense he'd mocked her for not having right out the window. "I can't blame you for me acting like an idiot, but I knew I should trust my gut.

You're exactly what you seemed the first time around, manipulating a situation to get what you want. And I'm dumb enough to feel sad about that even though I've only known you for twenty-four hours."

Holden's left eyebrow shot up. "I'm not going to apologize for *taking* what I want. I don't do that. But I do get what I want because I make a point of reading the situation and thinking about what the other person wants too and giving it to them. I'm about creating the win-win situation. It's the smartest and most efficient way to operate, and it's what makes me not just effective, but successful. It's one of the best things about me."

His confidence was sexy where it should have been off-putting, and Abbie wanted to slap herself the second she felt that twinge of wanting that started in her abdomen and raced along her nerve-endings. She knew better than this. She'd been here before. Except . . . not exactly. Suits #1–3 had all started out with a version of, "I want to change; I need to open up to new experiences." And each of them had been sincere. But it wasn't in the nature of someone who was wired for achievement and ambition to slow down. Abbie had been a phase for each of them.

By the third time, she'd begun recognizing the signs when she saw them, and although that relationship hadn't toasted her emotionally the same way the earlier ones had, it cemented her decision to never again go the Way of the Suit. Didn't matter about broad shoulders or blue eyes, or the stories she suspected lurked inside of them. Didn't even matter that Holden had opted out of the suit again today.

She crossed her arms, a defensive posture, but she was going on the attack. "You read me and decided that what I really want is flowers?" She knew she sounded smug, and she didn't care. She was only thankful he was about to give her the ammunition she needed to prove that he was reading her totally wrong, that no sooner would he have any idea about her than she would change and frustrate him. And she didn't want to change that about herself. But he would want to.

He shook his head and pulled his hand out to give her a bouquet of . . . towels, maybe? And rubber bands?

She took it from him, studying it. It had a vaguely human shape—long, straight torso, what looked like arms and legs fastened with elastics to the trunk, topped with a knob that looked like a sock ball held on with more rubber bands. "You shouldn't have?" Who knew? She wasn't exactly sure what it was, so she had no idea if he should have or not.

"It's a voodoo doll. Turn it over."

She did and burst out laughing. He'd used a marker to draw some rough-looking eyebrows on the sock to give the "face" a quizzical expression. "It's you."

"Yes. I thought a woman who runs around in vintage fabrics and carries a handmade purse would probably prefer something handmade to a bunch of flowers from a grocer's bucket."

"How do you know my stuff is handmade?"

"It's too interesting to be mass produced."

She felt a swoon coming on.

He peered at her, looking as if he wasn't sure if he should go on, but he did. "Anyway, I figured you'd rather take out your aggressions on me than have flowers."

She waggled a doll arm back and forth, and he winced and rubbed his elbow, which made her laugh again. "Fine. You're right. You read me well."

"Good. So between that and the promise of a true story I never tell, is it enough to get you to come to a real dinner? Something not out of a wrapper?"

She should say no. The word formed in her head but not on her lips. "Yes," she said, and it floated out on a sigh. "Yes, I'll go to dinner with you."

Gentry let out an echoing sigh of relief. "Good. I told him it would be okay to come in and talk to you, and I don't want to tick off my favorite author. You're the reason the store lives and breathes."

Abbie waved his words away and colored, but Holden didn't want to drop it. "What do you mean?"

"I mean," Gentry said, "that when the economy was eating independent bookstores alive and taking down giants like Borders, Abbie came up with a plan to save us. She wrote a Miss Leona book where Leona goes to Wonderland Books and has an amazing adventure bouncing through stories. It put this store on the map, and a big part of our summer business is families on road trips who detour to Seashell Beach so their kids can see the bookstore."

Abbie held the voodoo man over her face and mumbled into it. Holden tugged it down so he could see her. "That's pretty awesome."

She shrugged. "I have to go. Dinner tonight. I know a place—"

"Er, I was thinking I might pick. I like the look of that Fortune Café down the way. The reviews are good, so are you up for some Chinese fusion?"

Uncertainty did a couple of quick somersaults through her stomach, and she almost suggested the Italian place instead, but she stopped herself. She loved the Fortune Café, and just because he would be getting his first fortune there, that didn't mean it would have anything to do with her. "Sure," she said, and Gentry smothered a laugh.

She turned to him with narrowed eyes. "*Now* I'm getting annoyed."

He didn't stop grinning. "What? It's a bold move."

"Is the food bad?" Holden asked. "Should I pick something else?"

"No, it's a bold move for Abbie," Gentry clarified. "You'll love the food. That place is one of my favorites."

"Seven sound okay again?" Holden asked.

"Sure. I need to get some work done, but I'll see you

157

then." She waved and walked out, trying to convince herself with every step to turn around and cancel. But her heart and that churny place in her abdomen were way louder than her head. So she kept right on going.

Eight

Holden watched Abbie bike away, his voodoo likeness sitting in her basket watching the passing scenery. The voodoo must be real, because instead of going back to the hotel, Holden wanted to take in the ocean view too. He put in a call to Dave, explaining that he wasn't skipping out of the next session to work. "I swear, I'm down by the waves right now, unwinding and reflecting on life, not strategizing or looking at phone specs."

"Then I'm fine with it, but speaking as your CEO, so help me if I find out that you did a minute of actual work this morning . . . See you after lunch."

Holden hung up with a laugh and strolled down to the waves, glad he had the stupid flip-flops on so he could enjoy the warm sand on his toes. He'd never been a relax-at-the-beach kind of guy. In fact, his last vacation, two years ago, had been to climb Kilimanjaro. Just coming and sitting in the sand for days at a time had never appealed to him.

But here he was, doing it anyway, his face turned to soak up the sunshine, one thought after another falling out of his head. And he didn't care. Let them. For a few minutes, he wanted to sit here and be. He looked out to the horizon, imagining the things he couldn't see: other continents floating, full of people living, working, doing, being.

For years he'd been thinking about them, but as projects, trying to figure out what technology they needed to help them move from wherever they were to wherever they wanted to be, metaphorically or otherwise. He'd spent hours thinking about that, imagining how to make a real change, do real good. And then the idea for the Apex had struck, and somehow, so fast that the transition was a blur, he'd gotten focused on the literal nuts and bolts of the thing, designing, developing, testing, getting more investors, designing some more.

But he sort of missed dreaming and the sheer grit it took to get from an idea to development. He wondered if that feeling was anything like the creative space Abbie found when she worked. It was one of the things he wanted to ask her.

That list of questions was growing longer. Why did she always smell a little bit like citrus? Did she eat any non-sugar foods? What other situations could provoke her to cut off someone's tie? And how did she have such an intuitive feel for business and marketing? And would her curls spring back if he tugged on one softly? Really softly.

Soft was a good word for Abbie. Not her body. Whatever sugar she was eating wasn't sticking to her. But despite her clenched jaw when she told him off, despite her crossed arms when he made her mad, there was a softness about her that didn't go away. Not a weak kind of softness. It was more the kind of softness that had to do with down comforters and broken-in jeans and cashmere sweaters.

160

Except none of those things was sexy, and Abbie was also that. Irresistibly that.

Holden leaned back and smiled. He had no intention of resisting.

Nine

Abbie smoothed on lip gloss and leaned forward to check it out in the mirror. It was a true pink shade called Kissy Lips, and it looked great. She scrubbed it off. She wasn't trying to look kissable.

But it had looked really good. She reapplied it and turned away from the mirror before she could change her mind. She scooped up her yellow cardigan in case the evening grew too cool for her strappy white eyelet sundress, slid on her favorite espadrille wedges, and refused to think about why she felt the need to arm herself with another four inches of height before she saw Holden again.

Five minutes later she was halfway to Tangerine Street with the top of her convertible down, a bright silk scarf defending her curls from the ocean breeze curling around her windshield and trying to tease them into afro proportions. She parked a couple of blocks from the restaurant and plucked the scarf off, giving her curls a quick tousle to settle them down.

She wished she could settle her stomach too. There was no reason to be nervous. Except she had accepted a dinner date with a guy at the Fortune Café. The *Fortune Café*. And not just any guy—Holden. How smart was that?

Not very. In fact, super dumb. On multiple levels.

She rested her hand on the door handle, ready to hop into the Mini-Cooper and drive home, maybe try to make her sparrow story cooperate. But she let go and turned down the street. Because she was interested in a different story, Holden's story, the one he'd promised her, with a smile that crinkled the corners of his eyes even when she could see the tiniest flicker of sadness inside them.

He was waiting for her at the door, and he leaned toward her as if he would drop a kiss on her cheek. She jerked back, then acted like she was swatting a fly away so they could both play the moment off, her in case she was wrong, and him in case she was right.

"You look great," he said.

She preferred that to "cute." She didn't like to be called "hot" either, even though she was guilty of describing Holden that way in her head at least a dozen times. When a guy said she was hot, it made her feel like they were somehow turning her appearance into something she had done for them. "Hot" was turning heads just to make people look. "Cute" was your cousin or a neighbor. But "great" or "pretty" were words for when you'd made yourself a canvas and done something interesting with it.

"Thanks. I like your shirt." He'd gone back to one of his white button-down shirts, but he wore it with no tie, the collar open, and a pair of jeans. Two days ago she wouldn't have believed he owned any, but they looked like each fiber in them was exactly where it wanted to be.

"So what exactly is Chinese fusion?" he asked as he held

the door to the Fortune Café open for her. "What's being fused here?"

"Good question. I think the answer is that it's the dishes Cái grew up with fused with whatever he's in the mood for this week. Sometimes you get pumpkin wontons; sometimes you get mu shu Cuban pork. You never know."

"Hey, Abbie!" a cute brunette called as she zoomed past them with a loaded tray in the air above her. "Be right with you."

"Hey, Emma. No rush," she called and smiled when Emma winked before setting down her tray beside a full table. It was fun to see what love had done for Emma. Emma had always been high energy, but it was a tightly focused energy, and she'd delivered more snarky jokes than genuine smiles. But now Abbie doubted Emma could hold back her smiles even if she wanted to.

"You're a regular here?" Holden asked. "Sorry. Maybe you want to try something different?"

"Relax," she said, resting her hand on his forearm because she couldn't resist, but a stage whisper in her brain repeated her *Relax* on a loop, a reminder of how many times she would be doomed to say that to him if they spent more than a dinner together. She dropped her hand. "Emma and I grew up together. I mean, I'm a little older than her, but we've both been in Seashell Beach our whole lives. And I eat here often because it's good. So we don't need to go anywhere else."

His shoulders dropped almost a full inch, and he smiled. "Good. You can be my guide through the Chinese-and-Whatever fusion dinner experience."

Emma hustled over. "Window seats okay with you guys?"

"Perfect," Holden said. Abbie nodded when he looked at her to confirm. His smile grew. "Good. I can't get enough of the ocean today. I was hoping we'd get a seat with a view."

After Emma left with their drink orders, Abbie fiddled with her chopsticks, wondering where the conversation would go. She never ran out of things to say, but she'd come here with the intent to listen.

Holden leaned back on his side of the booth, watching her. She only stared back, curious. His smile grew to a laugh. "I don't think I've ever dated anyone like you before."

"You're not dating me now," she pointed out. "We're having a dinner together. One."

"Two, really. There was last night."

"I ate dessert with you, not dinner. One."

"Noted. I'll rephrase. You're not like other women I know. If I stared at one of them, it would make them self-conscious; but it doesn't bother you."

"Nope. Remember, my profession makes vision my primary sense for exploring the world. I figure most things out with my eyes. Doesn't bother me when other people do it. But let's drop that for a second and back up a step. Are you saying you were expecting me to be self-conscious when you stared at me, so that's why you did it?"

He held up his hands like he was warding off her words. "No way. I'm not guilty of every bad motive, I swear. I caught myself staring because I couldn't help it. I wasn't trying to put you on the spot."

She leaned back, satisfied. "That's all right, then. But forget eyes. Let's switch to ears. As in hearing a story you owe me."

Emma stopped by again. "You guys ready to order?"

"We haven't even looked at our menus yet. Sorry," Holden said. "Probably should have done that first."

Abbie shrugged. "You said you were here for the experience. Let's just tell her chef's choice."

"All right. Chef's choice."

Emma grinned. "Cái's gonna be really happy to hear that."

165

Abbie laughed at the look on Holden's face as Emma walked away. "Don't worry about it. He's never let me down yet. Now. Your story."

"Yeah . . . the story."

He shifted in his seat. Was he squirming? Cute. Really cute, actually.

"I feel like I've built it up to something big, but it's nothing special. It might even be kind of boring."

"Life stories rarely are," Abbie said. "And I get to be the judge. It's the control every storyteller has to sacrifice when they give up a story: the right to decide how it's received. So you're going to have to trust me."

He nodded. "Weirdly enough, I do. So. The story. My grandfather had figurines exactly like that on his desk, and he passed them down to my dad. My grandfather was an army private in World War II. I used to wonder which one of the soldiers he was most like, but Grandpa never talked about the war. For my dad, it was enough to know that Grandpa was one of the Greatest Generation; my dad spent his whole life living up to that. He retired as a major general, and I'm pretty sure he thinks he still hasn't measured up."

He paused for a minute to drink, put his napkin in his lap, and drink again. "I know he thinks I didn't. The military was never for me. I founded DBR Tech instead. But that doesn't carry much weight with my dad. He doesn't see that as serving my country. So I've failed."

Abbie's hand crept back across the linen tablecloth to rest on his arm. She didn't know what to do except to offer him a light squeeze.

He tried to smile, but it didn't quite work. "I saw those figurines, and it took me back to childhood, when I was allowed to sit on the floor of my dad's study and play with the soldiers, before I became this permanent disappointment to him. I think he only let me play in there because my mom died when I was eight. Cancer. And he didn't know what else

166

to do with me. So the soldiers babysat me as long as I didn't distract my dad. So there you go. The totally unoriginal story of a boy who can't please his father."

Abbie listened without comment, his story drawing her in the way the ones in her imagination did. She could see it all too clearly, even in Holden's unembroidered recounting. And yet she pitied his father too, who was probably lost when his wife died.

A growing sense of alarm pulsed through her chest, a feeling she wanted to push away—because it made her queasy—but also embrace—because listening to it would keep her safe. She didn't want to be pulled inside Holden's life, because listening to him peel back these layers of himself, seeing inside of him, made it hard to picture him as the arrogant suit who'd lied to get the soldiers.

And hearing this story now, she knew the soldiers should have been his. Listening to him . . . aargh, his voice was *killing* her. He was trying to keep it so even, so casual, to back up his claim that the story was no big deal. But it was a huge deal. That need for connection had clearly driven him his entire life. It explained why this hard-charging guy, who could have been a hedge fund manager or a high-powered attorney, or any one of a hundred other money-making jobs that the smart, ambitious guys she knew flocked to, chose to focus on giving the world a piece of technology he truly believed could change it and make it smaller in the best possible way.

Maybe that explained why she tangled her fingers with his the way he had done to hers in the candy shop. She wanted to guide him out again, this time from the emotional thicket he was stumbling through.

"Anyway," he said, his eyes on their entwined hands, "that's the not very interesting story of the tin soldiers. So they went to the right person."

167

Emma walked up to set down their plates, and Abbie smiled up at her. "Not that I'm not thrilled to have you as my server, because you are the ever-loving best, of course, but I thought you'd be out of here by now. Isn't *Dragon's Lair* taking off?"

"It is," Emma said. "But Cái needs me every now and then, and sometimes I just like running tables. And besides, it's fun to spend my tips on totally frivolous things. I got a new set of Wacom pens, just because."

"Oooh," Abbie said, her eyes closing for a second as she visited the favorite feeling of opening new art supplies.

"Are we about to have a *When Harry Met Sally* moment here?" Holden asked, and she snapped her eyes open.

"You wish. It's an artist thing. Emma draws a comic called *Dragon's Lair*, and lately it's exploding. Sometimes she and I like to talk shop, one visual storyteller to another. We feel about new art supplies the way some women get about new shoes. Total bliss, is what I'm saying."

"Speaking of total bliss," Emma said, nodding at their plates, "it looks crazy, but you'll have to trust me *and* Cái when I tell you that's going to make you very happy. It's hamachi with sea beans and a black garlic ponzu sauce, and it's going to change your life."

"Not to oversell it or anything," Holden joked.

Emma placed an arm on his shoulder and bent so they were eye to eye. "I'm going to give you two truths right now, and they are eternal and unchanging: first, you can bank on this food melting you into a puddle of happiness. Second, you will never do better than Abbie. Ever."

And then she yelped as Abbie popped her on the butt with a snap of her linen napkin.

"Shoo," Abbie said, her face hot. "We're just having dinner. Go away."

Emma rubbed her backside and grinned, her right eyebrow doing as much talking as either of Holden's could.

"Just dinner on a first date at the Fortune Café? You know better than that."

Abbie's face went from a slight flush to a full blaze. "Shut up. He picked it. I said yes because I'd made a deal that it could be his choice."

Emma winked and walked away, and Abbie met Holden's gaze, which glittered with curiosity.

"What is the deal with this place?" he asked. "I keep hearing these hints, but I have no idea what they mean."

"It's nothing. Stupid local legend. It's dumb. Really." Except it wasn't. Everyone in town knew that your first fortune from one of Cái's cookies came true. Hers had. And it was a gamble to be sitting with Holden when he got his. Except that it wouldn't have anything to do with her, so there was no reason for her to worry about it. She breathed out some of the stress in her chest and decided to change the subject. "Emma walked up before I could tell you how much I liked your story."

He shrugged. "I told you it wasn't super great. Now you know why I borrowed your grandmother's."

"Your story is good. Perfect even," she said, sliding her hand away from his to pick up her chopsticks. "And now for dinner." She hadn't had this dish before, and she wasn't prepared for the creamy texture of the fish and the delicate flavor of the perfectly seared beans. Luckily, Holden let out a happy moan at the same time she did.

"I only want to eat this dish for the rest of my life," he said after several bites. "It will never be possible to eat enough of this. How does everyone in this town not eat in this place every single night?" Holden asked as he finished off his last bite. He chewed it slowly, like he was afraid for the moment when it truly would be all gone.

"Guess you appreciate it more when you don't have it every day. Plus, we have other good places to eat too." She almost added, "I'll take you to a couple," but she realized

THE BOARDWALK ANTIQUES SHOP

what that implied and kept her mouth shut. She was in danger of careening full speed into another dead end sign with this guy, him with his bright blue eyes and his sad little-boy past. Him with his big ideas and his good intentions and clear need for some freely given affection. Him with his sexy shoulders and a way of filling out jeans that shouldn't be street legal.

She should go. Her common sense was slipping away by the second, especially now that his eyes had half-closed in that food-coma expression which the stupid part of her brain was trying to read as "come hither." She blinked and caught Emma's eye as she passed a nearby table. *Check*, she mouthed, and Emma nodded.

Holden leaned back and sighed, one of those sighs that she could tell was coming all the way up from the soles of his feet. His smile wreaked havoc on her insides. It was his half-smile, a knowing smile, like he realized she couldn't keep her eyes off of him and he liked it.

"All right, word girl, find the words to explain how good that food was, because I feel like every adjective I've ever known falls short."

"Hamachi tastes like Cái carved up sin and served it up as heaven." She wanted to clap her hand over her mouth as soon as the words escaped even though they were true. It sounded like a come-on, as if that's exactly how she wanted to sample Holden. His eyes narrowed further, and she caught a glint in them. *He's leaving tomorrow,* she reminded herself. *He's leaving tomorrow, and you'll be safe.*

Emma dropped the check by, along with two fortune cookies. Holden reached for one, and she grabbed his hand, freezing the cookie he held.

"Wait."

He did, staring at her. "Something wrong?"

She didn't answer, not sure how to explain the irrational nerves licking at her. What would his fortune say?

When she didn't answer, his eyebrow went up in a challenge. "I'm not trying to be anti-feminist, but this dinner was my pick, my pay. I'm not letting you get the check."

She let go of his wrist. "Right. Your treat. I agreed. Thanks." *His cookie is no big deal. Quit being a weirdo.*

He cracked it open. "Do they do the lame advice cookies here, or do you get the good ones, like, 'A tanker ship of money is heading your way'? Because those are the best."

"Most people like their fortunes," she said and wondered if he noticed how faint her voice was. "Or they do eventually, anyway." She remembered how mad Emma had been when she'd gotten her first one, but it worked out pretty well for her. Thinking about it didn't help Abbie relax, though. She felt even worse when she realized Cái was peering at them from the open kitchen, waiting to hear Holden's fortune.

He tugged the paper from inside his and read it, his forehead furrowing.

"What's it say?" she asked, not at all sure she wanted to know.

He cleared his throat. "Uh, it's a little awkward for a first date. Meal. First meal. It's not a date," he said, to head her off when he saw her opening her mouth to object. "Anyway, it says, 'Your future is full of cupcakes.'"

The bottom of her stomach fell out. "What?" she croaked.

"I'm kidding. Thought I'd break the tension. It's one of those generic ones that says, 'True love is staring you right in the face.'"

She quit staring at him immediately, her stomach feeling a hundred times worse when she transferred her gaze to the kitchen in time to catch Cái's satisfied grin at her before he ducked out of sight. That's when she heard a smothered laugh behind her and turned to glare at Emma, who was delivering an order to the people in the adjoining

171

booth. "What does yours say?" Holden asked, and she turned back to pick up the other cookie. At least hers would be safe. It was only the first fortune that came true.

She pulled her paper out and read it before dropping her head into her hands with a groan. Holden pulled the paper from her fingers and read it aloud. "A dark-haired man with light eyes will be important in your future.'"

Cái or Emma had rigged this somehow. They had to. But Emma had once told her it was Cái's strict practice to let the fortunes fall where they may. He never rigged anything, according to her.

Holden's hands slid up her arms to wrap around her wrists, and he tugged her hands away from her face, leaning forward to catch her eye. "I like you, Cupcake, but I'm not ready to be your future yet," he said, his voice soft and sincere.

She shot straight up and smacked her hands down on the table, ready to push herself up and leave this ridiculous man behind. "No one asked you to—"

She stopped when she realized he was trying not to laugh. "Very funny."

He held his hand up in a Boy Scout oath. "I promised I wouldn't propose. I'm pretty sure I can keep that promise tonight. I was thinking maybe we could get ice cream. I'll eat whatever weird flavor you want me to."

He slid his credit card onto the check, and she considered. She'd been planning to cut out after dinner, her curiosity satisfied after hearing his story. But now she'd look like a high-strung psycho who was totally spooked by a fortune. Which she was. But Holden already found her eccentric, and she didn't feel like feeding that perception. So she nodded instead. "Sure, ice cream. I know a good place."

And then she told herself a truth that was overriding common sense and experience. She *wanted* to stretch out the evening with him. She sensed more stories behind his light eyes, and she was content to let the rest of the evening be the sum total of their future. Keeping him around a tiny bit longer felt far more right than sending him away. Tomorrow would do that soon enough for her. And knowing he was leaving made her staying okay.

Ten

Holden wondered if there could be a better feeling than wandering out into a sunset with a stomach full of the best food he'd had in years.

Yes, he decided, glancing over at Abbie, her curls drifting across her forehead in the breeze: wandering out into all of that with Abbie to keep him company. Automatic two million percent improvement, even though she'd grown suddenly skittish about the dinner tab. Maybe he should have let her pay, or split it with her, but he didn't even like letting his friends pick up a dinner tab. It felt downright wrong to let charming, whimsical Abbie do it when he already owed her more than he knew how to repay for entertaining him the last two days.

They meandered down Tangerine to the coast highway, their footsteps in sync, leading them to the ocean without any discussion. For the first time in two years, he didn't feel the weight of the Apex and its future on his shoulders.

The hours he'd spent with his team all day had made him realize that having the project in their hands was as good as having it in his own. They were as committed as he was, but they had all been doing a better job of striking a work-life balance. What he'd viewed as a lack of commitment, a lesser urgency, was them making their lives work. And Dave was right—Holden had nearly burned out some of the people he needed most by pushing them so hard over the last two months.

That wasn't the only clarity he'd gotten. The speed at which Abbie had gone from being a pain in his neck to turning his head for totally different reasons had given him emotional whiplash. He hadn't had the interest or even the energy to go out with anyone over the last few months.

There weren't enough hours in the day to squander on first dates that never went anywhere because his mind strayed back to the Apex. After dropping off a few irritated women who'd had to work hard to break him out of his work-focused daydreams, he'd realized it wasn't fair to date anyone.

No such problem with Abbie. It was the opposite, in fact. He'd sat in a strategy session yesterday with a graffiti artist Dave hired to teach them some creative problem-solving activities via a huge canvas. While the rest of the DBR Tech people had gotten more and more excited as they made visual connections with their graffiti, he'd kept getting caught in an Abbie loop, wondering what she could do with the same materials and her unexpected mind. He couldn't even begin to imagine what she could create.

He loved that. It sparked some massive jealousy, even. He missed that head space for innovation. That space had birthed the concept for the Apex. When had it become so walled off inside of him?

The Apex was almost a reality now, and he was beginning to realize that all of the pieces he could control, he had. There was literally not one more thing he could give toward its success than he had already given.

He smiled down at Abbie. She didn't notice. Her gaze was far out in the sunset. He wondered where she had gone. To the space he was trying to find, he'd bet. She seemed to live in that place where ideas were born. Man, he wanted to go there too.

He nudged her, a brush against her arm that sent the hair standing up on his. He wondered if she could feel it like he could, electricity he could measure in watts. She stilled beside him, and he smiled. She was feeling it.

She glanced up at him and then out again toward the ocean. "I don't even know where you live, but I'm guessing the sun doesn't set as prettily there as it does here."

"I'm in Cupertino."

A satisfied expression crossed her face, as if he'd confirmed something for her.

"The sun sets there too. I'm not always great at noticing it."

Her smile held a touch of sadness. "You're a Silicon Valley executive. I guess it's to be expected, right?"

"Maybe," he conceded. "But a lot of the people around me do a pretty good job of working their brains out and still taking the time to soak up life. Haven't you heard? We all have ping pong tables in our offices and skate parks on our company campuses."

"Something tells me you're not a ping pong and skate park guy."

"No. But there's no excuse for not being a sunset guy, is there?"

"Nope."

"Your face is judging me so hard right now. I can't even look at it," he said. Even as she spluttered that she wasn't judging him, he slid his arm around her waist and drew her in front of him and settled her there, her back against his chest. Her head barely reached his shoulder. She was stiff for a long moment, and then with a sigh, she relaxed, leaning against him, letting her arms rest on his.

"That's much better. Now I can't see your disapproving expression."

She pinched him without much conviction, and he laughed, loving the way her body magnified the rumbling in his chest, loving the way it made him feel his own laughter more acutely. They didn't say anything until the sun was gone and the colors it left deepened into indigo.

She spoke first. "You shouldn't be in your office when the sun sets. That's a crime against nature. But if you are in your office when the sun sets, then you should at least look out of your window to watch it happen."

"Yes ma'am. It's permanently on my to-do list starting now."

Her laughter vibrated against his chest this time. "Reason why the beach is better than the Valley: no one has to put stuff like that on a list."

"That so?" He tightened his hold around her waist, tugging her even closer. "Maybe I should be here more."

It was the wrong thing to say. She went stiff again and stepped away from him, turning to face him. "Thanks for dinner. I should go."

He slid his hands into his back pockets, every inch of his body she'd been touching missing her warmth. No. Her heat. "Did I say something wrong?"

She pushed her curls out of her eyes, tucking them behind her ear. He wished he had done that. He wanted to feel them. "You're trying to hit the accelerator on what I told you is not a smart drive. I've seen this before, remember?"

He tried to figure out why her words didn't frustrate him more. She was doing the thing he hated, throwing up obstacles when he had an objective. But inside he felt an easiness he wasn't used to. "I'd kind of like to hear about this

177

road since you seem to know exactly where I'm heading when I have no idea."

She met his eye and gave him a long, searching stare. "You're re-thinking your whole life right now, aren't you? You're evaluating your priorities, wondering if you should be doing something different. Seashell Beach has a way of doing that to people. And right now I bet you're thinking you need to slow down, change lanes, maybe even idle for a while." She pulled her cardigan more tightly around her. "Is it okay if we abandon this metaphor? It's wearing me out."

"Sure. Kill the metaphor."

"I live life on my own terms, I follow my whims, I do the things that make me happy, and I'm not driven toward one single goal. Unless that goal is being happy. For that, I see a whole bunch of ways to get there. And I pick whichever way suits my mood at any given moment. In the past, guys I've dated turned me into some kind of poster girl for living the life most opposite theirs. And I think because I'm happy, they want to try things my way. So they do. And it never lasts.

"They come down for weekends. But the drive gets old, and they want me to come up there, whether it's Sacramento or San Francisco, or Cupertino, and see their lives, the ones they thought they didn't like anymore. And they start applying this slow pressure for me to see myself there." She waved her hand out at the Pacific, which was putting on a great show for them, foamy waves crashing against the beach, spraying in the air like a choreographed water show. "This is who I am. I'm not wired to live the way you do. And it's what you'd want."

Holden tried not to laugh as he dropped to one knee and reached out for her hand. Panic scrawled itself across her face, and she tugged at his hold. "Abbie, you make me so happy. I solemnly swear to you that I'm not asking you to marry me. I'm not even asking you to be in a relationship

178

with me. Stay in Seashell Beach as long as you like. I'm only saying come out with me a time or two or ten."

She finally got her hand free and swatted him before tugging him back to his feet again. "You're not funny." But he could hear the laugh she was trying to hold back.

"I am," he said. "I mean, I forgot that. But I really am." He reached out for her, pulling her in but this time facing him, drawing her so close he could feel her warmth again even though they weren't touching anywhere but at her waist.

"I'm not trying to coerce you. And I feel like a jerk for even having to convince you. But give me one shot to show you that this, you and me spending more time together, is a good idea. A great idea." He tugged her closer, so close she had to reach her arms around his neck to lean back and still watch him. "The best idea I ever had."

One of the hands twined around his neck slid up into his hair, and a shudder ran through him.

"Go ahead," she said, her voice low, no laugh left in her eyes, only pure challenge. "One shot." And her hand pressed lightly on the back of his head, guiding him down to her. His lips found hers in the softest brush, but it shook him hard. He needed more, and he took it, her hand insisting on it, pulling him toward her to seal them so tightly, the ocean breeze couldn't slip between them.

His hands climbed higher, skimming from her waist to her back, appreciating that her petite frame packed such tight curves that softened as she melted into him. Her hands slid from his hair, down around his neck, and she rose to her tiptoes to press her mouth harder to his while her fingertips brushed his jaw, discovering it, and he deepened the kiss to explore her.

She moaned, the tiniest, sexiest sound he'd ever heard, and he didn't know if she'd collapsed against him or just pulled him to her as tightly as she could, but he was supporting all her weight. His stomach lost its center of gravity, and he couldn't have pointed to the direction of the highway or the water, but there was no way he was letting go of her. In a minute he was on his knees again, only this time she was with him, breaking the kiss only for whispers of seconds so they could explore from new angles.

He threaded his fingers through the curls he'd been dying to touch from the first time he'd seen one quiver at him indignantly in the antiques store. They were silk against his fingers, and this time it was Abbie who shook, a vibration he felt through every part of himself as he anchored her to him.

It wasn't enough. How could there ever be enough with this woman?

It was the distant shout of teenagers splashing in the surf that finally brought him to himself. He lifted his head and stared down at Abbie, completely wrung out and yet more full than he'd ever been.

She reached up to feather a fingertip down his eyebrow. "Nice shot." She smiled, her lips swollen from their kissing in a look every pouty Hollywood starlet dreamed of having. He groaned. He needed them again. Now. And she let him have them, for several long, perfect minutes when he couldn't tell whose heartbeat he was feeling pounding between them. Maybe his, because it was loud in his ears, the rhythm of his wanting for this perfect, maddening girl.

When he drew back this time, he leaned his forehead down to hers. "So. This means you'll do it? You'll pencil me in, give me my own alarm on your phone for weekends? You can set a Friday night, seven o'clock alarm, call it 'Dinner with Holden,' and schedule it for an indefinite repeat, because that's a sure bet."

She pushed against his shoulders, a touch as light as one of her curls, but there was no mistaking that she was trying to put some distance between them. He let go of her waist, and she sat on the sand, leaning her hands behind her and staring out at the indigo sky. When she looked back at him, she shook her head. "I'm sorry, Holden. I can't."

Eleven

Holden looked stunned. "Oh." He swallowed. "I feel like an idiot. Is that—was that kiss . . ." He swallowed again and scrubbed his hands down his thighs. "Is it always like that for you?"

"No." It would be easier to lie and let him believe it was, but those kisses demanded the truth from her. "It's never like that for me."

"Then why?"

She took a deep breath. "I thought I was going to give you your kiss, pat you on your head, and send you on your way. It's what we Seashell Beach girls like to do with you weekend boys. But I can't do that either. I don't understand why the first kiss to ever make me lose myself had to be yours, but I got lost in it the way I do in the stories I write."

He reached toward her, but she scooted back. "No, don't. I need breathing room to think."

He sat back on his heels. "It's strange to hear you say

182

that, like I should be the one talking about taking time to think while you'd be the one to jump right into something."

Irritation rose in her. Had he listened to her at all?

He must have read her feelings in her face, because his hands came up in a "wait a second" gesture. "Whoa, that didn't sound right. You've been clear as glass that you don't jump into relationships. Sorry. I didn't mean to imply anything different."

She let out a long, slow breath. "I think that's the problem. How would you know what I really think? What's going to set me off? What isn't?"

"Red ties do."

She burst out laughing. "My point is, you're not wrong; I'm impulsive a lot of the time. But I set my million alarms because when I get caught up in an impulse, they remind me to come back to reality. And I've had a million alarms going off since I realized you smell like chocolate chip cookies."

"I do?"

"Never mind. There's no way I can walk away from that kiss, but I'm not going down the dead end road."

"But—"

"I didn't finish," she said, quietly, and he gave her an apologetic smile and mouthed, *Sorry*. "Maybe we should try a different road."

His eyes brightened. "What do you have in mind? Because I say yes."

She allowed a smile to spread. "To anything?"

"Anything." He leaned toward her, and she met him almost halfway.

"Good," she said on a whisper she bet he could feel against his lips. "Because I think we're going to be great penpals."

"Penpals?" he asked, several inches away now.

"Yeah. We know we connect here," she said, running her fingers over her still tingling lips, a prickling matched by her insides when she caught him following their path with hungry eyes. She reached up to cup his head again and let her thumb brush against his temple. "We have to figure out if we match here." She dropped her hand, and he leaned back.

"Okay. Tell me the rules. Are we talking actual letters here?"

She shrugged. "If that's what you want to do. Or you can text or email too."

"Semaphore?"

"Boat flags? Definitely," she said, fighting a giggle. "But only with the brightest flags."

He rocked to his knees and moved his arms in a few symmetrical angles, his face totally straight as he flapped like a slow motion cheerleader. "Did you get that?" he asked.

"No. Probably because of the no-flags thing."

"Fair enough. But if I'd had the flags, you would be able to tell that I'd spelled out 'Holden Stratton, overachiever and uptight corporate suit, is about to get an A+ in penpalling."

"Penpalling? I'm going to give you a B- in word coinage."

"You laugh, Abbie Cupcake, but my letters are going to rock your world."

This time she did laugh, but only to cover up a truth that had kept her stomach doing acrobatics since the first touch of his mouth on hers: he'd already rocked her hard.

September

From: H.Stratton@DBRTech.com
To: Curlywhirl@abbielakebooks.com
Subject: Pen pal regrets

I had no idea I would feel so much pressure to be a penpal. I think I have penpal letter anxiety on account of my traumatic 6th grade experience. Maybe I need therapy before I can be a penpal.

From: Curlywhirl@abbielakebooks.com
To: H.Stratton@DBRTech.com
RE: Pen pal regrets

That's it? You're going to tell me you had an epic penpal disaster and then not tell me what it is? You corporate types love performance evaluations, right? Here's yours: Supplying crucial details=F. Building anticipation for the next penpal note in which you tell me what happened=A+.

From: H.Stratton@DBRTech.com
To: Curlywhirl@abbielakebooks.com
RE: Pen pal regrets

I don't get F's, Abbie. Ever. I'm an obnoxiously good student. (I know, you're shocked. Especially by the obnoxious part.) So here come the crucial details:

My 6th grade pen pal was Sergei, from Ukraine. We played chess online. I think I was too dumb for him though. After I lost about ten times in a row, he quit emailing me. He probably went and found a much smarter Chinese chess player to keep him sharp. I have pen pal abandonment issues now. It's up to you to restore my faith in this whole process.

What made you decide we should be penpals?

From: Curlywhirl@abbielakebooks.com
To: H.Stratton@DBRTech.com
RE: Pen pal regrets

I'm a good student when I care about something. Does it make you crazy to know that I got a C in trig and I didn't care because I don't care about trig? But I got an A in writing. That's why the penpal thing. I told you, I'm good with words. Thinking of them, yes. But I feel them the way I do my art: I can sense things behind words. It's hard to explain but since I just bragged that I'm good with words, I'd better try. I can see through words to who wrote them. I know when they've been carefully constructed to convey an image or put together with no thought. I can tell when they're heartfelt and when they're not. I can read people by reading their words. So there you go: now we're penpals.

No pressure, or anything.

SOLVING FOR X

From: H.Stratton@DBRTech.com
To: Curlywhirl@abbielakebooks.com
RE: Pen pal regrets

Yeah, none. Here is my completely spontaneous, authentic, totally uncontrived thought for the day (by the way, I just spent fifteen minutes contriving the exact right string of adjectives): I like that you are unapologetically good at things. No false modesty. And you joked about bragging, but you don't. I think you can back up everything you're saying, and when you state out loud what your strengths are, it's not to draw attention to them. It's like you deliver them as a plain statement of fact specific to the situation you're in.

I think it's terrible that you hate trig. Like that trig teacher, I'm giving you a C for your math attitude.

IM Chat
A: Can it be a scarlet C?

H: I feel like you're not properly chastened by your grade.

A: You would be correct.

H: I'm shaking my head at you.

A: Truth? You're going to do that a lot.

October

From: Curlywhirl@abbielakebooks.com
To: H.Stratton@DBRTech.com
Subject: Halloween

What are you going to be for Halloween?

From: H.Stratton@DBRTech.com
To: Curlywhirl@abbielakebooks.com
RE: Halloween

Home with the lights off?

From: Curlywhirl@abbielakebooks.com
To: H.Stratton@DBRTech.com
RE: Halloween

Your question mark implies that you know this is not okay. Careful, Holden. You're about to flunk my fourth favorite holiday of the year. You need a costume. And you need to wear it where people can see it. And if your office doesn't have a Halloween-dress-up day, you need to make one happen. You're a tech firm. It's practically expected that you all engage in hijinks. Here's my suggestion: you should go as a gorilla.

From: H.Stratton@DBRTech.com
To: Curlywhirl@abbielakebooks.com
RE: Halloween

Hahahaha.
Wait. That wasn't funny. And why do I have to do what you tell me? Name the consequences. Will you stop being my penpal? You can't do that! It's emotional withholding, and I revealed my childhood to you, so you know I'm kind of a pro at ignoring that anyway. So really, I guess what I'm saying is, MAKE ME.

From: Curlywhirl@abbielakebooks.com
To: H.Stratton@DBRTech.com
RE: Halloween

Please see attached. If you do not comply, I'm going to send this to everyone in your office.

From: H.Stratton@DBRTech.com
To: Curlywhirl@abbielakebooks.com
RE: Halloween

Let me get this straight. If I don't dress in a costume, you're going to email bomb my coworkers with a gorilla

sketch of me looking like my eyebrows got collagen and
extensions?

From: Curlywhirl@abbielakebooks.com
To: H.Stratton@DBRTech.com
RE: Halloween

Yep. Am I right in guessing that it would be printed off
and posted randomly everywhere around your office for
infinity?

From: H.Stratton@DBRTech.com
To: Curlywhirl@abbielakebooks.com
RE: Halloween

Yes. Fine. I will dress up.

From: Curlywhirl@abbielakebooks.com
To: H.Stratton@DBRTech.com
Subject: Halloween post mortem

Best picture EVER. Except . . . I don't know what that
costume is. I'm so sorry!

From: H.Stratton@DBRTech.com
To: Curlywhirl@abbielakebooks.com
RE: Halloween post mortem

It's a sheet over my head. I made the holes big enough
for you to see my eyes so you'd know it's really me. I'm a
ghost. The black squiggles you see all over it are Shakespeare
quotes. Consider the theory that he wasn't the one who
wrote the plays we credit him with, and you have a . . .?

From: Curlywhirl@abbielakebooks.com
To: H.Stratton@DBRTech.com
RE: Halloween post mortem

GHOST WRITER. Hahaha! I'm dying! That's the best. So much better than mine.

From: H.Stratton@DBRTech.com
To: Curlywhirl@abbielakebooks.com
RE: Halloween post mortem

Thank you. Speaking of costumes, what was yours?

From: Curlywhirl@abbielakebooks.com
To: H.Stratton@DBRTech.com
RE: Halloween post mortem

Please see attached.

From: H.Stratton@DBRTech.com
To: Curlywhirl@abbielakebooks.com
RE: Halloween post mortem

A cupcake? I don't even know how you made that, but it just moved Halloween up my list of favorite holidays.

November

From: H.Stratton@DBRTech.com
To: Curlywhirl@abbielakebooks.com
Subject: Fun with algebra

Let's start with the number 8. It's been eight weeks since I was in Seashell Beach. Let's move to the number 105. That's the number of emails we've exchanged. I don't even have a number for the IMs. I have faith in you that you can complete this math problem. Warning: it involves a variable, notwithstanding your feeling that numbers plus letters equals The Satanic Verses. I believe in you anyway. Here it is. You can do it, Abbie: THE NEXT TIME HOLDEN WILL SEE ABBIE = X WEEKS. Solve for X, Abbie. Solve for X.

From: Curlywhirl@abbielakebooks.com
To: H.Stratton@DBRTech.com
Subject: Down with algebra

Don't you like being penpals? I think it's going pretty well.

From: H.Stratton@DBRTech.com
To: Curlywhirl@abbielakebooks.com
RE: Down with algebra

I do too, actually. Which shocks me. But I want to hang out. No, wait. That's what these college interns say. I want to see you, take you out, spend time with you. Will you let me do that?

From: Curlywhirl@abbielakebooks.com
To: H.Stratton@DBRTech.com
RE: Down with algebra

Yes. But. I may have created a little situation here. The thing is, when I suggested this penpal thing, I wanted distance from you. Two hundred miles, specifically. Confession time: I can't think when you're too near me. Second confession: your emails have become a bright spot in my day. Maybe even the brightest. And it makes me nervous. I'm not someone who is often nervous. But these are big nerves, and now the idea of putting you, the guy behind these emails, back together with Holden, the guy who made my head a little fuzzy . . .

Uh.

I'm a chicken. I can't solve for X. But isn't now a bad time, anyway? Aren't you smack in the middle of a massive product launch for the Apex? I've turned on my TV three times in the last month, and every single time, I've seen an Apex ad. You should stay there and oversee that.

Right?

IM chat

H: Bock bock bock.

A: Was that supposed to be a chicken? Because as the author of books with talking animals, I have to tell you that you spelled it wrong. It's bawk bawk bawk.

H: You're still a chicken. Also, your emails are the bright spot in my day too.

A: You're being more patient about this than I thought you would be. Thanks.

H: I'm not patient at all. But I'm a good listener, and what I hear you saying is that if I push, you'll retreat. So I won't push. And the reason I'm not going crazy with all the Apex stuff is because I offloaded it. I handed it all over to the team. So just so you know, leaving work is not an issue for me whenever you do quit being a chicken.

A: And just so you know, I feel warm and fuzzy when you call me a chicken.

H: Hey, I'm good at words too. I totally read the sarcasm in that. But just to clarify, is the warmth and fuzziness because of the chicken feathers?

A: I'm leaving now.

H: But you're laughing. Right?

A: Fine. I am.

H: Good night. Happy drawing.

December

From: H.Stratton@DBRTech.com
To: Curlywhirl@abbielakebooks.com
Subject: Winning Christmas

Remember how I told you that I couldn't figure out what to get for my niece? Why didn't you tell me I'm the biggest idiot in the history of idiots? She's six. SIX, Abbie. I want to get her the whole Miss Leona collection, signed. And maybe with a picture of the author with a stuffed Leona holding a sign saying "Hi, Hailey" around its neck. Will you do that? Why did you not hit me upside the head with this idea two weeks ago when I was complaining I couldn't find anything for her?

From: Curlywhirl@abbielakebooks.com
To: H.Stratton@DBRTech.com
RE: Winning Christmas

Good morning to you too. Yes. I'll do that for you. And I didn't suggest it because I don't know your niece. Maybe she isn't a kitties-in-tutus kind of girl. Didn't want to assume.

From: H.Stratton@DBRTech.com
To: Curlywhirl@abbielakebooks.com
RE: Winning Christmas

You turned a whole corporate strike team into kitties-in-tutus kind of people this summer. Hailey is definitely going to love it. YES. I will win for favorite uncle. My brother-in-law's brother is always trying to win the kids over with dumb stuff like candy in his pockets, but he puts things in like Tootsie Rolls.

From: Curlywhirl@abbielakebooks.com
To: H.Stratton@DBRTech.com
RE: Winning Christmas

I mean, Tootsie Pops, and he might be on to something. But Tootsie Rolls? *Shudder* You're definitely going to buy her love.

From: H.Stratton@DBRTech.com
To: Curlywhirl@abbielakebooks.com
RE: Winning Christmas

That's what I'm talking about. Should I give you my work address to send it to? I don't want to tempt you past reason with my home address.

From: Curlywhirl@abbielakebooks.com
To: H.Stratton@DBRTech.com
RE: Winning Christmas

Funnnnnny.

How about I'll put together the whole deal down at Wonderland Books and you can just call Gentry with your credit card info and he can send it out to you?

From: H.Stratton@DBRTech.com
To: Curlywhirl@abbielakebooks.com
RE: Winning Christmas

Well-played. Can we talk numbers again? 3. We haven't talked about this in 3 weeks: You ready to solve for X yet?

From: Curlywhirl@abbielakebooks.com
To: H.Stratton@DBRTech.com
RE: Winning Christmas

... No ...

From: H.Stratton@DBRTech.com
To: Curlywhirl@abbielakebooks.com
RE: Winning Christmas

Ellipses. No, *double* ellipses. That means HESITATION. You're thinking about this? It's my turn for a confession. A creepy one. Brace yourself. Remember how I told you I've been working on a new idea? I'm blocked. So instead of figuring out how to build the perfect 3D printer, I've been sitting in my office all day, every day, bouncing a tennis ball against the wall and thinking about you. Are you scared now?

From: Curlywhirl@abbielakebooks.com
To: H.Stratton@DBRTech.com
RE: Winning Christmas

THE BOARDWALK ANTIQUES SHOP

Less scared. But not brave yet.

From: H.Stratton@DBRTech.com
To: Curlywhirl@abbielakebooks.com
RE: Winning Christmas

I had this secret hope that I would get to see you before Christmas. I'm going to Montana for three weeks. That's where my sister is, and that's what feels like home during the holidays. They still have dial-up Internet service. So I'm not sure how often I'll get to "talk" to you.

From: Curlywhirl@abbielakebooks.com
To: H.Stratton@DBRTech.com
RE: Winning Christmas

Wait. When do you leave for your sister's place?

From: H.Stratton@DBRTech.com
To: Curlywhirl@abbielakebooks.com
RE: Winning Christmas

Two days before Christmas.

From: Curlywhirl@abbielakebooks.com
To: H.Stratton@DBRTech.com
RE: Winning Christmas

Why does that make me sad?

From: H.Stratton@DBRTech.com
To: Curlywhirl@abbielakebooks.com
Subject: I don't know

But I get it. Looking at the bright side. I'll be out of your pretty curls for a whole bunch of days, so there's that, right?

From: Curlywhirl@abbielakebooks.com
To: H.Stratton@DBRTech.com
RE: I don't know

Right. There's that.

Twelve

Abbie stopped at the conference room door and took a deep breath, hitching her laptop bag over her shoulder. She put her hand on the knob, dropped it, and straightened her skirt instead. It was a good skirt. She'd gone with her own take on the corporate power suit, ending up with a look she called Boho Business Chic. Her laptop bag was made from a repurposed quilt, but it was in an understated black-and-cream toile print, a sophistication that appealed to her.

It complemented her tailored suit. She couldn't bring herself to do neutrals—part of her soul died just flipping through the gray suits on the rack. But she'd found a canary yellow one for a major discount online since it was leftover from the retailer's summer collection. She'd gone with a vintage shoe, a pump with a sixties mod feel to it.

Her hair . . . well, was her hair. She'd pinned the worst of her flyaways back with a tortoise shell barrette. Wasn't going to get much better than that. She patted it to make sure the curls were under control, and then with a deep breath, she put her hand on the door knob and opened it for real.

At least a dozen pair of eyes turned her way. Even though she could feel their weight, the only two she cared about were the bright blue ones staring back at her from underneath the most expressive eyebrows the planet had ever known as Holden turned toward her from the screen he'd been pointing to. He froze, and his eyes brightened.

Good. She'd half wondered if he'd recognize her if he passed her on the street. It had been three months since he'd seen her. And vice versa. He was in a suit again. Why had that ever bothered her? He looked amazing, like he was the reason suits had been invented.

"Abbie?" His voice came out in a croak. He cleared his throat and tried again. "What are you doing here?"

Dave Macklin answered for her. "I believe you all remember Abbie Lake from our corporate retreat this summer. Abbie reached out to me a few days ago to let me know she had some new insights she wanted to share with us, so I invited her to come up."

Abbie walked over to the projector. "You don't mind if I highjack your tech for a moment, do you, Holden?" It was hard to keep her voice even when it wanted to shake with the excitement of seeing him again.

"Uh, no."

"Sit down, Holden," Dave said, grinning. "I think Abbie's got something really good."

She plugged her jump drive into the laptop and navigated until her own PowerPoint took over the screen. "Solving for X," she read aloud as she walked toward Holden, her hand extended for the projector remote. He gave her the clicker, and she could feel his tremor. His fingers grazed her skin, sparking a jolt of electricity. It was all she could do not to fling the clicker aside and pull him out of the boardroom

THE BOARDWALK ANTIQUES SHOP

and away somewhere private where she could answer all the
questions flaring in his eyes, somewhere she could kiss his
hopeful half smile, explore the shape of his lips again.

She read the desire in his eyes, and her stomach flipped.
She cleared her throat and swallowed. His half smile turned
into a full-fledged grin, as if he knew what she'd been
thinking and couldn't wait to take her up on it.

She pressed the clicker, and a new slide came up. "The
primary obstacle in storytelling and life that shows up and
tries to steal your success is fear. And so you have to banish
it."

She clicked again, and the slide changed to the picture
of Holden she'd pulled off of the DBR Tech website. "For
example, I feared corporate guys in suits. Not because I
thought any of them would downsize me or put me out of a
job. I was smart enough to pick a profession that corporate
suits can't touch."

A laugh swept the room. She took a deep breath. "I
feared corporate guys because I dated a few, and each one of
them worked hard to change me. Not at first, but always by
the end." She shrugged and scanned the room, stopping at
Holden. "So I did a little extrapolation. If I dated three suits,
and all three of them did it, then all other suits I dated would
also do that." She pulled up the next slide, a sketch of a kind-
eyed gorilla that sent another ripple of laughter through the
room.

"Then I met a guy in a suit who asked me to solve for
X."

The next slide read, "Bock, bock, bock," and she'd
illustrated it with a scared-looking chicken. "But I wouldn't."
She clicked to an illustration of herself with a dunce cap.
Holden was laughing now. "And then he said he was leaving
during my second favorite holiday of the whole year. And
that he'd be gone for a while. And the pit that made in my
stomach was the missing variable."

202

She watched her final slide come up. "X = now. And tomorrow. And whenever you want." She turned to Holden. "So. Here I am. And I'm not going anywhere. When you get back from Christmas, maybe Dave will give you a little time off to come down to Seashell Beach."

"I don't think that's going to be a problem since Holden is already taking a six-month creativity sabbatical," Dave said.

Color appeared on Holden's cheekbones.

"You . . . What?" Abbie asked, not sure how to process that bit of news.

Holden pushed back from the table and walked toward her, and she felt his gaze like a physical touch, one that surrounded her and shut out everything else around them.

He stopped a foot away from her, and she could still feel the heat coming off of him. She swayed toward him, and he raised one hand, slowly, like he was giving her a chance to draw back. But she stayed, and he cupped her face, his thumb brushing over her cheek. "I can't believe you're here," he said on a whisper. "It feels like I should be making a joke about Christmas miracles, but there's nothing funny about this. This feels . . ."

She wanted him to finish that sentence, badly wanted him to, to see if it would reflect the same need that had been growing in her since the moment she'd walked away from him on the beach in September. But he didn't speak anymore, instead leaning toward her, his eyes intent on her mouth, his hand pressing her closer until the sound of a cleared throat intruded, and they both blinked and turned to look at Dave, who was grinning even wider, an expression matched by every other face at the table.

Holden straightened. "Dave, I think I'm done for the day. See you tomorrow?"

Dave waved him away, and Holden caught Abbie's hand and pulled her to the door, where they exited to applause, a

THE BOARDWALK ANTIQUES SHOP

few curious heads popping over the cubicles outside of the conference room as they passed.

They walked in silence, but she didn't need words as she savored the feeling of their hands tangled together, the warmth of his palm against hers, and wondered why she'd denied herself the sensation for the entire fall. A couple of times he squeezed her hand, as if to reassure himself that she was really there.

He opened the door to an office in the end stages of being packed up. "Are you quitting?" she asked, not sure what a "creativity sabbatical" meant, as she registered the bare walls and stacked boxes.

Instead of answering, he reached for her other hand and leaned down until their foreheads touched. "I'm so glad you came," he said, and she closed her eyes, soaking in the moment. Finally, he straightened, sighing as he glanced through the large window facing the inside office, where several employees watched them from their desks, blatant curiosity on their faces. "I really wish we didn't have an audience right now."

Another delicious shiver danced down her spine as she considered what he might do if they didn't. One of her curls had escaped the barrette, and she pushed it out of her way and took a step toward his desk, too wired to stay still, too tempted to ignore the audience and see what happened next. The desk held only a half-packed plastic bin full of photos and plaques that must have recently been on his walls. "So you're quitting here?" she prompted him again.

"Not totally. I'm going to stay on the board here, but I got unblocked on that project I've been thinking about, and it's taking on a life of its own. My niece Hailey, the one I always talk about? She has Type 1 diabetes. I've been trying to think about how to make things better for her and help my sister stress out less. And I've got ideas, but the tech is really different than what we're focusing on here. So I'm opening a startup. Again," he said with a grin, and the sound of satisfaction was clear in his voice.

"I love the Apex, but I've learned that once I have it in the right hands, staying around to pilot it taps my energy in a different way, and it becomes a drain." He glanced around the office. "Starting from scratch feels good in a way my life hasn't in a few years."

She nodded, understanding completely. The same thing had happened when she'd left her big LA graphic design job to tell Leona's story. "What comes next when you leave here? What does this new startup involve?"

A shadow of uncertainty crossed his face. "That's . . . complicated. Are you okay with going to my place to talk about it? I'm not sure you're going to love what I have to say next, and I want to be somewhere private if you decide to punch me or cut another tie off."

"Sure," she said, her stomach clenching with her first attack of nerves.

He led her to his car in the company parking lot, and she was too anxious to tease him when he unlocked a sleek black BMW. Of course he would drive a BMW. What Silicon Valley mogul didn't?

The short drive to his apartment was quiet, interrupted by only a few questions he had, wondering when she'd gotten into town and where she was staying. She followed him to his town home, wondering what it meant that he didn't take her hand. He opened his front door and stood back to let her pass him before closing it behind them and sliding his hands in pockets, bouncing ever so slightly on the balls of his feet.

She looked away from him, unsure what she was supposed to do. She'd made her one and only move already by showing up. Instead of meeting his eyes, she studied the bare beige walls, lined with more boxes. "You going somewhere?" Her stomach clenched harder. She'd waited too

THE BOARDWALK ANTIQUES SHOP

long. Why had she been so stubborn about this? When had avoiding risk *ever* gotten her farther in life? It hadn't, not once. Every good thing about her life was the direct result of taking a big leap, and now, the one time she hadn't, she was faced with losing someone she'd only barely figured out she needed.

He leaned back against the door, his legs crossed in front of him, but his fingers drummed a nervous rhythm behind him, betraying him. "I was going to wear you down on this through some incredibly worded email over the holidays. Only I wasn't sure where to start when you weren't even open to going on a date. Guess that problem is solved?"

"Super solved."

"Then I can skip to the part where I was going to tell you all my reasons why it's a good idea for me to move down to Seashell Beach for a while."

Her heart stopped. "What?"

"I leased a condo down there. I needed to be out of here. I'm moving toward something so different in my professional life that it doesn't feel right to be in Cupertino."

She stared at him, stunned.

He cleared his throat. "You know what being penpals with you feels like? Being real friends. Knowing what you like and what you don't, talking to you at the end of each day about what you did, IM-ing with you during reruns of *Zombie Apocalypse*. I love that. I feel like I know how you think and what your priorities are. And all of that feels really good. Is that just me?"

She reached out to take his hands again, to quiet the drumming, to pull him upright, closer to her. She slid her hands up his arms to rest on his shoulders. "No. Not by a long shot."

His arms tightened around her waist until there was no separation between them, and his voice relaxed. "I like being friends with you. But always in the back of my head is that kiss on the beach. It almost undid me. I haven't felt like that before. And the thing is, I'm pretty sure I'm not remembering it as better than it was. So my plan was to talk to you about how I'm always going to be a suit but the kind who is bent on chasing the idea and making it a reality, not on chasing the dollar or the promotion. And I was going to tell you about my job change and how I need a space to think and conceptualize outside of the Cupertino box. And I'd rather have that space be near you than anywhere. And if all of that failed, I was going to kiss you again. Because maybe you forgot how it was."

"I didn't." Her arms crept up around his neck now, her fingers toying with the soft hair above his collar, and he shuddered. "But I think you were saving your best argument for last, when really, you should have started there."

He bent down and kissed her, a hungry demand for recognition of the energy that crackled between them. It wasn't enough, and Abbie pulled him closer, needing to absorb him through every sense, tasting the skin stretched taut over his jaw, feathering her fingers against his eyelashes, listening to his breath speed up, and detecting ever so faintly, the whiff of chocolate chip cookies. The man was almost irresistible.

He brushed kisses down her neck, unbuttoning her jacket so he could shift the lapel to the side and continue to the trail across her shoulder before her collar interfered. He brought his mouth back to hers, fumbling to pull the barrette from her hair and free it to spill over his fingers. She was so dizzy she couldn't think any more, but she only deepened the kiss and got lost inside it, lost to time, lost to place, lost in him.

She had no idea how long it was before she dragged her mouth away from him, and when he made a sexy growl of protest and pulled her back again, she pressed against his chest and stepped away.

She crouched and slid her hand into her laptop bag. "I almost forgot. I brought you something, although maybe I should save it for your housewarming gift." She stood and handed him a package tied with The Boardwalk Antiques ribbon.

He opened it and smiled when he found the soldiers. "I need to tell you a secret. The goal has always been to butter you up enough that eventually these little guys ended up in shared custody." He took a deep breath and stole a peek at her. "Like on a mantel that belongs to both of us. I don't want to play games with you. That's what I want, Abbie. I'm all in."

She didn't think her heart could pound any harder than it had for his kisses, but it proved her wrong. "I think that you should check back with me in six months, because something tells me that's your best plan yet."

"I'd better pull in my secret negotiating big guns again."

"You'd definitely better do that."

And this time when his lips found hers, the kiss tasted like home.

Part Three

A Stitch in Time

One

Cate Pierpont pulled her car over to the curb and stopped, having finally arrived at her grandma's home in Seashell Beach. Cate sat for a moment, staring at the majestic two-story house overlooking the Pacific Ocean. To think that Grandma Evelyn had died, alone, in this house two weeks ago, made Cate's heart burn with anger.

The beauty of the fading blue sky turning to violet, with the setting sun casting gold streaks like an enthusiastic painter, did nothing to calm Cate. She'd missed her grandma's funeral.

Cate had been on a travel-writing assignment through remote parts of Ireland without the Internet for three days. Three days! Couldn't anyone go off the grid for three days? How ironic that out of all the weeks of Cate's thirty-one years, those three days proved to be the most significant.

Once her cell phone had downloaded the three days of missed e-mails, Cate had stared in surprise at the half-dozen e-mails from her cousin Amber, someone whom Cate had very little contact with. Amber was the only daughter of her grandma's son.

Amber's e-mails informed her of Grandma's death and subsequent funeral. The day Cate received the e-mails had been the day her grandma was buried. And being a continent away, Cate had no hope of paying her last respects to the woman who taught her that there was a world outside of pain and sorrow.

Amber ignored Cate's frantic reply e-mails, asking if there was any way the funeral could be delayed. While Cate was in the JFK airport on her way to California, Amber had e-mailed her about the estate sale, and did Cate want her to leave anything out or just receive her portion of the proceeds? Cate immediately replied to save grandma's antique sewing machine. A 1926 Singer.

Amber hadn't responded, which didn't surprise Cate. Amber hadn't responded to anything, and so Cate could only hope Amber had read the e-mail.

And now, Cate would visit her grandma's house for the last time, pick up the sewing machine, then drive back to her apartment in LA, leaving all of her memories behind in Seashell Beach. The next morning, it would be life as usual, working to compile her travel notes into an article for the upcoming issue of *Better Travel*.

As Cate climbed out of her car, she was surprised at the neatness of the property. She'd assumed that after an estate sale, there would be upturned grass, random bits of furniture lying about, and evidence that the yard had been full of shoppers the day before. But everything was pristine—the manicured shrubs and rows of flowers Cate remembered so well from the summer she'd spent at Grandma's after she'd lost her parents. She'd been twenty years old.

It had been a summer of healing. A summer in which Cate learned love was bigger than the heart and that she could find love beyond the darkness. That there was plenty of love to be found. Since that summer, Cate had spent her career traveling the world, writing, touring, and falling in love with one country after another.

She walked up the cobbled path. A couple of lights shone from the windows, spilling across the large wraparound porch. Cate knew it wound all the way around the back and overlooked the ocean. She'd spent a summer full of evenings with her grandma, drinking iced tea as they watched the sun set.

The front door opened, startling Cate.

A tall, dark-haired woman leaned against the doorframe, blowing out a plume of cigarette smoke. She wore a fitted black dress that showed off the angular lines of her thin body. Cate cringed at the thought of cigarette smoke filling her grandma's home. Grandma Evelyn would not have been happy.

"Hello, Cate, you made good time."

So Amber did read her e-mails—she just didn't bother to reply.

"Hi Amber," Cate said, coming up the stairs and stopping on the porch. They were the same height, but where Amber had straight dark hair and brown eyes, Cate's hair was blonde and wavy, her eyes blue like her grandma's. Cate took after the Pierpont family, and Amber took after her mother—a woman whom Cate used to imagine was a gypsy in a former life.

It was no wonder that coming to stay with Grandma in a beach house had expanded her imagination as a child. Before Cate started college, she'd visit a couple of weeks out of each summer with her parents. Frequently Amber was dropped off by one of her parents, so as children, the two cousins spent a lot of time together.

Cate never understood why Amber's parents didn't stay too. But as Cate grew older, she'd realized that adult relationships, especially in-law relationships, were complicated. Traveling and meeting new people in every city was so uncomplicated, it was no wonder Cate preferred her job over reuniting with relatives.

Grandma Evelyn had been an exception, of course.

"If you're hungry, I'm afraid the kitchen is empty." Amber took another draw on her cigarette. "I threw out all the perishables and donated the rest to the food bank."

What could Cate say to that? Even if she had been hungry, she didn't really want to eat here.

"I assume you're staying the night?" Amber continued, not seeming to care that Cate hadn't replied.

"Yes. I hope that's all right," Cate said.

"Doesn't bother me." Amber dropped her cigarette on the porch and smashed it with the toe of her shoe. "You can have one of the upstairs bedrooms. I'm staying on the main floor."

Cate stared down at the wisps of smoke rising from the dark ash that smudged her grandma's porch. "That sounds fine," she said in a faint voice. Was this what death brought out in people—disrespect for property?

Amber turned and walked into the house, and Cate followed, feeling numb. "Ignore the mess," Amber called over her shoulder. "The Salvation Army will come tomorrow and clear out the rest of this junk I couldn't even give away for free."

Cate scanned the front room with its high ceilings. It always felt like such an open, airy room, but now it was littered with stacks of magazines, lamps, several chairs that had seen better days, a broken bookcase . . . "And the sewing machine? Is it still in grandma's room?"

Amber was nearly to the stairs, and she paused with her hand on the rail, turning her head slightly to level her dark gaze at Cate. "Oh, that thing. I wasn't about to drag everything out on the lawn, so I invited everyone inside to tag their items. One of the first people here was some guy, and he said the sewing machine caught his eye. Said he'd been looking for one for a long time for . . . what did he say? *Personal* reasons."

Cate stared at Amber, hardly believing the words coming out of her cousin's mouth. She swallowed against the sudden tightness of her throat. Amber wouldn't dare . . .

"He was actually charming, and when he smiled—" Amber brought a hand to her chest and flushed. "—well, he offered three times my asking price, so I sold it to him."

"You're kidding," Cate said, disbelief jolting through her.

Amber gave a little laugh. "I know, can you believe it? Fifteen-hundred dollars for some old machine. Who even sews, anyway?" Amber went up a couple of steps, then turned again. "The strange thing is that he said he was an antiques dealer. I thought he'd try to bargain with me, but he was only too happy to pay top dollar."

"Amber," Cate said, barely keeping her anger down. "Didn't you read my e-mail? That's the one thing I wanted *saved.*"

Amber arched a brow that was as thin as the rest of her. "Even I'm not stupid enough to turn down a fifteen-hundred-dollar offer. If you really want the machine that bad, call the dealer. His card is on the kitchen counter. I kept it just in case you put up a fuss." Her cool smile implied she'd figured Cate would "fuss." "I guess I was right."

Too shocked to come up with an answer, Cate stared after Amber as she continued up the stairs.

It was too much. Her grandma's death, the mad dash back to the States, the unanswered e-mails, and now the sewing machine. Tears fell fast, and Cate brushed them away as she stalked into the kitchen. She snatched up the business card and read the block lettering, hating that she was the one who had to make this right.

HENRY LANCASTER III
LANCASTER ANTIQUES
DEALER IN FINE ANTIQUES
949.555.5555

Two

Henry Lancaster knocked on the front door of the Boardwalk Antiques Shop. He smiled as a woman bustled to meet him. It might be an hour before opening time, but he could count on Jennifer Day opening the door for him. She'd recently taken over the shop and had quickly grown used to Henry's unusual business habits.

He often used Boardwalk as a holding spot for some of his antiques. Although he had a decent-sized storage garage in the back of his home where he shipped out for his Internet sales, he also liked to have a few pieces at a brick-and-mortar destination. He'd advertise the piece, and customers who came to look would often browse the rest of the Boardwalk store and make other purchases. Win-win.

But today, he had an odd request.

"Good morning, Jennifer," Henry said.

She smiled and tilted her head. "Up before the birds again, Henry?"

He laughed. Jennifer was a good-looking woman but not Henry's type. Although he wasn't exactly sure what his type was anymore. Not since his wife of five years had left him. Henry and Adella had traveled the world together. She'd run his website and handled marketing while Henry negotiated with antiques buyers and sellers. They'd made a great pair; at least he'd thought.

Ironically, when he brought up starting a family, things crumbled fast between them. And Henry found out why a few weeks later, when he'd inadvertently used Adella's phone to look something up. A string of texts between her and some British soccer player caught his eye. But that was over a year ago, and Henry tried not to think about Adella anymore, and what had gone wrong.

"What are you after now?" Jennifer's voice brought him back to the present. "You didn't even bring me my favorite bagel."

Henry pulled an envelope out of his pocket. "No, not a bagel, but two tickets to Imagine Dragons. They're coming Friday to the Mariposa Hotel."

Jennifer clapped her hands together. "Wow. Thank you!" She took the envelope and peeked inside. "Uh . . . do you want to come with me?"

Oh. Henry realized what he might have been implying. "No—I mean, it would be great and all, but both tickets are yours. My mother will be in town, and let's just say I'm not making any advance plans."

"That bad, huh?" Jennifer asked.

"I love saying hi, and I love saying goodbye," he said.

Jennifer gave a knowing nod. "What's your price, sir?"

Henry took a deep breath. "I need to stash something top-secret here. It's a surprise for my mother's birthday, and she'll find it in an instant when she arrives at my house. It's either bring it here or bury it in the backyard."

She watched him with amusement. "Can I know what it is? Or is it too secret even for that?"

Henry leaned in even though there was no one else in the shop. "It's a 1926 Singer 15-30 Tiffany Treadle sewing machine. Just like my grandma used to own but had to sell during the Depression. It's one of the famous stories of our family."

"I can see just by the gleam in your eyes why you fell in love with antiques," Jennifer said with a broad smile. "I'd love to store it here, but you need to bring me its story."

He narrowed his eyes. Everything in Boardwalk Antiques had a nice little write-up of the story behind the antique. It drew people in and connected them emotionally to the pieces. The problem was, Henry hadn't taken the time to find out the sewing machine's "story" when he'd bought it at the estate auction the other day. He was afraid the woman at the house would change her mind before he got out the door. "It won't be on display—can't you keep it in your back room?"

"Ha," Jennifer said. "I'm not going to let a piece like that sit in my shop without being seen. That's sacrilegious to me, you know, goes against my values."

Well, that was putting it a bit dramatically. Jennifer was definitely related to Daisy. "I don't know the story, actually," Henry confessed. "Maybe I could write up something about the manufacturer?"

Jennifer folded her arms. "Good try. Who did you buy it from? Ask them."

Henry blew out a breath. "It was at an estate sale, and everything is probably cleared out by now."

"So go knock on the door."

"All right," Henry conceded. More likely he'd make a phone call, assuming the phone was still connected. There'd been a number associated with the estate ad, and he could pull it back up on his cell. "But the sewing machine is in the back of my van now. Would you mind if I brought it in now?"

"The story—"

Henry raised his hand. "I promise I'll get it to you—today, in fact."

Jennifer's lips twitched. "All right. Bring it in. But only because I'm in a good mood."

Henry laughed. "Thank you! I owe you a bagel."

Three

Cate grabbed her cell from the bedside table and checked the time. *10:35 a.m.* She shot up in bed. She hadn't slept this late in a decade. Then she let out a sigh, combing her fingers through her hair. *Jet lag, that's it.* She still wasn't happy with sleeping so long. After Amber dropped the bomb the night before about selling off the sewing machine, Cate spent a couple of hours stewing. She'd called the antiques dealer's number three times, but each time it went to voicemail.

Cate hadn't left a message, determining to call again this morning, every ten minutes if necessary to get Henry Lancaster III to pick up. She swung her legs to the floor and stood up, then stretched. What kind of name was Henry Lancaster III anyway? It was completely pretentious. Maybe it was a pseudonym in order to sound more officially antique-y.

She grabbed the water bottle she'd brought in from the car the night before and took a few swallows. She called the dealer's number again. After the first ring, it went to voicemail. Great, now her calls were being screened. Hanging up, she crossed the bedroom and opened the door to the hallway. The bathroom was one more door down, but she paused before going in.

Amber's voice came from somewhere inside the house, most likely the kitchen. And she was talking about the sewing machine.

Cate exhaled with relief. Her cousin was tracking it down for her. Who knew that Amber had a conscience after all? After using the bathroom, Cate walked down the hall. As she came down the stairs, Amber was just shutting the front door.

She hadn't been on the phone, but talking to someone at the door.

"Oh, there you are," Amber said. "I didn't want to wake you, so I just told the man the story behind the sewing machine." She gave a shrug. "I probably got it all wrong. Oh well, not that it really matters anyway."

"What man? What story?"

"The antiques dealer. He was insistent that I tell him about the history of it; he said it gives more meaning to—"

"You didn't buy it back?" Cate interrupted.

"Uh, no. You were asleep, and I just assumed—"

Cate ran past Amber and flung open the door. A van was pulling away from the curb in front of the house. "Wait!" she shouted, running toward the van, waving her arms. "Wait, please!"

She caught a glimpse of a man with dark hair in the driver's seat. He didn't even glance her way. She ran after the van as it accelerated, waving her arms wildly. Surely he'd see her in the rearview mirror. But the van continued faster, then disappeared altogether as the road bent out of sight.

Cate stopped running and stood in the middle of the street, oblivious to neighbors who might think she was crazy. She caught her breath, then turned and ran back to her grandma's house to grab her phone and redial the dealer's number as many times as it took.

"So?" Amber said, her voice grating on Cate's nerves as she entered the house.

Cate was too angry to speak. She just shook her head and went back into the bathroom to get into the shower. Her heart pounded with the mad sprint, and her breath was shaky. She hadn't been this upset since . . . well, since she discovered her grandma had been found dead.

I'm in a living nightmare, Cate thought as she stepped into the shower. She closed her eyes and let the warm water envelope her. Grandma Evelyn had grown up in the Depression, and her father had rented a sewing machine so Evelyn could make her own wedding dress. A picture of her grandma wearing the dress sat back in Cate's apartment in LA.

When Evelyn was married, her father presented her with the sewing machine, telling her it had really been a wedding gift. During the summer when Cate stayed in Seashell Beach after losing her parents, she'd found the machine. She'd asked her grandma if she could make some curtains with it. "If you can get it to work, you can make anything you like," Evelyn had told her.

Sewing had been healing—she was doing a task that took little thinking, yet she was creating something beautiful. The hum of the machine's motor had been soothing in an odd way. And when the feelings of grief were too intense, Cate abandoned the sewing for a day or two and walked the beach. But she always came back to her grandma. A lot of words didn't need to be spoken between them; their companionship had been comfortable.

"When I die, I want you to have the sewing machine,"

Evelyn told Cate one evening. "You brought it back to life."

Cate had smiled. "It's slow but steady."

Her grandma had given a thoughtful nod. "Just like you need to take life. Slow and steady. Don't push yourself faster than you should." Evelyn had reached over and grasped Cate's hand. "Grief takes a long time to heal. Don't ever feel bad about taking it slow."

The memory faded as the shower temperature grew lukewarm. Cate scrubbed shampoo and conditioner through her hair, rinsed, then turned off the water. It was time to make another phone call to Mr. Lancaster.

Four

enry brushed his hands together, not because they were dirty, but because it seemed the proper thing to do when looking at his handiwork. The sewing machine was situated in the corner of Boardwalk Antiques, and its story had been printed off on blue filament paper, framed, and propped on top of the antique piece.

The story of the sewing machine was an interesting one, and Henry wrote it up as best he could. At least it should make Jennifer happy. There were only a couple of customers in the shop, and Jennifer was behind the counter discussing WWII figurines with a customer.

Henry took a few moments to browse the shop. A couple of turn-of-the-century silver match boxes drew his eye. One of his clients collected them, and Henry was always on the lookout, but the ones here looked like the ones his client already had. Regardless, he inspected them for flaws and noted the manufacturer.

The front door chimed, and a blonde woman breezed in. Henry glanced at her as she crossed his line of vision, and he couldn't help but smell her freshly-showered scent. Another quick glance told him her hair that was wrapped into a loose bun was still damp.

The quick glance turned into a longer study. She was tall and lithe and had the look of a no-nonsense personality. She wore long, elegant silver earrings, and her summer dress might look simple, but Henry's practiced eye recognized its high quality. The woman's lips were pale pink, her lashes thick, her eyes blue, and . . . Henry blinked. She was staring straight at him.

"Excuse me, do you work here?" she said, in a voice lower than he'd expect such a pretty blonde woman to have.

"Uh, no," he said. "Jennifer's at the counter."

She was still staring at him, didn't even look over at Jennifer.

Henry's heart thumped. It was strange because if he didn't know any better, he'd just felt the first stirrings of attraction, stirrings that had been dormant for a long time. He quickly pushed down the possibility, deciding it was completely irrational. "Jennifer's the owner," Henry said, as if he had to further explain as the woman stared at him. "I'm just browsing."

The woman finally blinked and moved her gaze toward Jennifer. Maybe she was hard of hearing?

"Thank you," she said, brushing past him in the narrow aisle.

She didn't touch him as she passed, but her dress fluttered briefly against his pants. He knew he couldn't have really felt it, but yet, he had. He turned and watched her approach Jennifer.

The blonde woman looked around the shop as she waited behind the other customers. She wore a shoulder bag, another expensive item, and if Henry had to guess, it was

Italian leather. And not the kind purchased at Neiman Marcus, but directly from a designer shop in Italy.

His stomach knotted. Yes, he admitted he was intrigued by her, even attracted to her, but he knew enough to stay away. The last thing he needed was a woman as travel-wise as his ex-wife.

The first customer moved away, probably sensing that someone was now waiting behind him. Henry took a few steps closer, not really intending to listen to the conversation, but his curiosity was too strong. The woman seemed to be on a mission, and he wondered what she was looking for. If Jennifer couldn't help her, maybe Henry could. He told himself it was purely a business interest. He loved to find things for people.

The woman greeted Jennifer, introducing herself as "Cate, spelled with a C" . . . Henry mused over the unique name. Cate's greeting trailed off as she turned her head to stare at something in the shop. "There it is!" she practically shouted. Cate hurried over to the sewing machine Henry was storing for his mother's birthday.

If the woman liked it, he could help her find another one that was close enough.

"I can't believe it," Cate continued, her voice still raised as she ran her hands along the top of the machine. "My cousin said she sold it to a dealer. Did you buy it from him or something?"

Henry's stomach dropped as Cate picked up the framed story and read through the simple paragraph.

"Actually, I—" Jennifer began, casting a quick glance at Henry before following Cate.

But Cate cut her off. "I can't believe my luck! I thought I'd never see my grandma's sewing machine again. This story's a bit off, but that doesn't matter now." She dug into her satchel and pulled out her wallet. "I know the dealer paid fifteen hundred dollars for it, and you probably have a mark-up, but I'm willing to buy it back."

"Ma'am, it's not—" Jennifer tried again.

"You don't know what this means to me," Cate continued, her voice trembling. "I was in Europe when I heard of my grandma's passing."

"I'm sorry," Jennifer murmured.

Henry watched the interchange in disbelief. He wasn't quite sure how to handle this situation. But when the woman mentioned she'd been in Europe, obviously extremely far away from her ailing grandma, and probably buying the wallet she was now holding, Henry's compassion was at a low. He wondered if she watched soccer.

"She was in her late eighties, but I still wasn't prepared," Cate said.

Jennifer glanced over at Henry, then focused on Cate again. "It's just that . . ." Jennifer started. "Well, that sewing machine isn't for sale. I'm storing it for the dealer."

Cate's cheeks flushed. She chewed on her lip, her eyes narrowing as she considered this complication. If Henry wasn't so annoyed with her self-centered lifestyle, he'd have thought her expression adorable.

This was very awkward.

Cate held up her cell phone. "You mean Henry Lancaster III? The dealer who hasn't answered one of my many calls? I'm surprised you do business with anyone like that. He took a sewing machine that wasn't for sale, and now you are saying I can't get it back?"

"Wait a minute," Henry cut in.

Both women swung their heads around to look at him—Jennifer with a defeated expression, Cate with annoyance.

"I paid *three times* the worth of that machine," Henry said, before he could think better of it. "I didn't *take* anything, and if it wasn't for sale, then it shouldn't have been part of the estate sale."

Cate's mouth fell open. "*You?*"

"*Me,*" Henry said, just because he was completely annoyed now.

"*You're* Henry Lancaster III?"

Five

"**H**enry is just fine," the dark-haired man said, tilting his head and studying Cate like she was some insect.

Henry wasn't fine. He had talked Amber into letting him purchase the sewing machine, and now here it was, sitting in the dusty corner of the local antiques shop. Her grandma's machine—bartered back and forth like it was part of a swap meet.

This man was certainly as arrogant as his name. "Mr. Lancaster, I have the money with me," Cate said as she dug into her bag and pulled out the envelope with the cash from Amber. Cate had planned on using her credit card if possible to get the Skymiles, but she'd brought cash as a backup. Who knew if a small-town antiques shop took credit cards?

She held out the envelope, waiting for the man with hazel eyes to take it. If she wasn't so frustrated, she might be able to place where she'd seen him before. His wasn't a face

231

she'd easily forget. Maybe he bought antiques in Europe and they'd crossed paths somewhere?

Henry Lancaster III didn't move, didn't reach for the envelope, didn't take his eyes off of her face. It was unnerving. Jennifer moved back to her counter, effectively taking herself out of the conversation.

Cate took a couple of steps forward until she was within reaching distance of Mr. Lancaster. "It's all here. You're welcome to count it."

Finally, he reacted. Folding his arms, he said, "It's not for sale."

Seconds passed as Cate processed what the dealer was telling her. "What do you mean, it's not for sale? It's mine—my grandma left it to me—which makes it mine. It was never for sale."

Mr. Lancaster's lips thinned. "I bought it for a more-than-fair price."

Cate stared at him. Under her scrutiny, his jaw twitched, but his gaze was steady—no, more like steely. Did this man not have a reasonable bone in his body? "The sewing machine is a family heirloom, and my cousin wasn't supposed to sell it to you. It was left to me, specifically, by my grandmother—we'd spent summers together, and she taught me how to sew on it. I don't care about the money you paid for it. I'm returning your money, and I want my sewing machine."

Mr. Lancaster raised his hands and moved back. Cate hadn't realized how close she'd gotten to him. "Your cousin was running the estate sale, and she was more than happy to sell it to me. If I didn't need this sewing machine for a very important reason, then I'd consider selling it back. But as it is, the machine no longer belongs to you."

"What's the reason?"

"Excuse me?" the dealer asked.

"The *very important* reason. What can you possibly need so desperately with an antique machine?"

"I—it's . . ."

The man was actually stuttering, Cate marveled.

"It's personal," he said.

"I just told you why the machine is important to me; why can't you tell me why it's so important to you?"

"Henry?" Jennifer cut in. "Do you think you could discuss this outside?"

Cate looked over at the shop owner, then noticed that the other three customers in the store were soaking in every detail of the conversation.

"Of course," Mr. Lancaster said, then turned and walked out, not even checking to see if Cate agreed or would follow.

Jennifer offered a faint smile. "Please?"

Cate nodded. If she wasn't already blushing, she was now. She walked toward the front door, where Mr. Lancaster was holding the door open. At least he was a gentleman in one small regard, but Cate didn't have much hope for the rest of him. Wasn't there some legal term called buyer's remorse? Or seller's remorse?

Once she passed him, he moved off to the outside corner of the store.

"Look," Mr. Lancaster said, scrubbing his hand through his hair. The once-perfect waves were now a bit messed up. It made him look more human. "My grandma had to sell her identical sewing machine during the Depression. She was a seamstress, and it was the last thing she held onto until the family became so desperate for food they had to leave the state and go live with her parents."

He looked away, and his voice grew quiet as he continued. "The trouble was, she didn't have enough for a train fare to leave the state. She became desperate. She sold the machine here in California, then spent the next ten years in Nevada. She always regretted it, and my mother never forgot her stories about it. You could say that our family lore always settles around that lost machine, and so when I saw the same make and model at the estate sale, I wanted to buy it for my mother. Grandma died a couple of years ago, and it's been really hard on my mom."

Cate found herself nodding and sympathizing, even though she didn't want to. A sewing machine had been an important part of his family, too. "Did your grandma live around here?"

"Just up the coast," Mr. Lancaster said.

Something niggled at the back of Cate's mind, something she couldn't quite grasp. "What year did your grandma move to Nevada?"

He arched his brows as if he were surprised by the questions. "It would have been, oh, before my mother was born. I'd guess 1932 or 1933."

Cate felt something turn in her mind. "Do you know who she sold it to?"

"I—" He stopped and went quiet. "What are you thinking?"

"It might just be possible that the sewing machine my grandma owns was purchased from your grandma."

Mr. Lancaster blew out a breath and shoved his hands into his pockets. "That would be completely surreal."

His eyes had changed from steeliness to warm and amused.

"Did your grandma keep any records?" she asked. "A diary?"

One side of his mouth lifted into a half-smile. "She did," he said in a slow voice. "I even have a copy of her diary at my house."

Something fluttered inside her chest. Suddenly she was curious to know if it was the same machine. Mr. Lancaster seemed to be thinking along the same lines.

"Can we start over?" he asked.

She looked at him, not sure what he meant.

He withdrew his right hand from his pocket and held it out to her. "Hi, I'm Henry. Sorry for not answering your phone calls. I like to return calls to new clients when I'm at my computer so I can log in all of their information."

She grasped his hand. It was warm, strong. "Am I one of your clients, then?"

He smiled, and she found herself a little short of breath. "Would you like to come to my workshop and read my grandma's diary?"

It was easy to return his smile. "I'd love to."

Six

Henry checked his rearview mirror again, hardly believing that Cate was following him back home to his workshop. Her hostility had fled when he'd told her about his grandma's machine and how he hoped to give one just like it to his mother. It was strangely easy to talk to her, and she seemed sympathetic.

It would be an amazing coincidence if it was the same machine. But that presented a new dilemma. Who did the machine belong to? Well, Henry technically owned it, but if it meant so much to Cate . . . he'd give it back.

In the store, her demanding tone made him defensive. But now . . . another glance in his rearview mirror, and he could make out her blonde silhouette. The morning sun was bright, and the neighborhood street they'd turned onto was pleasantly shaded now. He assumed Cate was single—he hadn't seen a ring—and if she was, he might find a way to delay handing over the sewing machine.

Henry shook those thoughts away—what was he thinking? Cate was not the type of woman he was looking for. He didn't want to be fooled again by an opinionated, beautiful, world-traveling woman—a woman who didn't need him.

He turned into his driveway and pulled to a stop on the right side, giving Cate plenty of room to park next to him. She parked alongside the curb instead. He climbed out of his van and waited for her to approach. He couldn't help but notice her easy walk, the confident tilt of her head, and the way her eyes quickly assessed her surroundings.

"This is your home?" she asked as she drew near.

"Yeah, I converted the garage into my workshop/office." He led her around the side of the house, where he had a separate entrance for clients to come through. "The diary is in the house, but I thought you'd, uh, be more comfortable in here. Seeing that we just met, you know." He opened the door and flipped on the overhead lights.

"Wow," Cate said, stepping past him into the workshop. "This place is really small for all the stuff you have."

Henry laughed. "I guess it would look that way to some," he said, looking around with a fresh viewpoint. Two overstuffed chairs sat in the corner next to a table with his laptop. That was the nook where he'd sit down with a client. The rest of the place, well, it was a bit of a mess. He'd installed counters along the three walls, and the counters were piled with antiques. Display cases were randomly stationed throughout the area.

He was proud of the bookcases he'd built himself, which contained an impressive, yet tattered, collection of magazines and history books. "It's fairly organized, actually."

Cate was still standing near him, and she looked up at him with those ocean-blue eyes. "I suppose there must be some method to this madness." She walked forward a couple of steps, then stopped. "I *thought* I recognized you," she said, pointing to a framed picture on the wall.

Henry looked over. It was the picture from a televised antiques show in London he'd participated in a few times. The picture had been there for so long he'd stopped noticing it. Which was strange, because Adella was in the photo too. As soon as Cate left, he'd take it down.

"Oh, and that's your wife," Cate said, stepping closer. "I remember the pair of you now. I've watched a few antiques shows, but I was always interested in hearing what you and your wife had to say." She looked over at him. "I thought it was interesting that a married couple shared the same passion."

"Not exactly the same passion," Henry said, before he could stop himself.

Cate raised a brow, and Henry realized he'd backed himself into a corner.

"I discovered that Adella was passionate about someone else, and we divorced soon after," Henry said, trying to keep his voice nonchalant, but the bitterness seeped through.

It wasn't until Cate's hand rested on his arm that he realized he'd been staring hard at the framed picture. "I'm sorry," she said. "I didn't realize the two of you were divorced."

He nodded, not able to think of a response that wouldn't make him sound like he was too angry. He'd thought he was completely over it, but apparently not, since seeing the picture of Adella brought back the pain.

He flashed a brief, tight smile and said, "I'll go get the diary. Make yourself at home."

Inside the house, the dimness helped calm him. He went up the stairs to the guest bedroom, where he kept his grandma's diaries. He'd read through most of the entries but hadn't paid specific attention to the dates. Opening the guest bedroom closet, he gathered the three binders containing the photocopied pages of her diary. He was suddenly grateful for his insistence on getting his own copy.

Back downstairs, he grabbed a couple of cold water bottles from the refrigerator, then went back into the workshop. "Cate?" he said, stepping inside and not seeing her. She came out from behind the bookcase, holding a magazine. It was the special edition on antique sewing machines.

"Did you find the Singer in there?"

"Yes, it's exactly like my grandma's."

Henry crossed to her and looked over her shoulder at the page she'd turned to. "It was a fine machine, even for its day." He held up the water bottle. "Drink?"

"Thanks," she said, taking the water bottle. She eyed the binders in his arms. "Looks like your grandma was an avid writer."

"She was pretty thorough," Henry said. "But we can just focus on 1931 and 1932." He led the way to the two overstuffed chairs, and after she sat down, he took a seat in the next chair. He flipped open the first binder, saw that the dates started at 1928, and set it aside. The next binder pages started with 1930, and he handed that one to Cate.

"Are you sure this isn't too personal for me to see?" Cate asked, slowly turning the pages.

"I doubt my grandma wrote down anything she didn't want others to read," Henry said. "She was a pretty straightforward person, though, and never hid her thoughts or feelings. Not much mystery in her life." He caught Cate's gaze. "Like some people I know."

She lifted a brow. "Are you referring to me?"

"Possibly." He held back a smile.

"You think I'm *mysterious*, Mr. Lancaster?"

"Oh, please," he said in a sarcastic tone, "call me Henry."

"What would you like to know, Henry?"

THE BOARDWALK ANTIQUES SHOP

He hesitated. What did he want to know? It shouldn't be anything. He shouldn't allow himself to get caught up in this woman's life. "Are you married? Single?" As soon as he said it, he knew he was revealing too much. He almost hoped she was married; then he could stop staring at her.

"Single," she said. "And you, Henry?"

"Oh—single, but you knew that."

Cate shrugged, her eyes gleaming with amusement. "Did I? Just because you're divorced doesn't mean you don't have a girlfriend by now."

"Not even close," Henry said. When did this conversation become about him?

"That's a pretty strong statement," Cate said. "Care to explain?"

"I—no, I don't want to explain." He narrowed his gaze, wishing her eyes weren't so blue. "I was asking *you* the questions, remember?"

She blew out a breath and looked back at the binder in her hands. "Yeah, I get that a lot. I tend to take over conversations."

Henry laughed. "That's not a totally bad thing."

She looked at him from the corner of her eye, then turned another page. "To answer your upcoming questions, no, I've never been married. Engaged once for a few months, but I decided a professional athlete wasn't for me."

He stared at her. "You're kidding!"

"What? That I haven't been married before, or that I was engaged once?"

Henry still couldn't believe what she'd said. "You were engaged to a professional athlete?"

"Yeah?" She was looking at him like he was crazy, and maybe he was.

"What happened?" he asked, trying to keep his voice even.

"Do you happen to play beach volleyball?" she asked.

"No, unless you count a pick-up game when I was about fourteen."

She looked relieved and leaned back in her chair. "So, I was engaged to a guy playing on the AVP—the pro beach tour that goes all summer. Lots of traveling, lots of chicks in bikinis, lots of kissing up to the media, and, well, the rest of the year, just working out and focusing on your body."

"Sounds like quite the life," Henry said.

She nodded slowly. "That's one way to look at it. I supposed that if I played too, then it would have been a lot different."

Henry suddenly had a different perspective of who his wife had left him for. Was she happy with that lifestyle? Everything dependent on athleticism and fans and sponsors? He'd heard that Adella had married her athlete, but he hadn't heard anything since. There had been no communication for a long time.

"Why are you looking at me like that?" Cate asked.

"Like what?" Henry pasted on a nonchalant expression.

"Like you just discovered a treasure box of gold, or in your case, an antique box."

Henry laughed, then scrubbed his hand through his hair. "The thing is . . . well, it's kind of personal . . ." He broke off, suddenly self-conscious. Only his mom knew the truth about Adella.

"Henry Lancaster, I think you owe me an explanation. If only because you practically stole my grandma's sewing machine."

He flushed, and it was Cate's turn to laugh. But she sobered quickly, and said, "Never mind, I don't want to make you uncomfortable." She turned back to the binder and flipped through several more pages, scanning the paragraphs as she went.

Henry took her cue and looked through the binder he held. He started reading the first few sentences of each page but couldn't process anything. He looked over at Cate; she seemed intent on reading, but he sensed she was waiting.

"The guy Adella left me for is a professional soccer player."

Cate looked up at him, compassion in her gaze. "I'm sorry, Henry."

"Yeah, well, I didn't mean to start a pity party." He tapped the diary page he'd been reading. "All things considered, our lives are pretty decent. At least we're not living during the Depression."

They both went back to reading, and after a few moments, Cate said, "I think I found something. Listen."

Henry leaned toward her and followed along as she read.

"'I can no longer pretend that everything will be fine,'" Cate read. "'Tomorrow will not be better. It will be the same or even worse. Today I went to the train station and purchased tickets for Friday. We are going to Nevada to live with my parents until this horribleness is over. This morning I sold my beloved sewing machine. I hope it's not too long before I can buy another one. The man who bought it from me said it was a gift for his daughter's wedding. When he saw how upset I was, he assured me they'd take very good care of it.'" She looked at Henry. "There's no name listed."

He took the binder from her and re-read the paragraph, then turned the page. Nothing else was written about the sale in the entry. "May 18, 1931." He met Cate's gaze. "When was your grandma married?"

"June of that year."

He nodded and closed the binder. "Amazing. It appears very likely that it's the same machine." Her hair had dried, and a lock of it had fallen out of her bun. He reached over and smoothed the hair back. He dropped his hand quickly, realizing what he'd done. He swallowed against another impulse to touch her. "It also appears that I need to return a certain sewing machine to its owner."

$\mathcal{S}$*even*

enry was becoming sweeter by the moment; quite opposite of Cate's first impression of him.

"But the sewing machine was your grandma's to begin with," she told him. "Maybe it's right that it belongs to your family again."

Henry dropped his hand. She wasn't sure what to make of his gesture of fixing her hair. Maybe its disorderliness bothered him, although that didn't make sense because his workshop was anything but orderly. Maybe it was because of the confession he'd made about his ex and her confession about her broken engagement. As it was, the atmosphere felt . . . intimate. There was really no other word for it.

It was plain this guy was still hurting over his ex-wife's betrayal, which ironically, only endeared Cate to him. His pretentious name and his obvious prestige in the antiques world were quite opposite of the deeper layers she'd glimpsed. He'd seemed self-involved when she'd first realized who he was in the shop, but now . . .

"It sure makes for a coincidence that we should meet now—because of the sewing machine," Henry said in a quiet voice.

Cate's heart pinged at his somberness. She reached over and squeezed his hand, which was suddenly easy to do. "Your grandma went through a lot. Keeping the machine would bring her story full circle."

"My mother would be ecstatic, that's true." His gaze found hers. "But what about you?"

He was being sweet again. Cate gave a shrug. "I think I got about all the use I can out of it. I made curtains with the machine about a decade ago, and it definitely needs a tune-up."

"You made curtains with that machine?" Henry asked. "I'd like to see them."

Cate laughed. "Really? Why?"

It took a moment before he replied, his gaze intent on hers. "I think my mother would love to know that the machine was well taken care of," he said with a shrug.

But Cate could see the interest in his eyes. Was he hitting on her? Wow. She didn't know what to think about that. "They're in my grandma's kitchen—nothing fancy, believe me."

Henry set his binder on the table, then stood and held out his hand. "I'd like to see the *nothing fancy* for myself."

Cate placed her hand in his and let him pull her to her feet. When she stood, they were standing close enough that Cate was having a hard time denying her attraction to this man—his eyes were too absorbing, his shoulders broad, and that half-smile of his . . . But she wasn't looking for a fling in her grandma's hometown and definitely not with a man who was still upset over his divorce . . . besides . . .

"Oh, damn," Henry said.

"What?"

He squeezed her hand, then let go. "Someone's here. Most likely my mother."

Cate turned toward the garage door, and sure enough, she heard the sound of a car door slam, then women's voices.

"Your mother and . . . ?"

Henry closed his eyes for a second. "It's not what it looks like, I promise." His eyes opened and seemed to implore hers, but then his gaze was broken as, seconds later, the workshop door flew open.

"There you are, sweetie," a woman's voice trilled. "I didn't even bother with the front door, as you can see." Henry's mother stepped inside, looking like a brunette-haired model for Chanel. Behind her, another woman emerged. A younger model version for Chanel. It was clear they weren't related, but perhaps shopping at the same stores made them look like mother and daughter.

"Darling," the younger woman said, gliding across the floor and practically launching herself into Henry's arms.

"Erika insisted on coming," Henry's mother said.

Erika drew back from Henry, her arms still draped all over him. "I couldn't miss your mother's birthday. So sorry to tag along. I'm happy to stay in a hotel."

"And I told her not to be silly," Henry's mother said. "You have plenty of room for the both of us."

Henry hadn't spoken a word the entire time; but Henry's mother noticed Cate at the same time that Erika did.

"This is C-Cate," Henry stumbled on her name. "And this is my mother and a friend of mine, Erika."

Cate gave her best smile and held out her hand toward Henry's mother. "Cate Pierpont. Nice to meet you, Mrs. Lancaster."

Henry's mother shook her hand lightly, her eyes narrowing although her smile was plenty friendly. "Are you a client of Henry's?"

"No—" Henry said at the same time Cate said, "Yes."

"Not yet," Henry said. "She hasn't bought anything."

Erika was looking between the two of them, her right eyebrow raised. "What are you shopping for?" she asked, the gloss on her lips sparkling as she smiled. She was also standing quite close to Henry.

"Just something my grandma used to own." Cate knew a predatory woman when she saw one, and she had no interest in being in the middle of anything. "Thanks for everything, Henry, and nice to meet you, Mrs. Lancaster and Erika. I really must go."

She was out the door, pulling her keys from her bag, when Henry caught up to her.

"What about—" he started.

"Just call me when you have a free moment," Cate said, well aware that the door to the workshop was wide open and Mrs. Lancaster and Erika could hear everything they were saying. "I left you several messages, so you should be able to find my number in your phone." She turned and headed down the driveway, feeling his eyes following her.

It wasn't long before she heard the women calling out something to Henry. Something about getting an early start on their weekend.

Eight

enry held his breath as the phone rang and rang, finally transferring to voicemail. He hung up. He'd left a message the first time he called Cate— that was last night. Another call this morning went unanswered, and now it was late afternoon. He finally had a moment alone, since his mother and Erika had gone into town to shop.

He still couldn't believe his mother brought Erika along. It was so obvious what she was trying to do that it made his head hurt. Before he'd married Adella, his mother tried to get him and Erika to date. While Erika was a beautiful and talented woman, there had never been any spark between them. Too bad Erika didn't realize that. The more he thought about it, the more he realized he might have rushed things a little with Adella in order to escape Erika.

He slipped his phone into his arm strap and took off on a short run. The sun was setting, and the air cool enough, so he hoped to get in the exercise before his mother returned. He needed to clear his head. Tomorrow was her birthday. Was he or wasn't he going to give her the sewing machine? He knew she'd love it, but he also couldn't forget Cate's imploring blue eyes.

Thinking of Cate . . . Was she ignoring him? Giving him a taste of his own negligence by not returning his calls?

Twenty minutes later, he realized he'd turned into Cate's grandma's neighborhood. He slowed to a jog. Cate's car was in the driveway. Should he run past or knock on the door? After a brief hesitation, he walked up to the door and knocked. No one answered. So he waited a few moments, then knocked again.

He thought about calling her but then decided he'd wait a couple of hours.

Leaving the house, he caught a glimpse of the ocean view behind the house. A path led past the house down to the beach. It looked like it was more a public path, so he walked along it.

In the twilight hour, the beach was nearly empty. He'd started down the incline that led to the sand when he heard someone call his name. He turned back toward the house, surprised to see Cate sitting on a back porch that overlooked the ocean.

She lifted her hand, a question in her eyes. Henry walked back up the path and cut over to where Cate was sitting.

"Looking for something?" she asked.

Henry heard the melancholy in her voice. "Can I sit by you?"

Cate nodded and inched over, giving him some room.

"I happened to be running by and—"

"*Happened* to?" She gave him a faint smile. "Sorry I didn't call you back." Her eyes returned to the ocean. "I'm in the middle of some pretty important decisions right now, and it seems that debating over the sewing machine is last on my list."

Henry wasn't sure what she meant but assumed she was dealing with her grandma's estate, maybe selling the house or something. "I didn't mean to push you," he said. "It's just that tomorrow is my mother's birthday."

Cate pulled her knees up and wrapped her arms around them, balancing her bare feet on the edge of the porch. "Your mother would love it."

Her tone was far from convincing. "What's wrong?" he asked.

She glanced at him, then back to the beach. "Amber's dad wants to turn this house into a vacation rental. I can't stand the thought of a different family traipsing in and out every week. Everything will be taken out, cheap carpet added, and it will be turned into a renter's paradise of plaid couches and framed pictures of wildlife."

Henry nodded, although he wondered if Cate realized that most of the stuff looked like it was selling as part of the estate sale. The house was already different. "Are there any other options?"

"Selling it, of course," she said in a quiet voice. "But with the market at a low for sellers, my uncle doesn't want to sell at a loss."

Henry followed her gaze out to the moving ocean. It was a peaceful view, and he decided he should take advantage of living so close to the ocean more often. His running usually took him to the beach and back, but he never really lingered or appreciated the view as he should. "This is a beautiful view," he said.

"The view is killer, but the house means a lot to me because of my grandma."

"Maybe you could live here," Henry said, not really thinking of the full implications.

Cate looked over at him, and he smiled.

"Would it really be so bad?" he asked, warming up to the idea. "Having this fabulous view and a house in which you could . . . What *do* you do?"

A smile broke through her melancholy. "I'm a writer for a travel magazine."

"Which means you're gone a lot," he guessed.

"Yes, probably enough that I couldn't justify buying a huge house. I wouldn't be able to keep up with the maintenance with all of my traveling."

Another idea popped into his head. With a place like this, he could have a formal office to meet in with clients, use the downstairs rooms as display areas, and . . . "How much do you think your uncle would sell it for? If the market was stronger?"

She drew her eyebrows together. "Why?"

He gave a casual shrug. "Just wondering." When he'd gone into the house and spotted the sewing machine, he'd also noticed the charming traditional aspects of the house—the hand-carved banister, the glass doorknobs . . . With a bit of work, it could be brought back to its former glory. "It's a great house, you know."

"Yeah." She was looking at him again. "How's your mother and Erika?"

He tried not to make a face, but it happened anyway.

"That bad?" she asked.

"It would have been much better if Erika stayed home," he said. "Not to be rude, but there's enough disruption with my mother. Ever since my father died a few years ago, she's become the mother hen. And now that I'm divorced, she's keen on pushing Erika and me together."

"Oh, so there's a history with Erika?" Cate asked.

"Not in the way you think. Erika's parents were good friends with my parents. One night, and I'm sure they were all tipsy with wine, they thought it would be fantastic if their kids married each other," Henry said, feeling Cate's gaze on him. "I had just started seeing Adella, and, well . . ."

"Adella captured your heart, but now that she's out of the picture, Erika is back." Her tone sounded triumphant.

"Something like that." Henry leaned back on his hands and looked over at her. "Makes me sound callous."

"Well, you are horrible at returning phone calls."

Henry pulled his phone from his pocket and tapped on his phone log to show her the three unanswered calls to her number.

"Touché." She laughed.

The sound warmed him through, and Henry smiled. "Do you want to get something to eat?"

"What about your guests? What about Erika?"

He laughed. "I'll let my mom know I'll be late, that I'm working on her birthday surprise."

Her expression sobered. "I think you should give the sewing machine to your mother. It will bring your grandma's sacrifice full circle."

"Cate—"

Her hand grasped his. "Henry, please. It will be in a great home with your mother. I'll figure things out on my end, but this decision feels right." She removed her hand before he could react. "Come on," she said, standing. "Let's go get food. I'm starving."

He stood as well, facing her. The breeze stirred her hair, blowing it gently against her face. He couldn't help brushing it away. She blinked up at him.

"Maybe we should order takeout?" he said. "I probably don't smell so great."

A smile tugged at Cate's mouth, and her hand brushed against his. An accident? He hoped not.

"That's fine with me," she said. "I didn't want to get dressed up anyway."

Cate wore a silk tank shirt and tailored shorts. It might

be casual for her, but she looked classy regardless. Henry followed her inside. "Is your cousin around?"

"She went back to LA. But she'll probably return next weekend to finish sorting things out—her father's coming too, I guess," Cate said, picking up her phone from the counter.

"How long are you staying?" Henry glanced around the spacious kitchen. His heart beat faster at the thought of being alone in the house with Cate. He could sit here for hours, talking about everything and anything with her. And he was finding fewer and fewer reasons to stay away.

Nine

"I'll be here a couple more days," Cate told Henry. "I promised Amber I'd clean out the small stuff." She opened a restaurant app on her phone, then looked up at Henry. "Any recommendations for takeout?"

"Pizza?" he suggested.

She scrunched her nose.

"Chinese? The Fortune Café is always good."

"My grandma and I went there a few times," Cate said, tapping the search into her phone and pulling up the number. "What do you want?"

"Shrimp cashew and egg drop soup," he said.

She flashed him a smile. "Sounds good to me. I'll get large sizes, and we can share." When the person at the restaurant answered, Cate placed the order.

Henry walked over to one of the kitchen windows, eyeing the blue-and-white linen curtains at the windows. With the growing darkness outside, they gave the kitchen a bright, clean feel. Cate hung up, and Henry said, "Are these the curtains you sewed?" He reached up to examine one.

"Don't inspect the stitches too closely," Cate said with a laugh. She crossed the room and stopped next to him, gazing at the curtains.

"They look great to me," Henry said.

She was close enough to smell the ocean air on him. It was strange being in this house with a man, with Henry. They'd only just met, and yet seeing the house through his eyes made her feel closer to her grandma, somehow. It was so easy to talk to him. She glanced up at him, and her stomach fluttered. It was dangerous being close enough to touch him. "Do you want me to show you the house?" she asked, hoping to distract herself.

"Sure," he said.

The tour itself didn't take long, but Cate found herself sharing bits of information about her grandma. When they returned to the kitchen and each sat on a barstool, Henry said, "Tell me more about your job."

As she talked about the places she visited and wrote about, she was well aware of Henry's gaze on her, making her feel flushed and fidgety. It seemed the house was growing too warm. At one point, she rose and opened one of the kitchen windows, letting in the ocean breeze.

He continued to ask questions, as if really interested, and she told him about the museums and local historical sites of the towns and cities she traveled to. She told him she lived in LA to be near the magazine's home office. "But the traffic makes me want to become a hermit," she said. "There is no place else in the world with worse traffic."

"Not even Europe or the Middle East?"

"Well, the traffic might be bad in some of the major cities, but there are more interesting things to look at in those countries than miles of concrete freeway."

Henry laughed. "What's the angle of your articles?" he

THE BOARDWALK ANTIQUES SHOP

asked. "Family-friendly vacations? Exclusive hotels and restaurants?"

Cate leaned against the counter, propping her elbow on it. "It's changed over the years. This past year or two, I've started out with the travel facts, then I add two or three recommendations of hotels and restaurants. I conclude my articles with highlights of little-known historical sites."

"You sound like you love it." His hazel eyes were intent on her, warm and inviting.

It was easy to talk to him, Cate realized. "I do love it, although it can be tough living out of a suitcase and a bit awkward going to restaurants alone all of the time."

Henry nodded. "I didn't think about that."

The doorbell rang. "Speaking of eating," Cate said with a laugh and rose from her barstool.

"I'll pay for it," Henry said, following her to the door. "Wait, I don't have my wallet with me. Can I pay you back later?"

"Don't worry about it. You're lucky I'm nice," Cate said, opening the door. While she paid the delivery man, Henry grabbed the food and carried it into the kitchen.

By the time she made it into the kitchen, Henry had taken the containers out of the sacks and lifted the lids.

Steam rose from the food, and Cate realized she was quite hungry.

She reached for the fortune cookie, unwrapped it and broke it open.

"What are you doing?" Henry asked.

"Eating my dessert first." She popped half of the cookie into her mouth; then she read the fortune. "New challenges are on the horizon."

"That's pretty accurate," Henry said with a smile. He opened his own fortune cookie and read it with a raised brow. "Sometimes the best thing in life is right in front of you." He laughed. "These fortunes are uncanny."

"Especially if I'm being called the *best thing in life*," Cate said.

"Well, I'm not one to go against a fortune cookie's advice. I guess the next meal's on me." Henry said before diving in and taking a bite of the food piled on his plate.

Butterflies twisted in Cate's stomach. *Next meal?* She admitted to herself that she did like Henry, but they lived a few hours apart. "Do you ever come to LA?"

"Not unless I can't help it," Henry said between bites. Then he winked. "I'm there quite a lot, actually. Trying to commit me to a dinner?"

"You're the one who offered." She folded her arms, waiting.

Henry wiped his mouth with a napkin, then leaned forward, his gaze intent on Cate's. "I did, and I meant it. In fact, I'll be in LA next Wednesday for an antiques trade show."

The slow flush was back. "With a booth and everything?"

Henry grimaced. "I'm a bit past that stage, thankfully. I'm actually the MC for the auction. Don't know what's worse. Sitting in a booth or trying to keep everything legit."

Cate was impressed, but she supposed she shouldn't be surprised. After all, she'd seen Henry on the antiques shows from Europe, and he was a dynamic person. Maybe she'd just have to go to her first antiques show next Wednesday.

Henry's phone buzzed, and he ignored it. When it buzzed a second and third time, Cate said, "I don't mind if you get that."

He took another bite, seeming to enjoy his food more than most people. When he swallowed, he said, "I have a pretty good idea who it is."

"Your mom?" Cate said, then immediately regretted being so nosy.

"My mom doesn't text," Henry said. "I think we both know who it is."

"So, you're here with me? Instead of Erika? Is this a repeat scenario of what happened with your ex-wife?" Sometimes Cate couldn't believe what was coming out of her mouth. She was a direct, to-the-point-person, but this was going overboard.

Henry started to cough. Then he covered his mouth, his face turning red. He grabbed the water bottle on the counter and took a drink. "No," he said, meeting her gaze, his eyes watering from coughing.

Cate raised her eyebrows and folded her arms.

"Okay, maybe yes," he amended. "Only the part about wanting to be with *you*, and not Erika. But this meal, this night, has *nothing* to do with Adella."

She kept her gaze steady. "If you say so."

"I do." Henry said, pushing the plate away. He propped an elbow on the counter, studying her right back. "Ever since you started yelling at me in the antiques shop, I knew I wanted to get to know you better."

Cate let a small smile escape, a very small smile.

He leaned forward so he was close enough for her to touch. "What about you?" he asked. "When did you decide you wanted to get to know me better?"

Cate thought about teasing him, but she supposed he already knew she was interested. She could hardly keep her eyes off of him. "I think it was when my cousin told me you'd stolen my grandma's sewing machine." Okay, so she was going to tease him.

The edges of his mouth turned up, and he moved even closer. It was like he and she were unconsciously gravitating toward each other. "*Stolen*, huh? I said I'd give it back."

"You did say that," Cate said. Her heart thumped at his nearness. Henry smelled like a mixture of musk, light sweat, and the ocean. His eyes were a blend of greens and golds up close; his lashes were dark.

He raised his hand and touched her hair, twisting it lightly with his fingertips.

She let her eyes close. She didn't know if he was going to kiss her, but she was going to enjoy this—whatever *this* was.

Ten

Henry had always prided himself on his practical nature. Marrying Adella had been practical. She was beautiful, talented, smart, and loved antiques. Staying away from Erika had been practical. She was high maintenance, became bored easily, and shared a too-close relationship with his mother.

But Cate. Nothing about her was practical. She captivated him, stunned him, and he was finding himself thinking outrageous thoughts around her. Such as buying her grandma's house. Such as following her around the world as she wrote her travel articles. Or, at the more immediate present, sitting on a barstool, ignoring the fact that he was supposed to be hosting his mother. Instead, he was sitting in Cate's kitchen with every intention of kissing her.

"Can I steal one more thing from you?" he asked.

She opened her very blue eyes. Her voice was soft. "What's that?"

"A kiss?" Henry asked.

She didn't speak, just lifted her chin slightly. Henry took that as an invitation. He rested his hand on her shoulder, drew her closer, pleased when her eyes fluttered shut. When he brushed his mouth against hers, he took it slowly. He didn't want to forget anything about Cate, not the softness of her lips, not the warmth of her skin. Kissing her was like waking up and seeing the morning sunlight.

But when she wrapped her arms around his neck and kissed him back, his temperature rocketed, pushing his pulse higher than it had been while running. Her kiss was way beyond practical. He wanted to get closer, to pull her onto his lap and not let go for a long time. But he didn't want Cate to be a fling. So he ignored his instincts and gave her a final, lingering kiss, then released her slowly.

"I don't mind if you steal that back," he said, his voice husky. He didn't want to leave, but he knew he had to or it would be impossible to.

Cate's blue eyes peered up at him. "I think you owe me dinner first."

He grinned. "That won't be a problem." Reluctantly, he stood and took a few steps away from her, forcing himself toward the front door. "What are you doing Wednesday?"

"I'm really busy," she said, standing and following him to the front room. "I'll be going to an antiques show in LA."

"If you see someone there named Henry Lancaster, you should say hi." His hand was on the doorknob, but the last thing he wanted to do was twist it open.

Cate stopped a couple of feet away from him. Henry's body still buzzed from her kisses.

"I'll think about it," Cate said, her smile sweet. "Goodbye, Henry Lancaster. Drive safe to LA."

"You too, Cate." He opened the door, and the breeze

touched his skin. He stepped through the doorway, headed down the stairs, and turned to wave.

Cate leaned against the doorframe, and he felt her eyes on him as he walked down the path. Then he started up the street he'd jogged down two hours previous.

He made it back to his home in record time. As he walked up the driveway, Erika came out of his house, talking on her cell phone. She was wearing a tight-fitting teal-green dress, as if she'd planned on going to a nice restaurant tonight. When she saw him from the porch, she ended her phone call and gave him a pouty smile. "Didn't you get my texts? Your mom and I were wondering if we should order takeout."

Henry inwardly groaned. He knew Erika had texted him, but he'd forgotten to read them. "Sorry about that. I'm not hungry though," he said, "so you two can get whatever you'd like."

He reached the porch, and Erika's fingers snaked around his arm. "That must have been some run. Did you get lost?"

Her heavy-floral perfume made him want to sneeze, which Henry believed wasn't the intention of whatever perfume designer had created it. "I made a stop."

"Oh," Erika, raising her eyebrows, waiting for more of an explanation. When she didn't get one, she said, "Something to do with your mother's birthday?"

"Sort of," Henry said, then reached for the screen door.

"You're *so* sneaky," Erika said. "I know you're trying to surprise your mother, and I think you're sweet for doing that."

"That's me, sneaky and sweet," he said in a dry tone.

"Mmm." Erika moved her hand up his arm.

Standing this close to Erika, Henry noticed how perfectly applied her makeup was, and he wondered if he'd ever seen her without makeup. Tonight, Cate hadn't had a bit of makeup on, and she'd been more beautiful than when he'd first met her in the antiques shop. He realized that Erika was still talking to him, and he hadn't heard a word.

"All that running has kept you in *such* great shape," she said.

Henry pulled open the screen door to go inside. Erika couldn't be more obvious. He felt bad, though, for always trying to avoid her.

"Wait, Henry," she said, her voice soft, yet insistent.

He exhaled, and turned.

"I know you had a nasty breakup with Adella, but I just wanted you to know that I'm here if you need to talk. About her or about anything." Her smile was wide, perfectly shaped, filled with hope.

He felt like a jerk standing here with her on the porch, thinking of ways to avoid her when she was just being nice. Even though he hadn't invited her for the weekend, he felt responsible for her somehow.

"I'm all right, Erika," he said. "I've made my peace with what happened with Adella." *Mostly.*

"That's good to hear," she said. "Because there's something I've wanted to do for a long time."

Before he could realize what she meant, Erika leaned against him and kissed him.

Henry was stunned and didn't move for a moment. He wanted to tell her something, anything, even if it was that he was dating someone new—which wasn't technically true, but he hoped it to be true.

Erika pulled away. "There," she said, looking triumphant. "You can tell Adella that you're taken if she ever wants to come back."

Henry opened his mouth, unsure of what to say. He was *taken*? By *Erika*?

"Henry? Is that you?" his mother's voice called.

Erika gave a soft laugh. "I think your mother would

approve of us. She always talks about you and gives plenty of hints about how she'd like to see us together."

"Yeah, I know," Henry said, "but here's the thing—"

"There you are, Henry," his mother said, opening the door. "Erika and I were just wondering . . . Oh, you *are* with Erika. We're starving."

At least his mother wasn't dressed to the nines like Erika. Maybe they hadn't planned on a restaurant, and Erika was just being Erika.

"Henry's not hungry," Erika announced. She sounded put out, which only seared guilt deeper into Henry.

"Do you want me to go grab you some takeout?" he asked, hoping they wouldn't select Chinese.

"No," his mother said. "I can order from here and have it delivered. We don't want you disappearing into the night again. You get showered up, and the food should be here by then."

Henry knew he was in for a long night. "Sounds great," he said, moving past his mother into the house.

Once alone in his bedroom, he had a chance to process what had happened in the past few hours. Had he really kissed Cate? And had he really been kissed by Erika? He'd dated some since his divorce but hadn't kissed any of the women. And now, in less than an hour, he'd kissed two.

He sat on the corner of his bed, staring out the window into the darkness, wondering what in the world he was going to do now. Erika was downstairs, laughing and chatting with his mother, probably feeling like their relationship had just taken a positive turn. Cate was in that vast empty house on the beach, alone, and maybe, hopefully, thinking of him.

Amid his tumbling thoughts, he knew one thing for certain; he couldn't part with that sewing machine, not even for his mother.

Eleven

Cate hung up the phone with her uncle. She'd successfully kept her emotions in check while talking to him, but now she couldn't hold the tears back any longer. Crying about it was ridiculous, really, and she knew it. Henry had given her the idea of renting Grandma's place herself, even though it was completely impractical. The beach house was over two hours away from the LA magazine office and much too big for her alone. Although there was the fact that her grandma had lived here for years by herself . . .

Thus the phone call with her uncle. He hadn't taken to the idea. And no matter what his excuses were about not wanting to mix family with business, Cate knew it was about money. He'd want to charge top dollar for the place, even though Cate had assured him she'd rent it at market value.

With the new Mariposa 5-star hotel recently opened and attracting the who's who in California, real estate was predicted to start rising throughout Seashell Beach. And many of the shops and boutiques on Tangerine Street had been recently renovated. It was like the whole town was prepping for an upswing in the economy.

Cate offered to rent the house until it sold, but what if it sold quickly? She would have to move twice, and there was still the time it would take to sell her apartment in LA. "Grandma, why did you have to die?" she said aloud in the car, which only brought a fresh wave of self-pity.

"Cate, get ahold of yourself," she said. Now she was talking to herself. She flipped open the visor mirror and checked her appearance. Her mascara was still intact, but her nose was a bit red. Hopefully the lighting in the antiques convention would be mellow.

She grabbed her handbag and slipped her cell and keys into it, then climbed out of her car, a new set of butterflies entering her stomach. Henry Lancaster was in the building in front of her. She laughed to herself, a nervous laugh, as she realized she always thought of him as Henry Lancaster III, not just Henry. It was fitting for him somehow, not in the austere way she'd first thought of him, but because he was more than just a Henry. He was the complete package— intelligent, kind, interesting, vulnerable, real . . . not to mention the fierce attraction she felt for him.

And it seemed to be reciprocal, judging by his kiss in Seashell Beach.

Each time she thought of how he'd kissed her, her skin hummed with warmth. Each time he'd called or texted her over the last few days, she'd become more and more attached to him. His voice, his laugh, his interest in her life . . . Cate's heart thumped as she started walking toward the building. She couldn't wait to see him again. In fact, her heart was racing as if she'd run instead of driven to the convention center.

As she pulled open the heavy glass door and walked to

A STITCH IN TIME

the ticket line, she chastised herself. It had only been one meal, one kiss—well, several in a row—so was she making too much of it? Was Henry a flirt? He was easy to talk to on the phone, and his texting made her laugh out loud. But he'd had a history of relationships, with Adella, with Erika, and with who knew how many others he'd dated.

But he'd seemed to really want her to come to the convention. Of course that was after she'd said she was already going . . . She shook her doubts away as she stepped up to the ticket window to make her purchase.

"Name and company?" the dark-haired woman in the booth asked, ready to type up a name badge.

"It's just me," Cate said. "I mean, I'm not with a company. Do I have to be?"

The woman looked at Cate, peering above her reading glasses. "No, but if you were, I'd add it to your badge."

"All right, then. My name's Cate Pierpont."

The woman typed almost faster than Cate spoke. "Oh," the woman said. "It looks like you're VIP. You've been comped the full package."

Cate didn't know what the woman was talking about but accepted the badge and the bag of items she slid across the counter.

"There's a luncheon ticket in there for the VIP table as well some goodies from our main sponsors."

"Well, thank you," Cate said, wondering if there was some mistake. But the tag dangling from the lanyard she held in her hands said, "Cate Pierpont. Lancaster Antiques." Henry had done this.

She turned away from the ticket window, a smile tugging at her mouth. She slipped on the lanyard, but as she stepped into the main convention room, she realized she had no idea how to find Henry. He wasn't running a booth, she knew that much. She stood to the side of the entrance, letting others pass by her, and she pulled out the schedule. The

267

luncheon was taking place in one of the ballrooms off the main convention floor at 1:00 p.m., and the auction started at 2:00 p.m. in the same room. On the line listed next to Master of Ceremonies was the name of *Henry Lancaster*.

It was 11:00 a.m. now, so Cate decided to walk around and look at the various vendors and booths before heading into the VIP lunch. She could text Henry, she supposed, to tell him she'd arrived, but it might be nice to see what a convention was like firsthand, while staying a bit incognito.

She studied the layout map and saw that some of the vendors were organized by era or type of vendor. A section of booths drew her attention—they were private collectors selling only a handful of items. She walked over to the north section to check out the private collectors. The first man she approached was sitting with a woman at a table, their hands linked together. The couple looked to be in their seventies.

"Good morning," the man said, rising to extend his hand.

Cate shook his hand.

"I'm Jeff, and this is my wife, Bernice." He peered at her name tag. "Ah, you're from Lancaster Antiques. I'm afraid we don't sell to dealers. We're hoping to find a good home for our antiques."

"I don't work for Lancaster," Cate said. "I'm just a guest."

The man smiled. "Are you interested in coins?"

Cate wasn't particularly fascinated with old coins but loved the passion with which the man and his wife talked about their coin collection that had taken them over fifty years to create. When she left the couple, she couldn't help but think about Henry and his ex-wife. They'd shared the same passion for antiques, yet their marriage had ended. What kept this other couple together?

Her next stop was at a china doll booth. She greeted the vendor named David, a tall man with a goatee. It seemed

268

incongruous that this man was collecting china dolls. Cate examined the painted faces and the delicate silk dresses.

"How did you start collecting china dolls?" Cate asked, curiosity getting the better of her.

"My twin sister inherited them from my great-grandma, but when my sister died a few years ago from cancer, I stored them," David said, sounding a bit rehearsed, as if he'd been asked the same question many times. "I didn't think much about them until I watched an antiques show on television."

Cate found herself fascinated as David told his story.

"There was a china doll on the show that was appraised for over $1,000," David continued. "I was intrigued and started to do some research. I found that my great-grandma's collection was valuable, but as I was researching I ended up purchasing a few more." He spread his hands. "And I ended up with this."

Cate laughed. There had to be over a hundred dolls on display. "You ended up with a lot of dolls, but it seems like you're preserving some great memories as well."

David nodded. "Connecting the past with the present has been interesting."

Cate couldn't agree more and started telling David the story about her grandma's sewing machine. Before she knew it, she was leaning across the booth table and talking about the part Henry Lancaster played in purchasing the machine and about the connections between their families. "So you just gave up on it, then?" David asked, leaning on the table as well, as they talked conspiratorially. "Let Mr. Lancaster have it for his mother?"

"I insisted," Cate said with a shrug. "It seemed the right thing to do. I felt like my grandma's machine should be returned to the family who originally owned it."

"Still, I don't know if I would have been so generous," David said; then he tilted his head. "When you speak of Mr.

Lancaster, your eyes change. Is there more to this story than you're telling me?"

Cate flushed. "What do you mean, my eyes change?"

David smiled. "It's hard to explain, but I love to observe people. It's just something I've noticed as you've been talking." He lifted a brow. "So what is it? Why did you really let Mr. Lancaster have your grandma's sewing machine?"

Someone stopped at the booth, placed his hands on the table, and leaned toward David. "I'd like to know the answer as well."

Cate snapped her head around, coming face-to-face with Henry. "Henry Lancaster?"

He grinned, holding her gaze. "I hoped that by now you'd be calling me Henry."

Her body flashed hot. Cate was sure she was completely red. "I know—I wasn't expecting—"

"To see me here?" He glanced at her name tag. "You *are* wearing the VIP badge."

"I know, it's just that . . ." She started again. "Do you know David? Have you heard his china doll story?"

Henry extended his hand to David, and the two men shook hands. "Nice to meet you, David."

"And you, too, Mr. Lancaster. I've seen you on television."

Henry nodded, then said, "I read about your china dolls online."

David beamed, but Henry was quick to turn his gaze back to Cate. "So, what's the rest of the sewing machine story?"

Cate looked over at David, giving him a look of desperation.

David raised his hands. "I can't get you out of this. I want to know the real reason too."

Cate kept her voice nonchalant and her gaze on David, although she could feel Henry's eyes on her. "I felt like the

270

guy needed a break. I was pretty upset when I found out my cousin had sold him the machine, and I might have yelled at Henry a little bit in the antiques store."

Next to her, Henry laughed. "I appreciate the break, but I didn't give it to my mother after all."

Cate turned to face him. "You didn't?"

He smiled. "I didn't."

Another customer stopped at the booth, and David stepped aside to talk with him.

Cate moved closer to Henry and lowered her voice. "When did you decide that?"

"I think it was when you were pulling out the fifteen hundred in cash from your bag," he said, his mouth turned up in amusement.

"But that was when we first met," Cate said. "You told me—"

"Shh," Henry said, grasping her hand.

The sensation of his touch, and in such a public place in front of all of his peers, shut Cate up.

"I don't think I can ever resist your blue eyes," he said in a low tone.

Cate wanted to roll her eyes and laugh, but mostly she wanted to swoon. She decided to narrow her eyes. "Are you trying to butter me up for something?"

"I'm trying . . ." he started, then tugged her hand and led her away so that they were a safe distance from the booth and David's proximity. Then Henry leaned toward her and whispered, "I'm trying to get you to come to lunch with me."

He was close enough that she could smell his spicy scent. Close enough to imagine the warmth of his skin. She tapped her VIP badge. "Do you mean the lunch in the ballroom?"

He winked. "The very one. Then, I'm hoping, that at some point today, I can kiss you again."

271

The breath left Cate's lungs. "I can't guarantee that, but lunch sounds good."

Twelve

ate's eyes and sweet laughter had done him in, Henry decided. If only she knew how much of a spell she'd cast over him. He'd been thinking about her nonstop for several days now. He'd even made the dreaded call to Erika and met her for lunch the day before. Because of their long-term friendship and her closeness with his mom, he had to be completely upfront and transparent with her. When he told her he was dating another woman, someone he was extremely interested in, Erika had given him a brittle smile.

He couldn't ignore the tears brimming in her eyes, and he told her he truly hoped she could forgive him. When he gave her a good-bye hug, she held onto him for a long time. Then she walked away without looking back. Henry had felt deflated, but he knew it was the right and fair thing to do.

By the time he'd reached his car after leaving Erika, he was already looking forward to texting Cate again. Over the past several days, it had taken every ounce of self-control in order not to call or text her every hour, on the hour, between last weekend and this Wednesday. He'd only called or texted her maybe every three hours. She had said she was coming to the antiques convention, but Henry didn't always believe in the good news until it actually happened.

He'd left her the VIP ticket anyway. When he saw her come into the convention center, Henry caught himself staring. She was elegantly dressed, wearing black slacks and a silk tunic. Her sandals had heels, which he knew would make her only a couple of inches shorter than him.

Her long blonde waves had been pulled into a clip at the back of her neck, making her look business-like yet effortlessly pretty at the same time. He fervently wished the entire convention center and all of its occupants would disappear so he could be alone with Cate. He wondered what scent she was wearing and if she'd let him kiss the violin curve of her neck.

She smiled at him now as they stood together a few yards from the china doll booth, and Henry couldn't remember a time when he'd felt more light-hearted.

"Are you going to tell me why you didn't give the sewing machine to your mother?" she asked.

Henry had to focus on her words to hear them. Watching her mouth move only made him want to kiss her. "I almost did," he said, finally answering her question. "I even brought my mother to the Boardwalk Antiques Shop, with the intention of showing her the sewing machine . . ."

"And?" she prompted.

Henry exhaled. "And . . . I couldn't do it. I knew that if I gave her the sewing machine, she'd take it to her house, put it in a corner, show it off to a neighbor or two, and that would be it. She'd love it, but she wouldn't love it as much as I do."

Cate's mouth quirked. "*You* love it?"

Henry could get lost in her eyes; he knew he could

definitely get lost in her kiss. If only everyone would disappear for a few moments. "I do."

She tilted her head, studying him in that way of hers. "Henry Lancaster, have you fallen in love with a sewing machine?"

Her choice of words sent a thrill through him, and he laughed. "The bottom line was that I didn't want to give something away that reminded me of you."

Cate looked down and was quiet.

"Hey, are you all right?" He linked his fingers with hers. "Cate?"

She looked up at him, and he thought her eyes appeared moist, but he wasn't sure.

"You might get that kiss after all," she said, squeezing his hand.

The day couldn't have turned out any more perfectly.

"So what did you give your mother for her birthday?" she asked.

Henry's senses had slowed down, so it took him a moment to remember what Cate was talking about. "I told her to choose any antique she wanted, regardless of price."

Cate's eyebrows raised. "What did she choose?"

"An antique cash register, if you can believe it." He shook his head. "Said her grandkids would love it someday—playing store, I guess."

"Grandkids?" she said. "Your mother will be an indulgent grandma."

"She can't wait," he said, then felt a bit awkward, realizing what he'd said.

But Cate didn't seem to notice. "So . . . Are you going to show me around, Mr. Lancaster?"

"Only if you call me Henry."

She laughed, and he decided he wanted to hear her laugh every day. "All right, *Henry*, have it your way. Now show me the wonders of the antiques world."

And so he did. Cate seemed interested in everything they looked at together, and he got more than a few interested looks from others he'd known a long time—likely speculating if Cate was his girlfriend. Most of the vendors had known Adella.

Henry introduced Cate to one of his favorite vendors, All About Hats. Karlene had been a great friend over the years; Henry even knew the names of her kids and grandkids. She kept a fascinating collection of antique hats.

"Oh, wow," Cate said, picking up a straw hat decorated with faded ribbons.

"That's from the Regency Romance era—early 1800s," Karlene said, beaming. "Just don't touch the ribbon. Your fingers have oil on them, even though you can't see it." She looked over at Henry and winked her approval.

Everyone seemed to like Cate. And she was personable and genuinely interested in those he'd introduced her to.

"Can I try it on?" Cate asked.

"Not that one, I'm afraid," Karlene said. She picked up a wide-brimmed felt hat that sported a fake bird's nest and bird. "This one is less valuable. Do you want to try it on?"

Cate smiled. "Sure." She placed it on her head, then tilted it at an angle. "How do I look, Henry?"

"Gorgeous, darlin'," he said in a thick Boston accent. He picked up a top hat and put it on his own head. "Care for a stroll?"

Karlene clapped her hands. "Stand together. Let me take your picture."

Henry slid his arm around Cate's shoulders, and Karlene took a picture with her phone.

"Text it to me," Cate said and gave Karlene her cell number. She looked up at Henry. "You should wear that as MC."

He lifted his eyebrows. "Maybe I will."

"That one's not for sale," Karlene said. "It's display only."

"I thought everything was for sale," Henry said, giving her a beguiling smile.

Karlene placed her hands on her hips. "That might work with the younger vendors, but not me."

"All right, all right," Henry said, acting sheepish, although he was anything but. He looked over at Cate; she'd taken her hat off.

"Ready for lunch?" she asked.

"Yes," Henry said, then looked over at Karlene. "Are you coming to the auction?"

"I'm planning on it," Karlene said.

As Henry walked with Cate across the convention floor, she said, "Have you known Karlene long?"

"Almost as long as I've been in business," Henry said. In fact, Karlene had introduced him to Adella, but he didn't want to share that with Cate yet.

Several other vendors greeted Henry, and he stopped to talk to some of them for a few moments each. He couldn't help watching Cate charm everyone she'd met. She'd certainly had a lot of world-traveling experience and likely had to deal with people of all nationalities and interests. Her personality and skills served her well at this type of convention.

They finally made it the outside corridor that connected the various rooms. Only half the building was in operation, and the corridor past the ballroom was dark save for the west windows.

Henry checked the time on his cell phone. Still twenty minutes before seating would begin at the lunch. Plenty of time to show Cate around.

"Come on," Henry said, grasping Cate's hand and leading her down the corridor, past the milling people moving toward the ballroom. "There's some pretty cool artwork this way." Cate's hand was warm in his, and he was glad she didn't resist. It wasn't as if they were an official couple, everything was so new, but the fact that she'd shown up at the convention was definitely a large step in that direction. That, and the flirting she'd done with him, and the way his heart tugged as she seemed to easily fall into step with his acquaintances.

"I'm surprised this part of the building isn't rented out," Cate said.

"The antiques show used to be a lot bigger, but with the overseas conferences sprouting up, the Europeans who collect Americana don't feel the need to trek to LA anymore." They turned one corner and then another until they reached the north lobby. Instead of a row of ticket windows like the south lobby, this one was dotted with lounge chairs, statues and a huge mural on the wall.

Cate came to a dead stop. "Oh, wow." Even in the dim lighting, the floor-to-ceiling mural of a rock band holding instruments was impressive. "It's a Kent Twitchell, right?"

"Yeah," Henry said.

"I once spent an afternoon looking at all of his work online," Cate said. "It's amazing. I'm always impressed with artists. I am not artistic at all."

Henry looked at her in surprise. "Writing isn't artistic?"

She bit her lower lip. "Maybe a little."

Their hands were still intertwined, and it was all Henry could do to not kiss her now. She'd promised after lunch, unless she'd been teasing about that. But they were alone here, finally. He focused on the mural, trying to take his mind off the amazing woman holding his hand.

"Henry," she said, looking up at him and drawing his attention.

"Hmmm?"

"Kiss me."

Thirteen

It was bold to ask Henry to kiss her, but Cate felt bold. Maybe it was because they were in a room filled with inspiring art, art that soared from floor to ceiling, making her heart soar as well. She had never said anything close to that to a man before, and she wasn't sure why she'd said it to Henry.

It was too late now to take back her words.

He'd hesitated, but Cate hoped it was because he was surprised and not reluctant. Her heart tripped with relief when he turned toward her and slid his arms around her waist.

"You're sure?" he asked, lowering his head close to hers.

She moved her hands up his arms, stopping at his biceps. "I'm sure."

"It's before lunch, you know," he whispered, pulling her closer still, torturing her with his teasing. Every part of their bodies was touching except for their mouths.

"Henry," Cate breathed. He was taking too long. She

didn't know when she'd become so impatient, when she'd become so demanding of a kiss. But Henry had that effect on her. Thankfully, he wised up and stopped talking.

He kissed her, and the heat of his mouth blocked out any other thoughts. She wrapped her arms around his neck, and he lifted her against him, closing the last bit of space between them. He kissed her long and hard, until she felt dizzy and a little bit crazy.

Henry drew away and laughed.

She still wasn't ready to let him go, but she opened her eyes to find him smiling at her.

"I like you, Cate," he said. Direct as always.

"I like you too," she said. Heat rose to her cheeks at her own directness. She stepped back, but he stopped her from moving too far by grabbing her hand.

"Where are you going?" he asked, his eyes glinting.

"I'm sorry," she said in a breathless voice. "I'm not usually that forward, at least with . . ." She pointed at him. "With this type of thing."

He nodded, his face growing serious. "I understand. And I'm glad you're okay with being forward with me."

She just stared at him, because the feeling had returned. She wanted him to kiss her again, but she wanted him to do it without being asked.

"I like that you can tell me what you're feeling," he continued, threading their fingers together, making her heart beat faster. "That you can tell me what you want."

"I guess I'm not the normal woman."

He laughed. "You're definitely not, but that's what I like about you, Cate." He stepped close to her and kissed her lightly on the cheek. "Come on. Let's get lunch, and then maybe we can come back here and make out after, if you want to kiss more."

Cate groaned in embarrassment, and Henry laughed. He kept hold of her hand as they walked to the ballroom.

And he still kept hold of her hand as they were directed by the hostess to their table at the front of the room by the makeshift stage.

People had definitely noticed, and Cate found herself blushing more than once at the raised eyebrows and the hushed whispers. Of course she assumed they were all about her, the new woman being escorted by Henry Lancaster III.

It was a welcome relief when Cate saw Karlene, the antique hat dealer, at their table. Cate had felt comfortable with her from their first introduction.

Karlene grinned when she saw them approaching.

"I hoped you were at my table," Karlene said with a little clap of her hands.

Henry pulled out the chair next to Karlene and indicated for Cate to sit next to her. Cate was more than happy to sit down and take a break from all the stares and introductions.

Two men joined their table, and Henry fell into a conversation with them about vintage wine discovered in an abandoned cellar somewhere up the coast. Henry hadn't resumed holding her hand after she'd sat down.

Cate fidgeted, and she picked up the napkin from the china plate and twisted it in her lap. Sitting down and having a chance to look about the room made her wonder what she was really doing.

"You look a bit overwhelmed," Karlene whispered conspiratorially. "I'm sure it's not easy to follow after Adella."

Cate couldn't be more surprised at Karlene's comment. She realized Henry and his wife had been a great team and had been in the business for a while, but it was almost as if Karlene had been close to Adella. "Are you good friends with her?" Cate asked.

Karlene offered a sympathetic smile. "Not so good that I

THE BOARDWALK ANTIQUES SHOP

have to choose sides." She brushed at imaginary crumbs on the pristine table cloth. "Let's just say—"

"Welcome, ladies and gentlemen," a voice boomed over the speakers, drowning out whatever Karlene was going to say.

The man standing on the stage dabbed his forehead with a handkerchief. It seemed the bright stage lights were already making him too hot. It was no wonder, Cate thought; the man was wearing a three-piece suit.

Henry leaned over to Cate and said, "Hungry?"

She flashed him a smile, then turned her attention back to the man giving the introduction to the lunch event. He thanked several sponsors, gave a short history of the annual convention, then said, "Enjoy your meal, and in about forty minutes, we'll start the auction portion."

Cate glanced over at Henry. "Nervous?"

He gave her a half-smile. "Only because you're here."

"Oh, really?" Cate said with a laugh. "I don't believe that for a moment."

He leaned in again as the room buzzed around them with conversation and plates of food being delivered and drinks being poured. "I'm worried you'll find out that I'm not all that amazing."

"I never called you amazing," Cate said, leaning just a little closer.

He raised an eyebrow. "Maybe I need to kiss you again."

Cate hoped no one at the table had overheard him, although with her blushing, they might get the general idea. "I might need to take you up on that later," she said.

Two servers arrived and set down the plates of rosemary chicken, rice pilaf, and steamed veggies. Only five people were sitting at their VIP table, when it looked like most of the other tables were filled to their capacity of eight each.

Henry dug into his food like a starving man, and Cate followed suit. Maybe kissing so much had made both of them hungry. The conversation at the table centered around which conventions in Europe were the most reputable. Cate half-listened, interested, but also wondering how well Karlene knew Adella. And where was Adella now? Had she completely abandoned her career to follow after her professional-athlete boyfriend, or did she work someplace in Europe?

She supposed Karlene might know the answers, but Cate didn't want to ask them here. Especially since she should be asking Henry if she really wanted to know.

The conversation continued, with Cate paying less and less attention as she let her gaze wander the room. Then she noticed a woman walking toward the stage. She climbed the steps and crossed to the podium. The conversations in the room began to hush as people focused on the tall woman.

She made a striking figure on the stage. Her smooth chestnut hair was cut in a bob, and long gold earrings dangled from her ears, catching the brilliance of the spotlights. She tapped the microphone, and the room hushed even more.

"Hello," she said into the microphone, in a soft and husky voice.

A few members of the audience chuckled, and she smiled, displaying a perfect row of white teeth.

Cate was a slender woman, but the woman up on stage was positively model-thin. Her pencil skirt and tailored jacket only emphasized her figure.

"Mr. Phillips wasn't feeling well," the woman said, "so you're stuck with me for introductions."

The audience laughed.

The woman smiled again and tilted her chin up, lifting her eyes toward the ceiling. "I volunteered in Mr. Phillips place because I figured I could wing it pretty well. What can I ever say about Mr. Henry Lancaster?"

More laughter.

THE BOARDWALK ANTIQUES SHOP

Cate's eyes snapped to Henry. What was going on? Who was this woman? Was it an inside joke?

But Henry wasn't laughing with the rest of the audience. His eyes were riveted on the beautiful woman on the stage, his face like stone.

Cate's stomach did a sour tumble, and she looked back to the stage. Sure enough, the woman was looking directly at Henry, a smirk on her face. And then, Cate realized who the woman was, although her hair was a lot shorter than Cate had seen on TV. The woman said, "It might be awkward for some women to be invited to introduce their former spouses, but you all know I'm not the typical woman."

Laughter. The sound grated on Cate and made her feel ill. The woman on the stage, the stunning woman who ironically spoke like the famous singer named Adele, was *the* Adella who had been married to Henry, then dumped him for another man.

Cate didn't want to stare at the gorgeous woman, but she couldn't seem to look away either. Cate didn't hear a word she said. She only heard the rise and fall of the audience's laughter and felt the distance between herself and the man sitting next to her.

And then the audience was clapping, and Henry stood and set his napkin next to his plate. His gaze stayed on his ex-wife as he walked to the stage. She smiled at him triumphantly as he moved toward her.

The gleam in Adella's eyes was unmistakable. Cate recognized it in other women who were chasing after a man with full intentions of getting their way. It seemed Adella had returned, and her target was Henry.

Cate swallowed the lump in her throat. She felt a bit lightheaded as she watched Henry join Adella on the stage. The woman grasped his hands and leaned in for a kiss, which Henry promptly gave her on the cheek. Even though it was only on the cheek, Adella looked more than pleased. She stepped back, allowing Henry to take his place at the podium and clapped along with the audience.

Adella made her way down the stage and settled into an empty chair at a nearby table. Someone queued up the PowerPoint, and the lights were dimmed. Henry launched into dynamic descriptions of the antiques displayed on each slide. A second screen showed the live streaming of the bidding website, the items categorized, and the starting prices next to them, updated every few seconds. Each item was open for bid during the auction for only two hours.

It seemed with the rate of the increases, people from all over the world were bidding. Cate scanned the room, fascinated to see people with various electronic devices and tablets entering bids. Her eyes snapped back to the screen as Henry introduced an antique by saying, "This item comes from my collection, and I've recently received permission from Adella to sell it. You see, it was one of her favorites." He gave a laugh, and the audience joined him.

A photo of a vintage dress was on the screen—its tight bodice and billowing skirts made Cate think of the Victorian era.

Sure enough, Henry gave the background on the dress about it being from the Victorian era, created in London, and worn by a duchess.

"Go to the next slide," a woman's voice called out, interrupting Henry.

Cate's heart thumped as she realized it had been Adella.

Henry clicked to the next slide, and the audience gasped at the sight of Adella wearing the dress. Although her hair was piled on top of her head and she wore a decorated mask over her eyes, it was definitely her. And she had her arm looped through none other than Henry's. They were posing in front of a sweeping marble staircase, both of them all smiles.

Henry stared at the picture for a moment, and Cate

hoped that meant he wasn't happy about it. Suddenly, Adella's voice was speaking into the microphone. Apparently, she'd decided to climb back onto the stage.

"Sorry about this personal slide, folks," she said in a cheerful voice that sounded anything but apologetic. "I thought this would be a fun addition. I loved that dress and only wore it for a few hours at a masquerade ball in Paris. I promise I didn't sweat in it!" She grinned while the people in the room laughed. "But as you can see," she continued, as everyone quieted, "it's a gorgeous dress and would be a priceless addition to one lucky person's collection."

On the other screen that showed the bidding numbers, the amount for the dress jumped, then doubled.

Looking as satisfied as a cat who'd just captured her first mouse, Adella headed off the stage and back to her seat.

Before Cate could process everything she'd just seen and heard, Henry was on to the next slide. Cate couldn't seem to make herself look away from Adella. The woman perched elegantly on her chair, watching Henry with . . . rapture.

"Oh my goodness," Karlene whispered next to Cate, reaching over and patting her hand.

Cate had been so caught up in the Henry/Adella saga that she'd completely ignored her neighbor.

"What is it?" Cate whispered back.

"I'm so sorry you had to see that. I didn't want to say anything, because I am sure Henry can run his own life . . ."

When she trailed off, Cate leaned closer. She wasn't about to let Karlene get away with not finishing what she'd started. "What's wrong, Karlene?"

The woman hesitated, then bent her head toward Cate. "Adella has been e-mailing me. She asked all about Henry, if I'd seen him at the local conventions, if he was dating anyone. Of course I told him no because I hadn't met *you*."

No one had met Cate. She'd only just met Henry. "Did Adella break up with her boyfriend?"

"She and Raul were married, and now their marriage has been annulled," Karlene said. She grasped Cate's hand as if she were about to impart very bad news. "I guess it was all over the European papers. Her husband is quite famous over there, you know."

Cate could only numbly nod. "And now she wants Henry back."

Karlene nodded. "It appears so."

Fourteen

Henry felt numb. Angry. But mostly numb. How had Adella happened to show up at the convention without him knowing about it? Without him being able to prepare? Although he didn't know what he might have done in advance, at least he wouldn't have been blindsided. And at least he could have discussed it with Cate—warned her, or something.

He clicked to the next slide, trying to refocus. He hoped he sounded and looked professional to the audience, because inside everything had jumbled. Adella had been texting him for the last three days but gave no indication she was showing up today. He'd been surprised at her friendly banter but assumed she was halfway around the world; he figured her new husband was traveling and she was bored or reminiscing.

But when she greeted him on the stage, she'd whispered, "Raul and I split."

It rocked him to the core. Seeing her in LA. Seeing her on their home turf. Breathing in her familiar scent, kissing her all-too-smooth skin. Learning that the man she'd left him for was no longer in her life. Henry clicked on the next slide and tried to peer beyond the bright stage lights to catch a glimpse of Cate. What was she thinking by now? Especially after that picture of him and Adella at the masquerade ball?

That photo brought back a lot of memories, good ones tangled with the bad. The masquerade ball had been a riot of fun, but even then, deep down, Henry had known something was wrong between him and Adella. The night had proved magical, reigniting Henry's hope that his insecurities about his marriage were only the normal ups and downs of a relationship. But it was the week following that Henry discovered the texts from Raul.

He shoved the memory away and clicked to the next slide. The time couldn't move fast enough for Henry, but he stuck to his job and didn't hurry up his presentation, even though he could feel a pair of green eyes staring at him. Adella was here for a reason, and every bit of Henry would be on alert until he discovered why.

The last slide arrived, and Henry had never been so relieved at the end of a presentation. After he thanked everyone and gave them final instructions, Adella swept back onto the stage. Henry turned to give her the microphone and leave, but she grasped his arm and kept him in place. Smiling at the audience, she reiterated her thanks on behalf of the convention committee, then said, "I have a special announcement to make."

Henry stiffened, wishing he was off the stage and not standing in front of everyone. He didn't know if he could take any more public surprises today.

"I've been asked to chair next year's convention," Adella began. "Of course, I couldn't turn it down." Applause broke out as she beamed at the audience. "And I was hoping to convince Henry to be next year's MC as well."

Henry straightened and nodded. He wasn't too excited that Adella would be running things, which meant they'd have to do some coordinating together. But it was an entire year away. Her next words nearly stopped his heart.

"I was also hoping . . ." She paused and gave a nervous little laugh. "That Henry would also serve as my co-chair." Applause started up, but Adella cut in over the noise, "Our marriage may have ended, but we always made a great business team." The applause exploded, and Adella turned to Henry. "What do you think, Henry?"

He opened his mouth to say no, or at least to ask her to give him time to think about it, but the audience started to clap again, and a few people called out, "Say yes."

And it was with a flushed face and thudding heart that Henry found himself agreeing to co-chair with his ex-wife. The moment he said it, he regretted it. She wrapped her arm around his waist and waved at everyone, a huge smile on her face. He disentangled himself quickly, but Adella grasped his hand and clung to him.

The clapping continued as the stage lights finally dimmed, and Henry was able to see his table. But Cate wasn't in her seat. He stepped away from Adella, literally tugging his hand from hers. How was he going to explain any of this to Cate? Their relationship was so new, so fresh.

He moved down the steps, only to be stopped by Adella's voice, "Henry, do you remember Mr. Sanderson?"

Henry paused and greeted the man. He couldn't very well ignore the biggest donor to the LA Antiques Foundation. After spending a few minutes with Mr. Sanderson, Henry was able to make it off the stage without further interruptions. By the time he got to the table, Karlene was waiting for him, her eyes studying him carefully.

"She's gone, isn't she?" he said.

"Oh, honey," Karlene said. "No woman could watch that and stick around."

Henry looked past her, wishing Karlene had been wrong. Maybe Cate was waiting for him at the back of the room or in the corridor somewhere.

Karlene grasped his arm. "Listen to me."

Henry watched Karlene, wondering how much this woman knew about Adella's plans in advance. The two women had been friends longer than Henry had known Adella.

"You need to decide what you want," Karlene began, "or *who* you want, before you break both women's hearts."

Henry exhaled, trying to collect his thoughts and make sense of Adella's sudden reappearance. "Adella left me . . ."

Karlene nodded. "And now she's back." She lowered her voice. "People can change."

Henry didn't doubt that, but this was so unexpected, and he'd thought his heart had healed and turned away from his ex-wife completely.

But now he wasn't so sure.

Fifteen

C ate didn't let herself cry when Henry smiled at the audience and told his ex-wife he'd be her co-chair for the antiques convention next year. Cate didn't let herself cry as she hurried out of the convention center. And she didn't let herself cry during the twenty-minute drive back to her apartment.

But once her apartment door was shut and locked, her heels kicked off and her silk blouse and slacks stripped, she climbed beneath her down comforter and closed her eyes, allowing the stinging to turn into tears. Her closed eyelids didn't stop the replayed images of Henry and Adella on the ballroom stage.

Cate knew she was being ridiculous. She hadn't even been on a real date with Henry, and yes, they'd kissed a couple of times—a couple of *amazing* times—but she truly had no claim to him. She knew the risks of becoming attached to a divorced man, and it seemed she'd just felt the sting of that risk. Would Henry go back to his wife?

Cate could honestly say she wouldn't entirely blame him if he did. Adella was beautiful and accomplished, and she had a major advantage over Cate—a shared history.

She grabbed a tissue from her nightstand and blew her nose. Her head hurt, and her heart was raw. She wanted to talk to her grandma. Thinking of her grandma brought another round of tears, and Cate decided she needed a do-over for the day. It hadn't started out well, and it wasn't ending well. She turned off her lamp and burrowed into her covers, even though it was still the afternoon. She wanted to sleep, but all she could think of when she closed her eyes was Henry. She knew if she hadn't been dealing with the loss of her grandma, her emotions over Henry wouldn't be so raw. Her thoughts flitted through their first meeting in the antiques store, their Chinese takeout dinner at her grandma's home, the phone calls and texts leading up to the convention, and then the kisses in the art lounge.

She should have known Henry was too good to be true. Her phone buzzed, and her heart lurched. What if it was Henry? What would she say? But the text was from her boss. One of the other magazine employees was scheduled to write about bed and breakfasts along the West Coast, but he'd only visited about four or five before coming down with the flu.

It would mean Cate would have to leave the next day and be gone for several days. She finished reading the text and dropped her head against her pillow with a sigh. It might be the perfect assignment to clear her head and stop moping over Henry, or she might do a terrible job because she couldn't seem to focus on anything other than Adella greeting Henry with a movie-star smile and a kiss.

Another text came in, and Cate checked it, thinking it was her boss. But her heart nearly stopped when she saw it was from Henry.

Are you home?

She waited a few heartbeats before replying. *Yes.*

Can I come over to talk? he typed.

Her breath fled. If he wanted to break things off, what little they had to break off, maybe it could be a phone call where she didn't have to gaze into his hazel eyes. Or maybe he wanted to apologize. Cate couldn't stop the hope blooming in her chest. She typed back, *Ok.*

Thanks, see you soon.

Cate scrambled out of bed and rushed into the bathroom. Her mascara was smeared, so she scrubbed it off and started over. By the time a soft knock sounded at the door, she was ready, for what, she wasn't sure.

She opened the door to see Henry standing there, looking more handsome than she remembered. Maybe it was because she didn't know where she stood—if she stood in front of Adella or behind her.

"Hey," he said in a quiet voice.

His gentle tone made her want to crawl back into bed and pull the covers over her head again. She really didn't want to hear him tell her in person that they were finished.

"Hey," she said back, because she didn't want to start questioning him right away.

"I have an apology to make."

She couldn't read his eyes. Was this a *please forgive me* apology, or a *sorry we didn't work out* apology? "Come in," she said, opening the door.

Henry hesitated, which made her heart sink. But then he was walking past her, into her apartment, gazing at her walls.

"You like the beach?" he said.

Cate regarded her walls through what she thought would be his perspective. An old sea net stretched across one corner, and next to it, she'd glued bits of seaglass into a mosaic—glass she'd found when walking the shores with her grandma. She'd hung several paintings of seascapes, one of a stormy scene, the other two peaceful ones.

"They remind me of spending summers with my grandma," she said.

Henry crossed to the painting of the stormy sea and shoved his hands in his pockets.

His quiet didn't bode well, Cate decided.

She leaned against the door and folded her arms, preparing herself for the worst. At least he'd been man enough to do this in person, she supposed. She didn't say anything, just allowed him to take his time.

When he finally did turn around, his gaze locked with hers. "Adella wants to get back together," he said in a low voice.

Her body flinched at the statement. Although Cate had expected it, she'd hoped for something else. She tightened her folded arms as if she could protect her heart more that way. "I understand," she said, but it came out as a whisper.

Henry took a step toward her, and the space between them seemed to shrink tenfold. "I wasn't expecting her to show up. I didn't know she was coming."

Cate held up her hand. She didn't want to hear any of this. The room kept getting smaller and smaller, and with Henry here, she wouldn't be able to breathe. "It's all right. Don't worry about it. I get the poor timing, but maybe it was good that we . . . do this now instead of later."

Henry lifted his brows, studying her. "Do what now?"

"Break up." She couldn't believe *she* had to say the words, because something inside her was still hoping . . . hoping he'd rush to her and tell her things were completely over with his ex.

But he didn't. He lowered his head and exhaled. After a moment, he lifted his head again and, with those intense hazel eyes, said, "I don't think I'll ever get over how much she hurt me. So when she came to the convention and told me she wasn't with Raul anymore, something inside of me turned hopeful." He looked away from her, and Cate was glad he did. She didn't want him to see her building tears.

"I'm so sorry," he said at last, still staring at some unseen spot on the wall. "I wasn't prepared for what seeing her again would do to me, what hearing her apology might change in me." He scrubbed his hands through his hair, and then he was looking at Cate again.

She didn't bother to wipe away the tears that were spilling down her cheeks.

"I've made a mess with so many things, and now you're hurt too, and I don't know how to fix it." He took another step toward her. "I don't know what will happen between Adella and me. But I can't keep you hanging when I don't know. It's . . . not fair to you."

Cate wanted to shrink against the door, to pass through it until she was in the hallway beyond, away from his words and sorrowful gaze.

He continued to move toward her, not stopping until he stood right in front of her. His hand brushed against her cheek, and then he closed his eyes and leaned down and kissed her cheek.

Cate couldn't decide if she wanted to wrap her arms around him, pull him close and tell him to choose her, or if she wanted to shove him away and tell him to never speak to her again. She did none of these things. She didn't move, just memorized the feel of his lips on her cheek for one last time.

Then she turned and opened the door with a trembling hand.

He left then, disappearing out of her life almost as fast as he'd entered it.

Cate locked the apartment door, barely registering the hollow click of the lock in the dead-silent apartment. She walked into her bedroom and found her phone on the nightstand. With fingers still trembling, she texted her boss:

E-mail me the itinerary. I can leave in the morning.

Then Cate put her phone on silent, climbed back into bed, and pulled the covers over her head.

Sixteen

enry woke with a start. He'd been dreaming about Adella and Raul. They were sitting at a bar, laughing at him as he tried to wade through the gyrating crowd to reach the two of them. Henry shook his head, trying to get rid of the vivid images in the dream. His heart was still thudding with frustration.

Then he groaned to himself. Adella was back in his life, and he didn't know what to think. They'd spent the last couple of evenings together. The day after the convention, she'd driven up to Seashell Beach and checked into a hotel. That night, they'd eaten at the Mariposa, and Henry found himself laughing most of the meal as Adella brought up many of their shared memories. He'd also become lost in her gaze more than once when she looked at him with those killer green eyes.

And last night . . . Henry let out another groan . . . he'd kissed her. It was a brief, innocent kiss, but it had been enough to twist his stomach into a knot. They'd grabbed hamburgers on the pier and walked until the sun set. It had been the most relaxing evening they'd spent together, ever, even when they'd been married.

But after he'd kissed her goodnight, he couldn't stop thinking about Adella and Raul together—kissing, touching, and more—and apparently it bothered him enough that now he was dreaming about the two of them. His emotions still raw from his dream, he climbed out of bed and staggered into the bathroom. A shower would help clear his head.

But twenty minutes later, showered and shaved, his stomach was still in knots. Kissing Adella had been more like a habit, but he knew she wouldn't see it that way. She wanted him back; she'd made that very clear. And the Italian dinner and the next night on the pier had started to reel him in.

Even though Henry had just showered, he changed into his running shorts and started off down the street. He ran hard, toward the ocean, until he realized he'd arrived in Cate's grandma's neighborhood. Cate wasn't there, of course. There was a *For Sale* sign out front, and he stood in front of it for a moment. The house was amazing—two stories, ocean view, tons of windows. The neighborhood was quiet today, and he walked around to the back of the house. The memory of seeing Cate sitting on the back porch flashed through his mind.

Everything Cate was, Adella wasn't. When Henry had first met Cate, he'd thought she was too much woman-of-the-world like his ex-wife. But he'd been wrong. Cate was down to earth, tied to her family, and purely herself. She knew what it was to be hurt, had lost her parents, had broken an engagement, and now he'd hurt her even more.

Henry sat on the back porch, staring out over the morning waves. A couple of runners jogged on the beach, and a stray dog was bounding in and out of the surf. Seagulls dipped and soared, their cries drowned by the surf.

Henry's phone buzzed, and he checked the incoming text. It was from Adella.

Good morning, Sweets! Hope you slept well! Wanna grab breakfast together? xo

Henry stared at the word "sweets" for a long time. Adella used to call him that, and she'd also called Raul that same endearment. Henry had read enough of their texts to know. The deep ache returned, the one he'd felt in the weeks and months after discovering Adella's unfaithfulness. The ache that told him he wasn't first, that he was replaceable. That his heart was still broken.

Standing up, Henry walked down to the slope leading to the beach. He pulled off his running shoes and continued toward the wet sand and into the surf. The coolness of the water against his skin was refreshing. He closed his eyes, letting the rising sun warm his face and shoulders.

He stood there, alone, with just the ocean at his feet and the world spread before him, as he thought about where he wanted to be in life. Where he wanted to go. And with whom. Not every man had the choices he did, he realized, and he was grateful for that. But he'd been alone now for long enough that he knew he wanted companionship again.

He thought of Adella and her plea for a second chance. He thought about her enthusiasm, their shared life and memories, their passion for antiques. She'd hurt him, but who didn't make mistakes in life?

And then he thought about Cate, whom he was just getting to know. Being with her had felt so natural, like coming home to a warm kitchen on a cold day. She was full of life and promises of love, and when he'd kissed her, his pain had dimmed, and the darkness had fled.

Henry pulled the cell phone from his pocket again. Adella had sent another text: *Henry? Where are you? I came to your house, but you weren't there. Are you having second thoughts? Call me asap!!!*

A STITCH IN TIME

She was in full panic mode just because he wasn't at home? She knew he ran almost every morning. The text felt stifling, demanding, but it was more than that. Just each time he saw her name on his screen, darts of pain shot into him, pain he'd slowly overcome. It was back, raw and tangible . . . He reread her words. *Was* he having second thoughts?

Henry exhaled and typed back: *I'm on a run. Meet me at the boardwalk. We need to talk.*

Seventeen

"The house sold," Cate's uncle said through the phone.

Cate stared at the quaint bed and breakfast she'd just pulled up to. She couldn't believe her grandma's house sold so quickly. It had only been on the market for a few days. Her uncle had decided to test the sales market instead of renting it out. "That's amazing," she said, even though the announcement made her numb.

So many memories were in that house; if only she'd been able to afford it herself.

"The owner is planning to move in right away," her uncle said, "but he wanted to meet with a family member to ask some questions about the upkeep, things like that."

Cate's mind took a moment to catch up to what her uncle was saying. Didn't he know more about the upkeep than she did?

"We're going on our annual company cruise the day after tomorrow, which Amber is coming on as well," he continued. "So I was hoping you could meet with them."

"All right," Cate said automatically, even though she was still reeling from the news of the house selling. "When?"

"Sunday?" her uncle suggested.

"That works," Cate said. It was Friday now, and she had one last bed and breakfast to visit; then she'd be off for a couple of days. She could easily drive up to Seashell Beach and meet the new owner.

She hung up with her uncle and then climbed out of the car to visit the bed and breakfast inn she'd pulled up to. As she walked up the cobbled path, her phone rang. Her breath caught when she saw it was Henry calling . . . again. He'd called twice in the past three days, but he'd never left a message or sent a text. Cate didn't know what to think about it. Since she had hesitated answering the first time, she'd been hesitating ever since.

Just answer the call, she chastised herself. *He's probably trying to return the sewing machine.* Still, she wasn't ready to hear his voice, no matter what he wanted. She turned off her phone and slipped it into her purse. Maybe if he'd leave a message or send a text, she'd know what he wanted, and then she could decide what to do from there. But as it was, she knew as soon as she heard his voice, she'd remember everything she was trying to forget.

Cate ignored her conflicting emotions and stepped into the bed and breakfast. She asked for the tour. It was a charming place, just north of Sacramento, and Cate loved the antiques situated around the old mansion. As she ate at their cozy café after the tour, her gaze stalled on an antique sewing machine in the corner. Cate rose from her chair and crossed to the machine.

It was a Singer, but not the same year, or at least not the same model, of the one that belonged to her grandma. Cate wasn't an expert, so she wasn't entirely sure. She bent closer to inspect the machine, and a feeling of nostalgia swept over her. This Sunday might be the last time she'd ever walk through her grandma's house again. Cate blinked back the encroaching tears. At some point she'd also have to get her grandma's machine from Henry; maybe she could tell him she'd pick it up from Boardwalk Antiques.

Cate straightened and made a decision. While she was in Seashell Beach on Sunday, she'd text Henry about her grandma's machine. And pride or not, she'd find some way to finally get it back.

Eighteen

Cate was ten minutes late to the agreed-upon 1:00 time her uncle had passed along to her. But as she pulled up to her grandma's home, there was no vehicle out front. Maybe the new owner was even later. Cate wished she'd at least gotten the family's phone number from her uncle instead of using him as the go-between. Hopefully the owner wasn't seriously delayed.

She stared at the house for a few minutes in the mid-day sun. The two-story home was framed by a brilliant blue sky and pure white clouds floating above. She bit her lip, holding back her emotions; then she climbed out of her car. Since the owner wasn't here yet, she decided she'd walk around the house and gaze at the view one more time . . . before it became the property of someone else.

She heard the seagulls before she saw them, and as she rounded the corner of the house, she breathed in the ocean air deeply, letting it calm her and strengthen her at the same time. She hoped she could handle the barrage of emotions that were sure to hit as soon as she stepped inside.

Cate stopped on the ridge leading down to the sand and gazed out over the water. The sail boats on the sea and the families on the beach looked perfect enough to be painted on a canvas. She was no artist, but maybe she could blow up a photograph and remember her last visit to her grandma's house. Pulling her phone out of her pocket, she snapped a few pictures of the scene below.

And then she released a sigh. She'd really miss this place . . . all the old memories and even the newer memories of eating Chinese takeout in the kitchen with Henry. She could now look at their flurry of a relationship with more objectivity. They had been a bit of a disaster from the first meeting, so it was no surprise that it burned hot and fast, then burned out even more quickly. She truly wished Henry and Adella all the best. As for Cate, well, she'd keep on writing and traveling, and who knew what the future might bring?

"Cate?"

She went absolutely still. Had someone called to her from the beach? No. The voice had come from behind her. And it had been *his* voice. *Henry's.*

She turned and saw Henry standing on the back porch. His hands were shoved into his khaki Bermuda shorts, and he wore a button-down shirt, sleeves rolled up. Her mouth fell open as she scrambled for something to say. To tell him she was sorry for screening his calls. To ask him about the sewing machine. But she said none of it. She just wondered how he'd suddenly shown up while she was here. Maybe he'd been running in the neighborhood again and saw her car?

No. He wasn't wearing running clothes. And . . . the back door was open, as if he'd just walked out onto the porch from inside.

"*You?*" She stared at him. "*You* bought the house?"

306

He nodded.

Cate clamped her mouth shut and looked away. It was unbelievable. She didn't know what to say.

He didn't say anything either. Giving her time to process this new development, she supposed. And then she let out a groan and snapped her head to look at him again. "That's why you were calling?" Not to tell her he'd made a huge mistake. Not to tell her he wanted her back. To tell her he'd bought her grandma's house.

Her face heated up, and anger sliced through her. It was all too much. First, he'd taken the sewing machine. Then her heart. And now, her grandma's home.

Henry could figure out the house on his own. She was done. She was leaving.

She turned from him and made her way around the house, trying not to run, trying not to let the tears fall. But she ran anyway, and the tears fell.

"Cate!" he called out. "Hang on!"

She didn't want to stop, didn't want him to see her tears, but her feet slowed anyway.

Henry caught up and moved around her so he was standing between her and the car. "Wait," he said, catching his breath.

Cate brushed at her cheeks, then looked up at him. His hazel eyes were intent on hers, pleading. She folded her arms and waited, not saying anything.

"I didn't want to leave the news on your voicemail, or text you . . . I hoped to have the chance to explain." Henry blew out a breath and scrubbed his hands through his hair, a habit she'd become familiar with. "I guess I should start at the beginning."

He stepped toward her, and Cate didn't know what to think. His gaze had gone from intense to soft and questioning. "Can you ever forgive a complete idiot?" he said in a low voice.

His question stunned her. Was this an apology, and if so, for what? Her thoughts were still colliding when she said, "Which part are you referring to? Holding my grandma's sewing machine hostage? Kissing me when you're still in love with your ex-wife? Inviting me to a convention so I could see just how great you two are together? Or dumping me an hour later? Or maybe you're an idiot for throwing out more money to separate me from what's most important to me— my grandma's house."

"Whoa," Henry said, putting up his hands and moving closer.

Cate took a step back. She'd pretty much covered it, and there wasn't much else to talk about.

"First off," Henry started, then shook his head. "There's a lot to say, but you have to know that I'm not in love with Adella."

Cate blinked. *What?*

"I made a mistake," he said, his voice was quieter now. "I thought she'd changed, and I wanted to give her another chance for some twisted reason. We went out to eat and had fun. It brought back the good memories. But I couldn't forget after all, and in the end I couldn't trust her with my heart again."

Cate felt a bit of the anger inside her slip away. She unfolded her arms, letting them drop to her side. "What did you tell her?"

"Good-bye." Henry shoved his hands in his pockets and looked down. "I felt like getting back together with Adella was like stepping backwards into a dark room I'd worked so hard to get out of."

Cate nodded. She hadn't been married and divorced before, but she remembered how it was when she'd lost her parents. Staying with her grandma had let the light back in.

"And I couldn't let go of you," Henry said, raising his gaze.

Her heart buzzed at his words. They had a long way to go before really getting to know each other. How could he be so sure?

His hand reached for hers, and she let him take it. "I'm a complete idiot, and I'm sorry." He leaned down. "There's a lot more we need to talk about, though. Come inside, and I'll try to explain."

Cate was at a crossroads. If she followed him, she was opening herself to him again. If she got into her car, she might have regrets, but her heart would be safe.

"Ten minutes," Henry said.

She looked up at him. He was close enough to hug, yet she wanted to be closer. "All right. Ten minutes."

One side of his mouth lifted, and he led her toward the house—her grandma's house—their hands still intertwined.

"Where's your van?" she asked as they walked up the front porch.

"In the garage."

"Oh," Cate said, giving a little laugh. "I guess it got cleaned out?"

"Part of the estate sale." Henry opened the front door.

Cate walked inside and stared at the transformation. She released Henry's hand and turned around in the room. The carpet had been torn out, and the old wood floor beneath had been sanded and prepped for refinishing. "Wow. It's beautiful." Her grandma had loved the hardwood but gave into a trend in the '80s when wall-to-wall carpet was the thing. She hadn't ever changed it after that.

"I have quite a few plans, actually," Henry said, "But this was my priority."

Cate scanned the front room, seeing that efforts had been started to take down the wallpaper. Then she stopped and stared. Her grandma's sewing machine was sitting against the far wall. "You brought it from the shop?"

"Yes, and I'll deliver it to your apartment, or . . ."

She looked up at him. "Or what? Are you changing your mind?"

"Not exactly." He linked their fingers together. "I'm turning this room into a display room of sorts. I'll be setting up my office in the main floor bedroom, then I'll meet with clients in here. If you don't have room for the sewing machine at your apartment, I can store it here for you. But not because I'm trying to keep it."

"Sure you aren't," she said, giving him a small smile before she crossed the room to trail her fingers over the machine.

"So," Henry said, coming to stand by her. "The other stuff I wanted to tell you . . . Buying this place wasn't totally planned. It was more of an . . . inspiration."

"Impulse?" Cate offered.

"Not impulsive." He was staring down at her. "I want to restore this house back to its original form where possible. It's like an antique in itself."

Cate found herself nodding. "I guess it's better in your hands than in a stranger's."

Henry laughed. "I'll take that as a compliment?"

She lifted a shoulder. Being inside, seeing what he'd already started to do to the house, wasn't making her upset that he'd bought the place.

"Come on," he said in a quiet voice. "Let me show you the rest, and you can tell me what you think of my plans."

Cate followed Henry up the stairs and into the different rooms and bathrooms. She listened in awe as he described the renovating he planned. He was going to do a lot of the finish work himself and hire other parts out.

"Where did you learn carpentry?" Cate asked as they stopped on the upper landing before going back downstairs.

He placed a hand on the banister, the one he said he was going to strip and refinish a dark walnut. "Summers between college semesters. I worked on plenty of older houses, and you could say I fell in love with the old stuff."

His grin was contagious, and Cate found herself smiling back. "So this really is your dream house?"

"Almost."

Cate raised her brows. "What more could you want? I think my grandparents designed this house to near perfection."

Henry threaded his fingers through hers and pulled her closer. "It's only perfect with *you* in it." His gaze held hers, and Cate admitted to herself that if she was going to get lost in someone's eyes, she wanted them to be Henry's. "So, do you forgive me?" he asked.

"For taking the sewing machine?" she said, holding back a smile.

"Yeah, and for letting you go, and for buying this house." He tugged her even closer. "And for wanting it all."

"All?"

"This house, and you," he said. His other hand moved to her waist, and she knew she was blushing, but she didn't care. "And maybe even a kid or two one day."

His lips were so close that Cate felt like she had to whisper. "Don't you think you're getting ahead of yourself, Henry Lancaster?"

"I'm just speaking from my heart." His lips brushed hers, and Cate moved her hands up his chest, then clasped them behind his neck.

"I think I like your heart."

He smiled and stole another kiss. "It's all yours."

Cate pulled him tightly against her, kissing him back. For a moment, she was going to forget all of the complications of the future. For this moment, she was going to be . . . with Henry. Breathe him in, kiss him, and hold him. Henry had been right. This was perfection.

Dear Reader,

We hoped you enjoyed *The Boardwalk Antiques Shop*! This has been a fun project, and reviews help us spread the word. Please consider reviewing *Boardwalk* on Amazon, Goodreads, Barnes & Noble, or iTunes. Or if you'd like to contact one of us personally, our websites are listed in our author bios.

Sincerely,

Julie, Melanie & Heather

Check out *The Fortune Café* from the Tangerine Street Romance series:

Julie Wright

Julie Wright started her first book when she was fifteen. She's written over a dozen books since then, is a Whitney Award winner, and feels she's finally getting the hang of this writing gig. She enjoys speaking to writing groups, youth groups, and schools. She loves reading, eating, writing, hiking, playing on the beach with her kids, and snuggling with her husband to watch movies. Julie's favorite thing to do is watch her husband make dinner. She hates mayonnaise but has a healthy respect for ice cream.

Visit her website: JulieWright.com
Twitter: @scatteredjules

Melanie Jacobson

Melanie Bennett Jacobson is an avid reader, amateur cook, and champion shopper. She consumes astonishing amounts of chocolate, chick flicks, and romance novels. After meeting her husband online, she is now living happily married in Southern California with her growing family and a series of doomed houseplants. Melanie is a former English teacher and a sometime blogger who loves to laugh and make others laugh. In her downtime (ha!), she writes romantic comedies and pines after beautiful shoes.

Visit her website: MelanieJacobson.net
Twitter: @Writestuff_Mel

Heather B. Moore

Heather B. Moore is a *USA Today* bestselling author of more than a dozen historical novels and thrillers, written under the pen name H.B. Moore. She writes women's fiction, romance and inspirational nonfiction under Heather B. Moore. This can all be confusing, so her kids just call her Mom. Heather attended Cairo American College in Egypt, the Anglican School of Jerusalem in Israel, and earned a Bachelor of Science degree from Brigham Young University in Utah.

Heather's email list: http://hbmoore.com/contact
Blog: MyWritersLair.blogspot.com
Website: HBMoore.com
Twitter: @heatherbmoore

CPSIA information can be obtained at www.ICGtesting.com
Printed in the USA
LVOW01s2134100615

442027LV00012B/284/P